THE
THIRD
SISTER

ALSO BY SARA BLAEDEL

THE LOUISE RICK SERIES

<u>The Missing Persons Trilogy</u>
The Forgotten Girls
The Killing Forest
The Lost Woman

<u>The Camilla Trilogy</u>
The Night Women
The Running Girl
The Stolen Angel

<u>The Homicide Trilogy</u>
The Midnight Witness
The Silent Women
The Drowned Girl

THE FAMILY SECRETS SERIES

The Daughter
Her Father's Secret
The Third Sister

PRAISE FOR INTERNATIONALLY BESTSELLING AUTHOR SARA BLAEDEL

"Blaedel is one of the best I've come across."
—Michael Connelly,
#1 *New York Times* bestselling author

"One can count on emotional engagement, spine-tingling suspense, and taut storytelling from Sara Blaedel."
—Sandra Brown,
#1 *New York Times* bestselling author

"Sara Blaedel is a remarkable crime writer who delivers a solid, engaging story that any reader in the world can enjoy."
—Karin Slaughter, *New York Times* bestselling author

"Crime-writer superstar Sara Blaedel's great skill is in weaving a heartbreaking social history into an edge-of-your-chair thriller while at the same time creating a detective who's as emotionally rich and real as a close friend."
—Oprah.com

"If you like crime fiction that is genuinely scary, then Sara Blaedel should be the next writer you read."
—Mark Billingham

"Sara Blaedel is at the top of her game."
—Camilla Läckberg, #1 international bestselling author

PRAISE FOR THE FAMILY SECRETS SERIES

"Compelling and unique, [*The Daughter*] delves into a dark and fascinating world rarely explored in suspense fiction. Sara Blaedel knows how to reel in her readers and keep them utterly transfixed."
  —Tess Gerritsen, *New York Times* bestselling author

"Denmark's Queen of Crime, Sara Blaedel, is back...If Scandinavian noir is your cup of tea, you'll want to check out Blaedel's newest venture. Blending Scandinavian sensibility with an American mystery...Blaedel uses her sharp storytelling and endearing character development to craft a compelling mystery that will keep readers turning the pages."   —Criminal Element

"This well-crafted dive into family secrets will appeal to fans of Lisa Scottoline."   —*Booklist*

"Blaedel does a fine job hooking the reader early, delivering another page-turner that packs a wicked cliffhanger ending that'll have her readers begging for the next book. Expertly written and deftly plotted, *Her Father's Secret* is a wild, fun mystery that shows once again why Sara Blaedel is fast becoming one of the premier mystery writers in the game."   —CrimeReads

"This series started off with a bang and just gets better and better."   —The Real Book Spy

"Blaedel does a fine job of fleshing out each of these characters, and readers will enjoy watching Ilka transform from frustrated and confused to utterly confident in her sleuthing as she discovers some of her father's painful secrets...the book's cliffhanger ending will make readers look forward to the next set of secrets for Ilka to unravel."
—*Publishers Weekly*

"A great start for mystery lovers looking to dip a toe into international intrigue."
—*Library Journal*

"Ilka is a complex and interesting character."
—*RT Book Reviews*

"[An] exhilaratingly morbid tale of a 40-year-old Copenhagen widow who travels to Wisconsin to run her dead father's funeral home—and is forced to confront the enemies he left behind."
—Oprah.com

PRAISE FOR SARA BLAEDEL'S INTERNATIONALLY BESTSELLING LOUISE RICK SERIES

"I loved spending time with the tough, smart, and all-too-human heroine Louise Rick—and I can't wait to see her again."
—Lisa Unger

"Sara Blaedel is at the top of her game. Louise Rick is a character who will have readers coming back for more."
—Camilla Läckberg

THE THIRD SISTER

SARA BLAEDEL

TRANSLATED BY

MARK KLINE

GRAND CENTRAL
PUBLISHING

NEW YORK BOSTON

Copyright © 2020 by Sara Blaedel
Translation copyright © 2019 by Sara Blaedel; translated by Mark Kline

Cover design by Elizabeth Connor. Cover copyright © 2021 by Hachette Book Group, Inc.

Grand Central Publishing
Hachette Book Group
1290 Avenue of the Americas, New York, NY 10104
grandcentralpublishing.com
twitter.com/grandcentralpub

Originally published in Denmark as *Den tredje søster* by People's Press in November 2018
First U.S. edition published in hardcover and ebook in April 2020
First U.S. mass market edition: October 2021

Grand Central Publishing is a division of Hachette Book Group, Inc. The Grand Central Publishing name and logo is a trademark of Hachette Book Group, Inc.

The publisher is not responsible for websites (or their content) that are not owned by the publisher.

The Hachette Speakers Bureau provides a wide range of authors for speaking events. To find out more, go to hachettespeakersbureau.com or call (866) 376-6591.

ISBNs: 978-1-5387-6331-5 (mass market), 978-1-5387-6330-8 (ebook)

Printed in the United States of America

CW

10 9 8 7 6 5 4 3 2 1

For my son, Adam
—because I can always count on
you

1

Ilka woke up and squinted against the bright light. The floor was marked by a triangle of sunshine. When she raised her head, she found herself staring straight at an automatic weapon.

"I was beginning to think you weren't ever going to wake up." Sister Eileen rose from the chair. "We need to go."

Ilka was the one who had insisted on staying the night in the funeral home. She rolled onto her side and watched the slender woman disappear through the doorway, the long-barreled weapon dangling from her hand.

She wanted to pull her comforter up over her head and pretend that everything she'd heard the evening before was none of her business. Everything. That Sister Eileen wasn't actually a nun, that her real name was Lydia Rogers, that she'd gone underground and had been in hiding for the past twelve years to escape a death sentence in Texas. She wanted to convince herself it didn't matter that Artie lay in the hospital, hovering between life and death, because of Sister Eileen—*Lydia*.

Ilka was the one who had found Artie. Lydia must have had her suspicions, because she'd called and asked Ilka to drive out to his house, but regardless, Ilka had sensed something was amiss when she pulled in, and she'd been right: Lydia spotted him lying on the sidewalk with a black hood pulled down over his head. At first, she had thought he was dead, but she'd detected a weak pulse in his neck beneath the blood streaming down from under the hood.

Later, Lydia had explained that the people searching for her were unscrupulous and dangerous. "They won't hesitate to kill someone to get their hands on me."

And Ilka had understood: These people, these killers, were Artie's assailants.

If Ilka hadn't found Artie herself, she probably would have thought Lydia was being dramatic. But she had seen him, and she'd waited outside intensive care at the hospital in Racine while they fought to save his life. Lydia hadn't exaggerated, no doubt about it.

There was another reason she didn't want to get out of bed. It had been a shock to learn that her father was still alive and, according to Lydia, had also gone underground, and Ilka needed time to let that sink in.

"But he should be the one to tell you about it," Lydia had said.

She was right about that, Ilka thought. He was definitely the one who should tell her. But finding out he was alive had shaken her, and now she struggled to get everything clear in her head. It was hard to accept that he and Lydia had been lying to her.

Suddenly she shot straight up in bed: She hadn't inherited the failing funeral home after all, since her father wasn't dead! Finally, something positive in all the turmoil.

"Are you coming down?" Lydia yelled up the stairs.

Ilka grabbed her jeans off the floor and picked out a clean blouse while mentally going over their conversation from the previous evening.

She'd been enraged because nothing the woman she had known as Sister Eileen had revealed made any sense. The only thing Ilka was sure of was that her father had done it again: He'd run off, and everything he'd left behind had become her problem. Just like back when he left Denmark, leaving her mother alone with the funeral home on Brønshøj Square.

"Where is he?" she'd asked. The question now echoed in her head. Lydia had known he was alive since before Ilka arrived in Racine, and for weeks she'd stood by watching Ilka struggle without saying a word, until she was forced into it.

For what felt like an eternity they'd sat across from each other in silence, while Ilka tried to calm herself down. "In Key West," Lydia finally answered. Living in Artie's house, she added.

"So Artie's known about it the whole time?"

Ilka thought back to the night she'd spent in Artie's bed. He'd said nothing, even though she had opened up to him, exposed the part of herself that missed her father terribly.

But Lydia shook her head. Artie had believed his friend and employer for the past nineteen years was dead, that he'd died while Artie was up in Canada fishing. Lydia was the only one who knew the truth. She'd faked a death certificate by copying a signature from the many certificates the funeral home had handled. And she hadn't needed to ask Artie for a key to the house in Key West, because she knew it hung on a hook in the prep room.

Ilka had shaken her head in astonishment, but Lydia had refused to answer any more questions.

"He helped me," was all she would say. Instead she'd warned Ilka again that the men from her past would return, which was why it had been too dangerous for Ilka's father to stay in the funeral home. And she'd pleaded with Ilka, told her they had to get out of there too.

None of this felt plausible to Ilka, and finally she'd stood up and announced that she was tired, she needed to think, and she was going to bed. Too much had happened. She wouldn't give in and agree to take off at once, even though the fear in Lydia's voice had made her skin crawl, on top of the shock of knowing her father was out there somewhere. She'd rolled into bed praying that all this would somehow disappear during the night. Or at least not feel as horrifying when she woke up.

But it was every bit as bad today. In fact, she'd half

expected the sister would be gone when she woke up. The sister—Lydia—yelled up at her again.

Ilka pulled on a sweater and buttoned her pants, then she dragged out a weekend bag from under her father's bed. She jammed some clothes into it and grabbed her toiletry bag from the table. She had no idea how long it took to drive to Key West, but she was ready to go.

Downstairs Lydia had made coffee and put out crackers, a picture of normalcy that seemed absurd against the backdrop of Ilka's chaotic thoughts. But she took the cup that was handed to her. Her phone rang as she was about to sit down: the hospital. Ilka had added their number to her contacts list after Artie's admission.

She sat down slowly and listened, ignoring the other woman as she stared at the table.

"Okay," she said. "I understand. Of course you should do whatever can be done; absolutely."

She swiped at her damp forehead as she spoke.

After hanging up, she said, "The hospital needs the name of Artie's insurance company and the policy number, otherwise they won't keep treating him. And they need an okay from the insurance company or money in his patient account so they'll know they'll get paid."

Ilka shook her head. Her thoughts were too foggy; she couldn't think straight.

"How much is the bill?" Lydia asked.

"Almost fifty thousand dollars. And that's only for intensive care up to now."

It sounded completely absurd to her. Artie was in a coma. What was the alternative if they stopped his treatment?

Lydia stared straight ahead for a moment, then turned and walked out the back door. When she returned, she took out a thick wad of bills from the travel bag in her hand and gave it to Ilka. "Open a patient account for him and tell them we'll be paying in cash, until we clarify the situation with his insurance."

Ilka stared, her eyes wide open, at the thick bundle of hundred-dollar bills in her hand. But Lydia ignored her bewildered expression. Truth be told, Ilka didn't want to know where they came from. She didn't need any more loose ends or sketchy explanations. All she wanted was assurance that the doctors would take good care of Artie, and when she got it, she would take off to look for her father.

Ilka had said she was going to drive to Key West, and without hesitation Lydia had said that sounded perfect for her; there was something she needed to take care of before moving on.

At that moment, the nun peered through the window out at the parking lot and suddenly stiffened. She quickly stepped to the side.

Ilka stood up. Two men were walking toward the funeral home, one of whom she recognized immediately; he'd come by the funeral home and asked about Javi Rodriguez—as well as about her father.

"Who's the other guy?"

"It's the man we met at the hospital," Lydia said.

"And you think they're coming for you?"

Lydia nodded silently. She stared blankly, squeezing the bag's leather strap so hard that her knuckles turned white.

The two men focused on the funeral home's front door as they approached. One of them led the way, while the other tossed away a crumpled-up sack that the wind caught and flung across the street toward the school.

Ilka grabbed Lydia and pushed her into the hall leading to the garage. "I'll talk to them. You wait here—and keep away from the windows, there could be more of them out there."

Ilka checked to make sure the back door was locked before walking past the closed doors of the prep room and the memorial room. She reached the reception just as the men began knocking. A few seconds later, they rattled the doorknob. Only when they knocked again did she casually walk over and open the door.

She nodded graciously at the men. "Good morning. What can I do for you?"

One of them stood at the door while the other stayed on the sidewalk, unwrapping a sandwich. The wind whipped the paper around in his hands, and strands of lettuce fell to the ground.

"We're here to talk to Lydia Rogers." The man's black hair was graying at the temples, and his nose was broad. He wore a vest and a knee-length leather coat. Ilka noticed a square diamond in his left ear.

"She's not here right now." She kept smiling politely even as he put a hand on the doorframe and made a move to elbow past her, but she stood her ground. "I expect her back within half an hour, and you're more than welcome to come back then."

"We'll wait here," the man with the diamond stud said, his eyes darting around the reception behind her.

Ilka stalled a few moments. The other man had finally liberated his sandwich and was holding it with the paper around the lower half. He stared at Ilka as he chewed, and she stared back. A tattoo circled his neck like a wreath.

"Come in." She backed away from the door and straightened up to her full height. She towered over both of the short, stocky men. Their chests pushed out like shields as they glanced around. The guy eating the sandwich was younger and taller but had the same broad nose. Obviously brothers, she thought.

"We know Lydia Rogers works here," the older one barked out, as if he expected Ilka to deny it.

Streamers of lettuce kept falling from the sandwich, but the younger brother didn't seem to notice the trail he was leaving. Now that he was closer, Ilka recognized him from the hospital. Something about the way he stared straight at her made her feel smaller, but she ignored his intimidating manner.

"Have a seat." She gestured at the two chairs for visitors.

They didn't budge.

She walked around behind Lydia's desk. "You're sure this isn't something I can help you with?"

"She's the one we want to talk to," the older brother said. His diamond gleamed as he turned and walked to the window.

"Would you like a cup of coffee while you wait?"

The sandwich paper crinkled when the younger brother peeled it down and took another huge bite. He still ignored his mess on the floor. "We don't give a shit about your coffee," he said, his mouth full.

The punch came out of the blue, and the paper and sandwich flew out of his hand. The older brother then turned back to Ilka and said they would both appreciate a cup.

His brother stared down at the chicken and bacon littering the floor. A small dab of mayonnaise dotted the corner of his mouth. She watched the almost imperceptible aftermath play out between them, and for the first time she spotted fear in the younger brother's eyes—which in turn scared her.

But she pulled herself together and pointed again at the chairs. This time they sat, and she went out to get cups and the pot from the coffee machine.

"I'm sure she'll be here soon," she said as she handed each of them a cup. She made a show of picking up the mess from the chicken sandwich.

Neither of them answered. One brother sat leaned over with his cup in his hands; the other leaned back and again peered around the room. Ilka glanced at her watch.

"You'll have to excuse me, I need to deliver a body to the crematorium. You're welcome to more coffee. And again, I'm sure it won't be long before the sister is back."

They didn't seem particularly interested in what she said, though they exchanged a few short sentences in Spanish.

"You're also welcome to come back later," she said. She didn't want to leave them there, but she needed to get going, now.

The older brother stared at the front door. "We'll wait here."

Ilka nodded and left the room as casually as she could, but the moment she was out of sight she grabbed her travel bag and the keys and ran out to the garage. Lydia was standing by the hearse with her bag at her feet, and Ilka couldn't help noticing the gun underneath the coat draped over her arm.

"Give me the keys," Ilka said. Before she knew what had happened, the nun had tossed her the keys, opened the rear door, and jumped into the back. She shoved the lid off the coffin, and in one swift movement she was inside. When Ilka reached the back of the hearse, she was lying with the automatic weapon resting on her chest. She didn't come close to filling the large coffin.

"Let's go."

Ilka checked her watch again. At best, they would have a twenty-minute head start, and they had to stop by the hospital before leaving town. She closed the coffin as fast as she could, slammed the rear door shut, and opened the garage door with the remote.

On the way out of the parking lot, she glimpsed the shadow of a broad figure standing in the reception window. She grabbed her phone, and when they reached the street leading to the hospital, she called the police and reported that the two men almost certainly responsible for the attack on Artie were in the funeral home.

2

Ilka drove the hearse to the rear of the hospital, far from the visitors parking lot and front entrance. She spotted the loading dock, then the drive-in entrance, the one she'd been told undertakers should use when picking up a corpse. After parking in a spot where she would not block anyone bringing out a stretcher, she grabbed her bag and stared at the bills inside. Well over fifty thousand dollars, she guessed. Maybe closer to a hundred thousand. She stepped out of the hearse and glanced back at the coffin with Lydia inside, then walked over to the door beside the entrance.

She stopped to get her bearings when she entered the dim basement, but there were no signs telling her where to go. The heavy odor of cauliflower hung in the air; the hospital's kitchen had to be nearby. Ilka tried a door, which opened up to a wide, brightly lit hallway filled with empty hospital beds. Some of them lacked mattresses; others were filled with stacks of hospital linen.

She hurried past all the beds to the ELEVATOR sign, her footsteps echoing the entire way. Artie was on the sixth floor, but she didn't know if this was the right section of the hospital. The elevator clanked loudly when it stopped and the door opened. It rose slowly, and when she stepped out, she recognized the waiting room. She'd reached his ward by the service elevator.

She smoothed her hair, which was easy enough; the hair she'd been born with was straight as a string. Like a rag doll's hair, as one of the catty girls in her class had once said. Back then she'd felt bad about it, but it was true. She squared up her coat then walked to the ward's office, where a middle-aged woman sat behind a computer screen, talking on the phone.

Ilka had slipped a rubber band around the bills, and when the woman hung up, she held the bundle out. "I'm here to see Artie Sorvino. Maybe you're the one who called me earlier today, about paying for his stay here?"

The woman nodded. "Yes, I'm the one."

"I'll have to get back to you about his insurance; we haven't found the information yet. But this should be enough for his treatment so far. Put the rest in his patient account."

The woman accepted the bills without batting an eye and slipped them into a machine. A moment later Ilka heard a hectic rustling sound as the money was counted at lightning speed. She handed Ilka a receipt, confirming that eighty-seven thousand dollars had been deposited in Artie Sorvino's patient account.

Ilka sent a silent thank-you to Lydia in the coffin.

The woman's face was still blank. "Would you prefer the patient be moved to the hospital's private patient unit?"

Ilka didn't doubt the level of service was much better there, but for the moment she just hoped the doctors and quality of treatment were the same where Artie was. She shook her head and explained that the money in his account was solely for his treatment.

"Can I go in and see him?" Twenty minutes had already passed—their head start was almost certainly wiped out—but the real question was whether the men looking for Lydia Rogers had been arrested, or if they'd caught on before the police got there. She had to see Artie before leaving for Key West, though, if for nothing else than simply to stroke his cheek.

Just outside his room, she spotted the head doctor who had treated him when he'd been brought in. He'd been unconscious, and the doctor said they'd found a significant accumulation of blood in the back of his head. A tube had been inserted to drain the blood, which the doctor said should help. She'd also told Ilka and Lydia that Artie would be put into an induced coma to help his body recover.

"Is he awake?" Ilka wanted so much for the crisis to be over, but the doctor shook her head. They'd decided to keep him in the coma the rest of the week, after which they would reassess when to bring him out.

"He's stable," she said, and then assured Ilka that his condition hadn't worsened. "But his injuries are serious, and we can't know how they will affect his brain when he wakes up."

"Does that mean nothing will happen this week?" Ilka explained that she planned on being gone. "Maybe four days."

"That won't be a problem. And I promise, you will be contacted if there's any change in his condition."

Her voice turned serious. "But you should know that he'll need extensive testing and medical treatment going forward. And he'll also be in for an extended rehabilitation. Both from the injuries he sustained and from his time in a coma, which will weaken him. A physical therapist will be treating him daily, moving his arms and legs, but that doesn't maintain muscular strength."

Ilka nodded. She was enormously relieved that the doctor was thinking long-term, which surely meant they expected him to make it, she thought.

"And you have my number?" she asked, even though the office had already contacted her for money.

The doctor nodded. Ilka mentioned that Artie's bill had just been paid, and she asked her to please not hold back on any treatment.

Artie lay by the window. The first day in intensive care he'd had a private room, but now he was in with two other patients. One of them slept with his head leaning back and mouth open—it was abundantly clear he was still breathing. The other lay in bed reading. He watched her pass by, and when Ilka nodded at him, he immediately hid behind his book.

Someone had folded Artie's hands on top of his blanket, and his shaved head was covered with a bandage that also shielded from sight the tube in the back of his head.

Ilka stroked his cheek and cupped her hands gently around his face. It was so nice to feel the warmth of his skin. She ran her finger over his lip. He looked peaceful, and without thinking she leaned down and kissed him. She felt she was letting him down by leaving him behind all alone, and she was ashamed when the thought crossed her mind that his coma gave her a convenient excuse—that she was practically leaving with the hospital's approval.

She had no idea how she'd tell him that her father wasn't dead. That it had been a cover-up. But that was something her father would have to do, she decided.

Ilka kissed him one last time before walking out without a glance at the other two patients. She hurried to the elevator and took it down to the foyer, where she jogged over to the kiosk and bought water and a few sandwiches for the trip.

She glanced around the large area by the entrance, at the sofa groups on both sides of the information desk, but no one resembled the two men she'd left behind at the funeral home. A crowd was waiting for the next elevator up, and she squeezed through to a door beside the porters' elevator. Moments later she was in the basement, making her way past the empty hospital beds.

Outside, another hearse had pulled up and parked behind her. A young guy behind the wheel was talking on his phone. Ilka hesitated, but she decided she didn't have time to wait for him to leave. She walked to the rear door and opened it, then tapped on the coffin a few times and lifted the lid a crack. She tried to make it look as if she were arranging something inside while she spoke to Lydia.

"Are you okay in here?" The nun peered up at her, and for the first time Ilka wondered if she was getting enough oxygen. Should she even be in there?

"There's a guy parked right behind us, but I can drive off to the side and you can get up front."

But Lydia wanted to stay in the coffin. She rose on her elbows and unscrewed the lid of the water bottle Ilka handed her.

"Do you need to pee before we leave?"

Ilka glanced at the guy behind them. He was staring directly at her now, with no phone in sight.

Lydia shook her head and drank more water, then grabbed the sandwich and said she was ready to go.

Ilka ignored the guy and quickly shoved the lid in place, though this time she left it open a crack. She walked around the car and got behind the wheel.

Forty-five minutes had passed since they'd left the funeral home. She punched in their destination on the GPS and was informed it would take twenty-four hours to reach the tip of the Keys.

3

Seven hours later, somewhere in Kentucky, they ran into road work. Ilka had left the freeway to find a rest stop. They'd already paused once for Lydia to stretch her legs and go to the bathroom. She'd insisted on keeping out of sight while they drove. Ilka felt it was unnecessary, that they were far enough away from Racine, but Lydia had just looked at her blankly before crawling back in and getting settled.

They were behind a long line of cars at a temporary stoplight, waiting to cross a river bridge with one lane closed for repairs. The line of cars zipping past them from the other side was endless. Ilka felt sure many more of them were allowed to cross than from their line; whenever it was their turn, they advanced only a few short spurts before stopping. She noticed woods on the other side of the river they'd have to drive through to get back to the freeway.

Ilka rolled her window down and swore. They were wasting so much time. Her phone rang, and she checked the display. Her mother. She thought about answering but put the phone on mute and waited for the silent ringing to end. It still boggled her mind that her father was alive, and she couldn't imagine how her mother would react to the news. Telling her would have to wait until she'd found him.

She was still holding the phone when the line began moving again, and she straightened up in her seat, expecting to cross the bridge this time. But again, the line stopped, and she yelled out the window.

She googled Lydia Rogers and stared in astonishment at the number of articles that popped up. Had she spelled the name correctly? She checked; yes, she had. After enlarging the photos on her phone's screen, she saw it was the sister, with longer hair that fell gently onto her shoulders. In other photos her hair had been styled up, and her face was of course younger, but it wasn't difficult to recognize her. Ilka clicked on the first article and gaped at the headlines.

"The Baby-Butcher of San Antonio." Shocked, she scrolled down through the first row of headlines. "Baby-Butcher Wipes Out Own Family," "Rogers Behind Stolen Bodies of Babies," "Fleeing from the Police," "Drug Smuggling."

Ilka enlarged the text to find out what these gruesome acts had to do with the photos of Lydia. A moment later the drivers behind her began honking—cars in front of her were already crossing the bridge. She tossed her phone aside, and when she floored it the hearse lurched forward.

She stared in the rearview mirror at the shiny lid of the coffin. Her knuckles were white from gripping the wheel, she noticed. She badly needed cigarette smoke deep in her lungs; she craved the dizziness that would dull her growing nausea as her brain processed the short headlines.

The cars behind them had long since passed her when Ilka spied a rest stop ahead in the woods. She turned in and sat motionless for a long time, staring again in the mirror at the coffin while considering whether to call the police or get in the back and lock the coffin. Instead she reached in her bag and grabbed her pack of cigarettes, then pushed in the cigarette lighter—one of the advantages of driving an old car. She opened her window a crack, closed her eyes, and leaned back against the headrest, waiting for the tobacco to reach her nerves. A wave of dizziness finally rolled over her, and she savored the moment. After stubbing the cigarette out, she reached for her phone.

The events described by the headlines had taken place in Texas in 2005, and there was no doubt they referred to Lydia. Among other things, she had been accused of killing infants and stealing baby corpses from the morgue and out of graves, after which she filled them with drugs and smuggled them over the border from Mexico.

One of the photos was of a ten-month-old baby, Gina, one of Lydia Rogers's many victims. The baby was obviously dead in the picture, but she was dressed in red pajamas with small bears. She'd been taken from a morgue and was found by the police when a younger woman (not Rogers, the article stated) attempted to cross the border into Texas with the baby "asleep" in its baby buggy.

"Stuffed Babies" was how the journalist described them. Ilka was dumbfounded. There was also a photo of the house where Lydia was said to have lived before fleeing. Two gutted baby corpses had been found in her backyard. Two pouches for drugs.

Another headline, "The Brutal Baby-Butcher Strikes Again," was followed by a long article about how Lydia Rogers had shot her brother and his wife and their two daughters. She'd also shot several men who had tried to rescue the family. A manhunt was formed, which led the authorities to the two baby corpses. The article named Lydia as the head of the dead-baby smuggling ring that had been operating for several years.

Ilka was so absorbed in reading the articles that she didn't hear the car pulling into the rest stop. Nor did she hear the footsteps approaching. She was startled when a man flung her door open and dragged her out onto the ground, her phone flying through the air. Before she could react, he'd bound her hands behind her back with plastic cable ties that cut into her wrists.

A bandanna covered the lower half of the man's face.

As he was about to slide into the hearse, she kicked him and screamed, "What the hell are you doing!"

In a second he was all over her again. He opened her mouth with hands that stank of motor oil, ripped off his bandanna, and stuffed it into her mouth. She gasped for breath and tried to kick him again, but he grabbed her ankles and bound them with another thick cable tie. He began going through her coat pockets, and when he came up empty, he rolled her onto her back and pressed against her, hard.

"You have a wallet?" he hissed. He sounded younger than he looked.

Ilka shook her head.

He was wearing a denim jacket and torn jeans. He worked his hand into her pant pocket, which reminded her of the twenty thousand dollars in her bag, money she had taken from Raymond Fletcher's office the day before. The old man had originally given her the money to help her—a welcome-to-the-family gift, as he put it—but when she found out what an asshole he really was, she threw the money back into his face. After he was killed, though, she had entered his office and grabbed it out of his desk drawer. No one knew she'd returned the money to him, so no one would ever know she'd reclaimed it. The bills were in an envelope in her bag.

Was this guy somehow reading her mind? He jumped in the front seat of the hearse and started rummaging through her bag. He smiled in satisfaction as he pulled out the envelope, then he leaned across the seat and went through the glove compartment and side pockets of the doors, checked underneath the seats. Finally, he turned his attention to the coffin in back.

"Nnnnn! Nnnnn! Nnnnn!" Ilka struggled to yell through the handkerchief in her mouth, but by then he'd already opened the rear door. From the ground she watched as he prepared to pull the coffin out. Suddenly the lid opened, and Lydia sat up with her gun pointed at him. He stepped back in shock, and a second later she shot him first in one knee, then the other. He fell to the ground screaming in pain.

Ilka stared in disbelief as Lydia crawled out of the back, still holding the gun. The man looked up at her, silent now, his mouth contorted, his eyes wide with terror.

Lydia walked over and pulled the bandanna out of Ilka's mouth. The guy started screaming again.

"Shut up," she snarled, pointing the gun at his chest.

Ilka could barely breathe, but she managed to say, "He took my money." She explained about the twenty thousand dollars.

The man clamped his mouth shut as Lydia approached him. She found the bulging envelope in his denim jacket, then went through his pockets and fished out a black wallet, cell phone, and Ilka's cigarettes.

She pulled out a knife and cut Ilka free, then helped her to her feet. "Did he steal anything else?"

Ilka shook her head and took the money, all the while watching Lydia out of the corner of her eye. Nothing about this woman resembled the nun she'd known from the funeral home, and Ilka was still so shocked by what she'd read that she couldn't look her in the eye. Lydia made no attempt to hide the gun; on the contrary, she wielded it as if she might start shooting again at any moment.

Ilka rubbed her wrists as Lydia looked around inside the hearse.

"Where's my bag?"

The guy was beginning to moan again, loudly, as he crawled toward his car. He left a trail of blood behind him.

Ilka didn't understand. "What bag?"

"The one I packed, my travel bag."

"I didn't load any bag," Ilka said. She thought a moment, then she remembered the dark-blue bag with the leather handle. "It must still be in the garage."

"You can't be serious." For a moment Lydia looked like herself again. "You didn't bring it along?"

Ilka shook her head. "No—it must be in the garage," she repeated.

"Take me back to the funeral home." Now Lydia was sneering at Ilka. Her eyes were black, and she pushed the barrel of the gun against Ilka, who staggered back against the hearse. "Now!"

Lydia's face was contorted with rage. The gunshots from a few minutes earlier were still ringing in Ilka's ears, and she knew she should follow the woman's orders, but she shook her head.

"No." She kept shaking her head. "I won't. If you want to go back to Racine, you're on your own."

The image of Lydia from the newspaper articles was frozen in Ilka's mind. She wanted nothing more than to tuck her tail between her legs and run.

"Give me the keys." Lydia held out her hand and stepped close to her, so close that they were touching.

Ilka's head began spinning; Lydia was short, but her fury made her seem ten feet tall. She glared up at Ilka with a look on her face she'd never shown as a nun.

Ilka caught herself breathing in short spurts, and she straightened up. She wasn't about to let Lydia see how frightened she was. "No," she said, as calmly as she could. "Go ahead, shoot me. I just want to go down and find my father, I don't want to get mixed up in this."

They stood for a moment, staring at each other.

"I hope for your sake I never see you again," Lydia spat.

She's going to shoot me after all, Ilka thought. But Lydia turned on her heel and walked over to the man at the car. Ilka slumped against the hearse, shaken but alive. She didn't hear what Lydia said when she bent over the man. He shook his head and said something as he started to hand her his car keys, but the woman stood up and walked away. Back in the direction they'd come from.

Ilka slowly got to her feet when Lydia disappeared behind the trees. Her legs were shaking, which annoyed her. She clasped her hands tightly in front of her.

"Who the hell was that?" The man was leaning against the rear tire of his car now, crying. All of his tough-guy act was gone, and he looked like a boy. A big one, but still just a boy.

"She's a nun." She looked at his bleeding knees. The shots had been bull's-eyes, both of them. She walked over to the open coffin, took out the lining, and tossed it over to him along with his wallet and phone.

"She was going to steal my car," he said, whining now. "She just about shot me, again. But I got a flat. That's why I pulled in. If I wouldn't have gotten that flat, I'd never have run into you." He made it sound as if it were all Ilka's fault.

She had no pity for him. "You shouldn't have robbed me."

That angered him. "I needed the money. For a new tire. I can't get to work without my car, and they'll fire me!"

"Call nine-one-one, and get something wrapped around your knees."

She pushed the coffin back into place. She felt his eyes on her back as she walked around the hearse and got in, but he kept his mouth shut. She glanced in the rearview mirror; he was wrapping strips of material around one of his knees.

She closed her eyes a moment and leaned her head back. Her phone beeped: a text from her mother. Ilka felt like calling her, she needed a shoulder to cry on, but she knew the moment she heard her mother's voice, it would all come out. And that wouldn't be good for either of them.

How's the weather in Racine? Is it cold? her mother wrote.

No, the weather's been great, and it's lighter than it is back home right now. She sent a sun and a kiss, then she started the car and checked the side mirror, in the direction Lydia had disappeared.

The man with the bleeding knees was still sitting on the ground when she pulled out. Darkness was falling, and Key West still lay far away.

4

The next morning, after sleeping five hours, Ilka tossed the key card into the motel's checkout box beside the reception door. She'd paid for the room in advance, so the night manager couldn't have cared less when she left, as long as she dropped the card off. And when she had asked if she would be able to buy a cup of coffee early the next morning, he flashed her an indulgent look and said she couldn't buy a cup of coffee there at any time. The motel offered no service, only rooms.

It had been dark yesterday evening when she'd pulled in, and what she'd seen of Georgia mostly were the reflectors on the road's center line and the lights of Atlanta as she passed by. At first Ilka had planned on driving to Key West in one stretch, thinking she could handle twenty-four hours behind the wheel with a few breaks along the way. But that was before she'd read about the Baby-Butcher from San Antonio, before she'd witnessed Lydia rising up in the coffin and shooting out the robber's kneecaps. After collapsing on the motel bed, fully clothed, she'd tried once more to pretend that none of what had happened concerned her. Unlike the day before, she'd almost succeeded. The day's events had seemed so implausible that part of her brain refused to accept them.

It took a few moments to get the hearse started in the damp morning air. It wasn't nearly as cold here as in Racine, but the dew lay heavy on the hood. The engine wasn't much for waking up.

As she drove out, she was surprised to notice that the parking lot was almost full. If she hadn't begun nodding off at the wheel last night, she'd never have chosen this dreary little motel. Again, she thought about telling the police that Lydia Rogers was likely headed for the funeral home in Racine. But something held her back. Not loyalty to the woman, definitely not, because Ilka hadn't the slightest idea who she really was. But if she called the police, Ilka would be delayed even more; the cops would want to hear what she knew about the wanted woman.

She had about thirteen hours of driving ahead of her, if she drove nonstop and managed to avoid any rush-hour traffic. Which, she realized, was seldom the case. She needed a cup of coffee, but instead she rolled the window down and lit a cigarette. She thought about

Artie. Did he know what Lydia had done? No way. She inhaled and focused on the six lanes of the interstate.

All morning long, chains of enormous semis boxed her in. The old hearse didn't have enough horsepower to slip past them, so she resigned herself to the situation. Even though respect for the transport of the deceased wasn't the same nowadays as it had been, the trucks gave her room when several hours later, with her heart practically in her throat, she weaved her way through three lanes and exited onto Florida's Turnpike. She set course for Miami.

It was hot in the car. Ilka dangled her arm out the window. She had been expecting something else, something better from the Keys. She'd imagined a long stretch of surfer paradise with exotic, charming restaurants, but Key Largo wasn't much more than old stores spread out along the highway and a single trailer park. Plus, hotels. Her disappointment lingered until she finally could see water on both sides. Then, for a moment, she was spellbound by the view opening up in front of her.

She still had over a hundred miles to go, but the uneasiness she'd felt since leaving Georgia early that morning was growing. She was nervous, to say the least, about meeting her father. And with every sunny bridge she crossed, it got worse. The magnificent view seemed to fade into the background, until she hardly even noticed the historic Seven Mile Bridge, standing like some old ruins, or the fishermen lining the bridges with their extended poles and large buckets, or the small roadside shacks selling clam chowder and renting out boats.

She was out of cigarettes when she finally pulled into Key West. She felt like absolute hell. What if her father wouldn't have anything to do with her, or if he'd forgotten her? What if he was angry about her arriving out of the blue? What if he threw her out?

While making her way through the long string of islands, she had come to realize that what she most feared was rejection. But she'd told herself that she had at least as much right to walk away from him, if she didn't care for the person he'd become.

And she was angry too. Hugely angry, she kept telling herself out loud, hoping that the feeling would shoo away some of her anxiety. She tried to convince herself that she was the one in control. That she was there to give him a thorough cussing-out, that it didn't matter how he reacted. Thirty-three years was a long time, but he was still a father who had abandoned his daughter, and he owed her an explanation. So said the voice in her head. An explanation of what actually happened back then, as well as what the hell he had been thinking this time, disappearing again and dragging her back into his life. She did feel a sense of relief, though, at the prospect of getting some answers to what had happened since she arrived in Racine.

Many of the houses lining both sides of the street resembled majestic old Southern homes. Traffic was now so heavy that Ilka assumed she was close to downtown. She had no idea how to find Artie's house, so when she noticed a man tying a short surfboard to the back of a scooter, she parked and leaned across the seat.

"Main Street?" she called out.

He walked over to the hearse and eyed her T-shirt and jeans, then he raised his eyebrows at the sight of the coffin.

She ignored his unspoken question. "I'm looking for a gallery. Or at least a place that used to be a gallery."

"Most of the galleries are down on Duval Street." He pointed straight ahead. "Just keep going into town, you can't miss it. It's where all the tourists hang out."

Ilka thanked him and took off. It had been a long time since she'd seen so many motorcycles on a town's streets. There was a vacation atmosphere in the way people walked around, most of them wearing shorts; Artie's Hawaiian shirts would fit in perfectly here. When Ilka reached Duval Street, she was momentarily astonished by the crowds of people on the sidewalks, all the souvenir shops and bars, with a gallery on every street corner, literally. And not a parking space in sight.

The hearse was proving much too large as she crept down the street, desperately looking for anywhere to park. She finally found a space, but only after she'd driven far out from the crowded part of town. It felt somehow rude, disrespectful even, to leave behind a coffin in a tourist parking space, but she decided it would be almost as bad on a residential street, where BED-AND-

BREAKFAST signs had been set out in front of most of the beautiful wooden houses.

She decided to leave her travel bag in the car, even though she was very much aware of having slept in the clothes she was wearing, and that it had been a while since her last shower. It wasn't exactly how she'd imagined she would look when she and her father met. She found a pack of wet wipes in the glove compartment, and pulled one out to swipe her face and throat. They weren't particularly fresh, but she felt it was better than nothing. She took off in the direction of Duval, pushing herself to walk fast so she wouldn't have time for second thoughts.

Once she was out on the street, Ilka heard "Born to Be Wild" booming from speakers inside a bar. She knew she was stalling when she walked over to a food stand and ordered a hot dog and cola, but she couldn't think straight until she ate something. She also needed to rinse the taste of tobacco out of her mouth. Maybe she ought to go back for her bag and find a hotel room anyway, then start out fresh and clean in the morning to find her father.

She paid and chugged half the cola. She ate the hot dog on the way. It amazed her what was being sold as art on Duval Street; there were practically no limits. The one thing the displays in the gallery windows had in common was the artists' enthusiasm for wild colors. Yellow, green, blue, and red were the favorites, preferably a combination of them all. There were paintings on coconuts and on tiny wooden surfboards, paintings of fish, flamingos, turtles.

She finished the hot dog and decided to walk over to Art Gone Wild and ask if anyone knew a gallery formerly known as Artie the Artist, but before she could toss her ketchup-smeared napkins into a trash can, she saw the sign.

Across the street stood a wooden house painted turquoise, with a red roof and a driveway almost hidden between palm trees. A sign hung on the front above the plate-glass window: ARTIE THE ARTIST, carved into weathered wood. It looked as if it had been hanging there forever. A gate closed off the driveway, and another sign in the window informed her that the gallery was open by appointment only.

Ilka walked over and peeked in the window. She recognized the style from the work she'd seen in Artie's house. A lamp base carved from wood, intricately carved frames, and elegant wooden animals, as if a Scandinavian hand had guided the design. Which set them apart from everything else in the surrounding shops. The colors in Artie's gallery were muted too.

She stared a long time before stepping over to the door, which of course was locked. The sign said as much. She walked to the gate, opened it, and yelled out, "Hello!"

She called out once more before walking around the house. A hammock was tied between two trees, and a boy's bicycle lay on the ground. A clothesline had been strung at the far end of the backyard; dresses and several sets of underwear, panties, and bras hung from it, along with striped boys' pajamas and a light-blue T-shirt. Ilka leaned against the house. The noise from the bars and the crowds on the street faded out. She gazed at a soccer ball and a skateboard lying beside the house. Lives were being led here that she knew nothing about. Finally, she steeled herself and walked to the door. A table and four chairs stood in the middle of a small patio, and beside the wall was a big electric grill, though not as big as the one at Artie's house on Lake Michigan.

She knocked on the back door; no answer. She knocked harder. At last she sank down onto the back step. The late-afternoon sun wasn't nearly as warm as before, and Ilka rubbed her bare arms. She felt empty. And alone. There was no sign of her father, only of this woman with a child who seemed to be living in Artie's house.

She thought about her father. What if he suddenly walked around the corner, what would she say? She no longer knew. The air had gone out of her balloon now that there was no sign of him here. She'd been naïve to believe Lydia, especially now that Ilka knew the woman had reasons aplenty to protect herself—she would have sent Ilka practically anywhere if it could help her vanish.

But Lydia had also wanted to go to Key West, she recalled. Though again, it could have been something she'd said just so Ilka would take her along. She might have run off anyway, once they were far enough away from the men hunting her.

Ilka was surprised how shaken she was at seeing a woman's clothes on the line. She'd never considered that Artie might have a life she knew nothing about, or that he might know a boy with a skateboard, who let his bike fall to the ground.

She imagined Artie's face, the line running down along his cheek, and suddenly she felt tender, bruised inside. She glanced around the empty patio and realized how keyed up she'd been about seeing her father, and how little she now believed it would ever happen. She stood up and walked away.

After closing the gate behind her, she headed farther into town. More people were milling around, standing in flocks listening to music or checking menus. Couples walked along, their arms around each other; older couples held hands. Everyone was with somebody, in the middle of a dream vacation. Ilka stood off to the edge on the sidewalk to let a small family get by. Suddenly all she could see were kisses and smiles from people who belonged together. People hugging; a man carrying his wife's beach bag. She belonged nowhere, and her loneliness was suffocating as she strolled down Duval Street. She knew she would never fit into this picture. It struck her that she would always feel alone, always a bit adrift.

At first, she thought about asking around in the bars and restaurants, if anyone had ever seen her father or possibly knew of him, but she decided against it. She turned down a side street with no idea of what she was looking for.

A few houses down she noticed a dimly lit bar with no loud rock music or tourists. Three or four roosters strutted around in the dusty entryway. A man, late middle-aged maybe, stood behind the bar and greeted her when she walked in. The place was nearly deserted. She ordered a beer, then laid two one-hundred-dollar bills on the bar and asked for change to play the slot machine beside the door. All she wanted was to forget herself, head out on some back road accompanied by John Denver's "Country Roads," the song playing in the bar.

The bartender nodded and picked up the bills. He pointed at the row of beer taps and asked which one, and if she wanted a small or large.

"Large. And it doesn't matter, choose one for me."

He handed her a small stack of tens. The machine also took twenties, he said.

"Do you sell cigarettes here?"

He shook his head, but he reached under the bar, brought out a pack, and offered her one. A man at the end of the bar was eyeing her, but she ignored him. She grabbed her beer and the money and walked over to the machine.

After feeding it thirty dollars she took a long swig. It had been quite a while since she'd drunk beer, and she closed her eyes for a moment while the bitter taste spread inside her mouth. She took another drink, then she laid the glass aside and turned to the one-armed bandit. Its arm had been amputated and replaced by several large buttons. Though it wasn't the same, she didn't really care. She began playing.

Ilka nodded and held out her glass when the bartender came over and asked if she wanted another one. The cigarette he'd given her was on the windowsill, and he handed her a lighter and brought over an ashtray.

"Is it okay to smoke inside?" she asked, her eyes still glued to the colored fruit and crowns whirling in front of her.

"Not really." He flicked the lighter. "But once in a while I make an exception. Where are you from?"

"Denmark."

She sensed somehow that he nodded.

"I thought so," he said.

Ilka turned to him. "What do you mean?"

"You two look like each other. Tall, those blue eyes. A person wouldn't think you're Viking stock, though, you're both too skinny."

"Us two? Who are you talking about?"

"You look like that Dane who got hurt." He held his hand up high to indicate they both were very tall.

She set her glass down. "What Dane?"

"This old guy who showed up here several months ago. I sure don't mean to offend you, it's just that you both have this way about you."

"Do you know him?"

The bartender nodded and said that at first, he hadn't

known the man had come from Denmark. "I found out when he tried to explain that crazy game they have going. Or maybe it's more like a contest, I never really did catch on. He asked if they could do it here, he thought it would be good for my business. I told him I didn't want to get involved in that sort of thing, stupid me. People love it, and he was right, it brings in the customers."

Ilka was standing now. "Do you know where he is?"

"Who's asking?"

"I think the man is my father."

He nudged the ashtray and moved her glass before sitting down in the windowsill. "Are you the one who handles the racehorses, or the one who takes care of his wife in the wheelchair?"

Ilka glanced out the window a moment then shook her head. "Neither one. I'm his daughter from Denmark."

The man raised his eyebrows. "So you came all the way from Denmark to visit him?"

Ilka nodded. "How is he?"

"Now that he's got a cane and gets around by himself, he's doing better. He's a social type of guy, always a crowd of people around him. At first, he mostly stayed at home, though. When he asked if he could use my patio, he said he needed a few hours' nap every afternoon. I didn't want to pry too much. It sounded like he hurt his head, maybe a bad concussion. But there's nothing wrong with his spirits, and he sure has lit a fire under the seniors down here."

He laughed and shook his head. "They're probably getting after it right now."

"Getting after it?"

"I heard them yelling a little while ago. They meet over behind Mudville. It's a bar a little ways down the street."

He nodded to the side.

She still had beer in her glass and money in the machine when she stood up and walked out to find her father.

5

Ilka saw the sign when she stepped out on the sidewalk. Mudville was down where the homes with the broad wooden porches were set back from the street, like small oases, amid palms, green lawns, and densely crowned trees. It all looked lush, even though winter was just around the corner.

A bell rang somewhere, followed by loud cheering, but she couldn't see anyone close by. Finally, she realized the noise was coming from the bar. It was dim and empty when she stepped in, so she walked to the open back door, where a broad-shouldered man stood with his back to her.

She excused herself and squeezed past him. A group of old men were gathered around a low fence, jawing excitedly among themselves as a voice began counting down. The bell rang again. A new game was starting up.

Ilka stepped forward and peeked in between and over the shoulders of the men circling the fence. Small numbered squares had been drawn on the cement. The only differences from the first time she'd seen a chicken-shitting contest was that there were fewer squares here, and they were drawn with chalk instead of paint. They were also betting on a rooster, not a hen. Ilka hadn't known before that roosters held some sort of special significance in Key West, but she'd caught on after seeing figures of them everywhere.

She recognized her father at first glance. He was the one ringing the bell, leaning forward as he sat on a wooden box. He wore a white shirt open at the collar, and his straw hat shaded part of his tanned face, but she knew it was him. Not so much because of his face, but everything about him. Ilka reached back and supported herself against the doorframe. He was following the action enthusiastically as a new rooster was lowered into the circle. Unlike a horse race, the betting was on the squares and not the animal.

Her father leaned his head back and laughed at something one of the men said. For a second their eyes met, but he didn't react. He held a small glass and pointed at the rooster in the circle while the babble around him continued. Another guy walked around taking the bettors' money, jotting down on a notepad which squares were being played. The man who had been standing at the door earlier came out with a new round of refreshments.

Ilka had first seen this bizarre contest a few years after she'd met her late husband, Flemming. They had planned to bicycle around the island of Bornholm, and had ridden from where the ferry docked in Rønne to the town of Svaneke about twenty miles to the east, but that's as far as they got. It had been so laid-back and fun, so *hyggeligt*, that they stayed there the entire week. In a small square in the middle of town, people crowded around to watch the hens shit; it had been right up Flemming's alley, at least until he saw that Ilka had put money on thirty of the one hundred squares.

He was scared she was having a relapse, even though she insisted she wasn't. She kept trying to convince him, but he didn't buy it. He claimed she couldn't control her addiction. So she quit every form of gambling, just as she steered away from alcohol. Not that she'd ever drunk very much, but she knew that after downing a few, not only could she not stop drinking, but her decision-making abilities took a hit. Which meant that then she couldn't stop gambling either.

She called over the man holding the notepad and was told that each square cost five dollars. She kept an eye on her father as she handed him ten dollars and told him she wanted squares number two and twenty-three. One was on the edge, the other right in the middle.

She felt totally adrift, overwhelmed, and frightened. Her father's hair, visible from underneath his straw hat, had turned white, but she recognized the shape of his face. He seemed exuberant, alive. He was sitting practically right in front of her, and she kept staring at his hands and sinewy arms. He wore a gold ring on his right hand and held his glass close to the rim.

Memories began popping up. She'd been five, maybe six, and he and her mother had invited friends over for dinner. Ilka had been allowed to take her plate into her room so she didn't need to sit and listen to the grown-ups talk. But after the table was cleared and her mother made coffee, she went into the living room, nestled on the sofa under a blanket, and fell asleep to the sound of their voices. Before nodding off she'd watched her father at the end of the table, holding his glass exactly the same way as he did now. She'd completely forgotten those evenings, the cigarette smoke, the wine, the voices rising in their Brønshøj home. Her mother's laughter.

She felt someone's eyes on her, and she looked over at the man standing just behind her father. He'd been watching her since she arrived, and now he leaned over to him and pointed her out.

The moment he looked up at her, Ilka instinctively wanted to pull back. She wished she'd had more time to study him, to consign to memory everything about him she hadn't managed to catch before he left them.

A shock wave swept through her from head to toe, and more than anything she wanted to delay meeting him, but she couldn't move. Several of the men standing around now glanced at her, and she straightened up a bit when her father took off his hat and wiped his brow, staring at her all the while. At first his expression was open and friendly, but soon it became more intense. He held his hat in both hands and studied her thoroughly.

Someone called out that the rooster had shit in square number two, and the bell rang.

Ilka didn't move a muscle, even though the men began clapping and yelling, as if she personally had done the deed on square number two. She couldn't hear her father's voice in all the noise, but she saw his mouth forming her name. He rose from the wooden box a bit feebly and reached out for his cane, which he'd leaned against the fence. Ilka's throat clogged up; she felt close to sobbing.

The men were too focused on catching another rooster and getting ready for the next round to notice him wobbling on his feet. Ilka quickly elbowed her way through the crowd and grabbed his arm to keep him from falling.

The man holding the notebook called out behind her, "You won forty-five dollars."

"Is it really you?" her father whispered. Ilka could barely hear him, but she immediately recognized his voice, even though she hadn't heard it since she was a little girl.

"When I saw you standing over there, this feeling hit me; it's what I always feel when I see somebody I think is you. If you only knew how many times I've believed it was you."

Ilka gripped his arm, and they walked away from all the noise.

Her father turned to look at her face. He must have noticed her skepticism, Ilka thought, because he said no more. After all, he was the one who'd left. The one who hadn't answered her letters, even though she now knew he'd received them. He'd even written letters meant for her, but they'd never been sent. Raymond Fletcher had made sure of that. Ilka had found them in her father's desk drawer.

She knew exactly what he was talking about—that feeling! All the times she'd glimpsed someone and mistaken him for her father.

He reached up and cupped her cheeks with his hands; she'd done the exact same thing, the exact same way, in the hospital with Artie.

Another rooster had crapped, but all the yelling faded out as her memories took over. When she was young, she'd always felt safe when he'd held her face that way.

They stood silently. The feel of his hands made her remember how he used to pull her into him. His eyes were moist, and he was about to say something, but instead he shook his head weakly and slowly lowered his hands.

Ilka's throat began aching; it was pain from missing him her entire life.

"You look like your mother," he whispered, clearly overwhelmed. He reached out for her again, only to let his hand fall before touching her. "I can't believe it's you."

"How are you?" It was the only thing Ilka could think of to say.

He was looking at her now as if he was afraid she would disappear if he took his eyes off her. He nodded down at his cane and said he'd seen better days.

"How did you find me?" His voice was barely above a whisper, as if he still could hardly believe it really was her.

"Sister Eileen told me where you were." She noticed all the wrinkles around his nose when he took off his glasses and blinked rapidly. "And I came down here to find you."

Again they fell silent as they looked each other over. The noise behind them was part of a different world.

"I was thinking it was about time to go back," he said.

"Back? But you can't go back, you're dead!"

"Dead! What in the world do you mean?"

His voice was stronger now. She noticed that his face had gone slack, a serious look in his eyes.

"I don't blame you one bit if you gave up on me a long time ago," he said. "And I understand if I've been dead to you for many years. I want to explain." He took off his hat; the mild breeze rustled his thin white hair. "And to apologize."

He was tall, around six-four. Taller than she was, she noted as she took a step back, away from the look in his eyes telling her he wanted to wipe out all the years gone by with an apology.

"I'm sure my mother would appreciate your explanation." She turned and headed for the bar. Suddenly she needed some air, some space to catch up with the fact that he really was right there in front of her.

He followed her. "How is your mother?"

"Okay, as far as I know. But I haven't seen her since being called over here to take over your funeral home business."

He'd begun knocking the sandy soil off his cane, but now he looked up. "What do you mean?"

Ilka turned back to him. Why was he pretending he didn't have the slightest idea what had brought her to the States? "Haven't you been in contact with Sister Eileen?"

The bartender came over and asked what they wanted to drink. Ilka shook her head and said they were about to leave.

"Yes, of course. We talk once a week."

"But didn't she tell you I've been in Racine?"

Her father hesitated, as if he was trying to understand where she was going with this. Finally, he shook his head. "If I'd known that, I would've come home."

When he reached out for her again, she stepped back. She was about to yell at him, cuss him out for all the problems he and his funeral home had caused her, but she caught herself. "Haven't you heard about Artie being in the hospital either?"

His arm fell as he slowly shook his head. "Why? Is it serious?"

Something in her face might have given it away, because he obviously was preparing himself for the worst. She nodded slowly. "Yes. It's serious."

They sat down at a table just inside the door. She explained that Artie had hovered between life and death, but now his condition was stable, according to the doctors. "He hasn't regained consciousness yet," she added.

Her father folded his hands in front of him, his eyes closed. He was clearly in pain, and Ilka feared he was about to cry, but he straightened up and gazed at her. "What happened?"

He stretched his fingers out on the table, as if he needed support to hold himself up.

"He was assaulted. And Sister Eileen thinks it's the men looking for her who did it."

"She didn't tell me about this."

Ilka studied his face. "It sounds like there's quite a bit she hasn't told you." She wondered how much of the sister's past he knew about.

"How long have you been in Racine?"

She stared at him. "But...I came a few weeks after you were declared dead."

Now it was him staring at her; it was obvious he was confused.

"Everybody thinks you're dead," she said. "Even Artie."

Her father shook his head a moment before struggling to get to his feet. "Let's walk home. You have to tell me what's happened."

He grabbed his cane and reached out for her arm, then headed for the door.

6

Artie was attacked a few days ago." As they walked, she described how she'd found him, and she tried to give her father a complete account of what the doctors had said. When she told him the chances the doctors had given Artie, and that they'd put him in an induced coma, he stopped and turned to her. All the life she'd seen in his face earlier had vanished.

"But it can't be the same one," he said, his voice low again. Ilka had to lean in to hear him. "The man who came after Sister Eileen that night is dead."

He looked away.

"Dead?"

"Sister Eileen shot him. That's how she saved my life."

Ilka had a firm hold on his arm. She gave him a moment before starting again. Neither of them spoke

as they slowly approached the milling crowd on Duval
Street.

He was limping, and he seemed tired, but his voice
picked up as he told her about the night Javi Rodriguez
found the nun.

"It was almost midnight, I'd just gone to bed when I
heard her scream. At first, I thought it was someone out
on the street, but then I spotted them through my upstairs
window. He'd dragged her out of her apartment and was
hauling her over to the car. I ran down for the baseball
bat I keep in my office."

He closed his eyes a moment. "I thought someone had
broken into the apartment to rob her. I doubt he suspected anyone was in the funeral home, and either he
didn't hear me, or else he just let me get close before he
turned around. He held a rifle under one arm and was
towing Sister Eileen with the other. He'd wrapped a thin
nylon cord around her throat, I saw. She was fighting
him, but he was a lot bigger. He swung at me with the
rifle, but it must have surprised him I was so quick, because I managed to smack him in the head with the bat.
He fell, and I hit him again, but then he rolled away and
got to his feet."

Every step seemed to be an effort for her father, so she
helped him as best she could. "What did he look like?"

He described the man as strong, stocky, and completely unaffected by being clobbered by a bat.

She nodded. "So it *was* his brothers who attacked
Artie. What happened then?"

"He hit me with the rifle stock. I remember getting hit the first time, and I remember falling, but then I halfway blacked out. I heard shots; at first I thought he'd shot Sister Eileen. I tried to pull myself up, but there was no way—I might not even have been fully conscious, not really. I lost all sense of time, but when I came to, he was lying there a few feet away, under a blanket. We'd killed him."

"Sister Eileen killed him, you mean."

Her father shook his head. "We both did."

They stopped. He gazed at her a few moments.

"She'd never told me much about her past. But I've always known she was putting something behind her when she came to me. And that night she finally told me about what happened down in Texas. I'm the one who said we should keep the police out of it. She may be the one who pulled the trigger, but I'm just as guilty. If we'd called the police, they would have found out who she was. And she would have spent the rest of her days on death row. She saved my life. Javi Rodriguez would have killed me without batting an eye to get hold of her."

Ilka could barely grasp that her father and Sister Eileen had killed a man. She listened in near-disbelief as he described getting rid of the body.

"I wasn't much help, but Sister Eil—Lydia—is a lot stronger than you'd think. She managed to stuff him into the coffin, and she also drove his car out of the parking lot. But then his brother showed up before she could leave with the coffin. She was wearing her nun's habit, and she got out to talk to him. Apparently Javi hadn't told him about her disguise, and he didn't recognize her, he just asked about his brother."

Which, Ilka remembered, was also what had happened when the other Rodriguez brother showed up at the funeral home during a memorial service.

"It turned out that Javi had sent him a message, telling him he'd found Lydia Rogers, and she was staying at the funeral home. I was lying in bed upstairs, in bad shape after the attack, but I heard the sister say it had to be some misunderstanding. That we didn't know any Lydia Rogers. And that I hadn't even been around lately, that I was at some coffin showcase in Massachusetts. It sounded like the man believed her, but after he left she said I had to get out of there. She was sure they'd be back looking for her, and it was way too dangerous for me."

"But what about your family? They think you're dead! They're grieving for you. *We're* grieving for you."

He held the gate open for her, and Ilka ducked to avoid the palm leaves.

"No one is proud of a man in rehab, but they know I'll be getting out," he said.

"Rehab?" She looked questioningly at him.

"I've been fighting a gambling addiction since I left Denmark. A vice, you could say."

Ilka closed the gate behind her. "I know."

"After I left Racine, Sister Eileen told my family I'd checked into a clinic in North Carolina. I've been in treatment there before, so we thought it would sound plausible. That way I could be gone for three months without my family starting to wonder about not hearing from me. I don't know how much you know about that kind of clinic, but once I was in one where you have a contact person outside the family, and that person is the only connection you have to the outside world. And my contact person was Sister Eileen."

"But you didn't go to that clinic!"

"No, but it was the only explanation we could think of, so I left without telling the family what had happened. And really, I did it to protect them."

Ilka gaped at him. "They haven't heard a word from Sister Eileen in all the time you've been gone."

He didn't seem to hear her. "Have you met my wife, Mary Ann?"

Ilka nodded.

"It hasn't always been easy, so she's in on this, the story that I left to go through rehab, and that Artie is taking care of the business while I'm gone."

They were in the backyard now; the bicycle still lay on the ground and the clothes still hung on the line.

Ilka sank down into one of the lawn chairs. "You really don't have a clue."

7

Her father didn't say a single word while Ilka spoke. She handed him her cell phone and showed him the articles about "the Baby-Butcher of San Antonio" while explaining how Lydia Rogers had stolen babies and stuffed them with drugs. How dead infants had been dug up from their graves or taken from crematoria and morgues. Clearly this wasn't what Lydia had told him that night about her past.

For a long time, he sat in silence with the phone in his hands, staring at the screen.

"Babies," she said, "taken across the border from Mexico by a couple, babies stuffed with drugs. They would put the dead baby in a stroller or baby sling and pretend it was asleep. They covered its face with a sun hat and hoped the customs agents and border police wouldn't try to wake it up. The nun you've been employing, the one living at your funeral home—among other things, she killed her own brother and sister-in-law and their two daughters."

Without a word he handed the phone back to her. Ilka leaned toward him.

"She shot them. And before she and I split up, she pointed an automatic weapon right into my chest. You can't trust the woman, and she hasn't enrolled you in any clinic. She's written you out of your life."

On her phone, Ilka showed her father his obituary from the *Journal Times*, the paper covering Racine and a large portion of Wisconsin. He rested his elbows on the table as he read his own obituary, then sat for several minutes staring into space.

"So my wife thinks I'm dead?" he finally said. "She doesn't know I'm coming back home?"

Ilka shook her head. "Mary Ann put your urn on the fireplace mantel after the memorial service for you."

He slumped in the chair; Ilka could see that the extent of Sister Eileen's lies was sinking in. She decided it wasn't a good time to tell him his wife was in jail after confessing to shooting her father. That would have to wait.

She straightened up when she heard voices out by the gate. Her father handed her phone back to her and glanced over at the sidewalk in the yard.

"I'd better get dinner started," he said. He wobbled a bit as he got to his feet, then he walked over to the gas grill and opened it. His movements were slow and shaky; he was possibly in shock from everything he'd been told. He began cleaning the iron grate while staring straight ahead at the wall. Ilka wanted to join him and put her arm around his shoulders, but she stayed in her chair instead and watched, trying to get used to the sight of him. To commit to memory the way he moved and leaned over the grill.

A blond-haired boy came around the corner of the house and stopped on a dime when he noticed Ilka. A dark-haired lady holding two grocery bags followed. She was younger and quite a bit shorter than Ilka.

Her father turned slowly with steel brush in hand and greeted them. He introduced Ilka and explained that she was his oldest daughter. "She lives in Denmark, but she just arrived from Racine. She's going to have dinner with us."

A guarded look flickered over the woman's face, and the boy walked over and stood behind her father.

The woman hesitated, then approached Ilka and held her hand out. "Fernanda." She glanced at Ilka's father, but he had nothing more to add.

"Nice to meet you," Ilka said. She had no idea how this woman fit into her father's life, though he acted as if she belonged there. The woman had pinned up her thick black hair. Even though her dress was simple, she radiated a femininity Ilka would never possess.

"What's your boy's name?" Ilka asked.

"Ethan."

The boy looked up at her from under a heavy curtain

of hair drooping over his forehead. Ilka smiled at him
to break the ice. Her father had turned away from them,
and the woman stood motionless with the two bags dangling from her arm.

"Can I help with anything?" Ilka glanced at the bags.

"No thank you," Fernanda replied quickly. "Would
you like something to drink?"

She headed for the door and nodded for the boy to follow.

"The grill's ready in five minutes," her father said.
"Do you want me to help with the meat?"

Ilka could see he was tired. She offered to help in the
kitchen, but Fernanda said the meat had already mari-
nated in barbecue sauce and was almost ready.

After she and Ethan went inside, he turned to Ilka and
explained that Fernanda had worked for Lydia's brother
and sister-in-law in Texas. "They came to Racine with
Lydia twelve years ago. At first, she hid them in her
apartment, but Artie found out."

"So Fernanda worked for the family Lydia shot?"

Her father ignored her question and said that initially,
he'd thought the boy was Lydia's son. "Artie and I figured she was running from a man who mistreated them.
Ethan was a baby back then, no more than three months
old. But it turned out he was her nephew, and that Fernanda was his nanny. Now she's his mother."

They ate most of the meal in silence. Several times Ilka
tried to start a conversation, but her father said very lit-

tle. Fernanda told Ilka she baked key lime pies in a small bakery close to where the cruise ships docked, and Ethan went to school in town.

"Tell her about how you help Theodor during the weekends," Fernanda said to the boy, but all he did was look up bashfully at Ilka.

"Ethan picks up fallen palm leaves for an artist in town. The man weaves baskets and hats for tourists." Even though Fernanda made the greatest effort to keep a conversation going, Ilka couldn't establish eye contact with her. Every time she tried, the woman looked away.

"Does Lydia know they're living here?" Ilka asked her father after they'd cleared the table and Fernanda and Ethan had gone inside. He sat with a cigar and a cup of coffee, exactly the way she remembered him sitting in the living room while her mother washed dishes in the kitchen.

He nodded and said he thought Lydia sent them money to help make ends meet. "A token of appreciation to Fernanda for taking the boy." He leaned forward and knocked the ashes on his cigar into a colorful ceramic ashtray.

Ilka tried to clear her head. Maybe it was the insecure look on the boy's face, or how the woman's eyes kept darting around, but for whatever reason she felt like they were hiding something. "Why in the world did they leave with Lydia, when she killed the boy's family? Did she force them to go along?"

Again, her father didn't answer. The sun had gone

down, but he still wore his straw hat. Ilka was getting annoyed at how he just sat there, pretending everything was marvelous.

"If Fernanda was the family's nanny, and they went along with Lydia—it doesn't make sense." All the questions in her head seemed jumbled up. "One of the articles said the couple's son was never found; he wasn't in the house with the rest of his family. The police thought she might have killed him too and used the body to smuggle more drugs. We have to contact them and tell them the boy's here."

Her father shook his head. "You can't call the police. Ethan has a good life down here, he's safe and has lots of friends. He and Fernanda are doing fine. Don't let what happened in San Antonio spoil their lives."

Ilka leaned forward and spoke slowly and emphatically. "Lydia Rogers is wanted for the murder of eight people. We have to call the police and tell them she's on her way to Racine. Her name is on the Most Wanted list. We can't just let her go. We could be charged as accomplices if we don't report her. And you can't know if Fernanda and the boy are safe here. Lydia is that dangerous a person! She shot a young man yesterday."

Ilka brought out her phone. The experience back at the rest stop was still fresh in her mind, so shocking that her hands shook when she began thinking about it.

Another silence fell between them.

"We have to report her," she repeated.

"Lydia saved our lives." Fernanda stood in the doorway holding a clothes basket. "She wasn't the one who shot her brother and his family, and she didn't smuggle drugs in the bodies of babies."

She walked over and set the basket down, then gathered her shawl closer around her shoulders. "None of it is true. Lydia is a good person."

"Lydia Rogers threatened me with a gun less than a day ago." Ilka described what had happened at the rest stop. "She almost shot me because we'd left without her bag! She's totally insane."

Something flashed across Fernanda's face, then she turned to Ilka. "What was in the bag?"

Ilka shrugged. "It was just a travel bag. Maybe her nightgown, a toothbrush, some clothes."

Fernanda shook her head. Her golden-brown face turned a shade lighter, and she began wringing her hands. "I don't think it was just a travel bag."

Ilka's father sat up in his chair. He'd finished his cigar, and his straw hat lay on the table.

"I think there were some important papers in that bag." Fernanda glanced over at him as if she needed his support. "It must be the notes her brother hid in Ethan's luggage the day the family planned on leaving. We found the papers later, under the mattress in the baby's carrier. They are important to her, very important. Lydia was a scapegoat. They blamed her for everything, lied about it all. The papers were her only proof she was innocent. They are her insurance if she gets caught and has to explain what really happened. She needs those papers."

Darkness had fallen; the gas grill had cooled off.

Ilka was about to say something, but Fernanda pulled out a chair and sat down. "If it hadn't been for the children, I think Ben would have reported it earlier."

"Ben?"

"Lydia's brother. He worked for the Rodriguez family, but he was always talking about moving away and starting a new life. You might not know, but he and Lydia grew up in a religious cult. There were four children in the family, but only Lydia and Ben got out."

Her father nodded; apparently, he'd already known this. And she had to admit, it didn't surprise her much that Lydia's childhood had been unusual.

"Ben and his wife, Jenny, planned to leave everything they had behind, to get away from Texas and the Rodriguez family. He wanted out of the life of a criminal. I packed the children's bags the morning they were leaving. They weren't taking much, just some toys and clothes for the first few days. The evening before, I heard Ben call Lydia to tell her they were leaving. He asked her to stop by early the next morning. I don't know how much they talked about it before, but Lydia and Ben were close. They lived close to each other too, in San Antonio."

Ilka was getting cold. She poured herself a cup of coffee and held it to warm her hands, all the while watching Fernanda as she told her story.

"Early that morning, we were packing the car out in the garage. I'd carried some of the load down the evening before, but we'd waited to pack the kids' things so they wouldn't ask questions. Ben and Jenny hadn't told them much; they didn't want them talking about it, it had to be kept a secret. I'd just picked up the carrier with Ethan in it as well as the bag Ben had laid beside it when they arrived."

She looked away for a moment. "I don't know how many of them there were; I was out in the garage stowing things in the back of the car. The front door blew open, I heard it through the door between the front hall and the garage. First they shot Cindy; she was the oldest girl. I'd sent her down to put on her shoes. Her little sister was still upstairs with Jenny, and I ran inside to go up to them, but Ben was already on his way down. He killed one of the men before they shot him, then he fell in the middle of the stairs. I'd set the crib with Ethan beside the bottom of the stairs, but they didn't even see it, they just ran upstairs, so I grabbed Ethan and the bag and ran back into the garage."

She squirmed a bit, rubbed her arms as if she was trying to hold herself together while she relived what had happened.

"Lydia showed up at the house right after they went upstairs, I heard her car outside. I was hoping the neighbors had called the police. Or that Jenny had. I think Lydia knew something was wrong right off the bat, because she came in through the garage, which she never did. She saw me and signaled to me to stay out there and hide with Ethan. I had to tell her Ben and Cindy had already been shot. Lydia walked inside, but she came right back out and said they were both dead."

Again Fernanda looked away; then she took a deep breath. "Lydia had her brother's gun. We listened to Jenny upstairs, pleading to save her daughter's life."

Tears began streaming down her cheeks. "Lydia told me to put Ethan and his things out in her car, then she went upstairs. I got in the backseat, then a car drove up in front of the house. I thought about running in and warning Lydia, so she wouldn't get caught in between, but she'd already heard the car. The door was open, I saw her standing just inside the doorway, and two men from the car started shooting at the house."

Fernanda fought to keep her voice under control. "Lydia stepped out and shot them both with her brother's gun, killed one of them."

She dried her eyes and stared down at the table a moment. "The men upstairs heard all the gunfire, and one of them came down. There was more shooting, and I thought Lydia was dead for sure, but no, she killed him. Then she came running out, said they'd already killed Jenny and Lucy and they were tearing things apart upstairs."

She wiped away more tears and shivered a bit in her shawl. Ilka's father hadn't moved a muscle since laying his cigar butt in the ashtray. Ilka was leaning toward Fernanda, and she realized how tense her body was.

"What happened," she said, "to make Ben want to run away with his family?"

Fernanda took a few moments before answering. "Ben was the financial middleman. And he was the contact for the people who crossed the border with the dead babies. I didn't know that at the time. He had nothing to do with the babies, but he would find people, a single person or a couple, who wouldn't attract much attention. And he wanted out of it."

"So Lydia helped him? Or how was she involved?"

Her father said nothing, but Fernanda shook her head.

"Lydia wasn't involved. I don't know how much she actually knew about her brother's connection to the Rodriguez family. She said she suspected he was involved in something not good for him, but she didn't know it was the dead babies and drug smuggling thing. And it shocked her, of course it did, but she was sure he'd done it to give his family a better life. Remember, none of them had anything to begin with after they left the cult."

She kept wringing her hands, but now her voice was clear as she told Ilka about the day she'd found out that Ben was working for the Rodriguez brothers.

"I was folding clothes when they came to talk to him. It was a few days before the tragedy, all the killing. Either they didn't think a nanny had ears, or else they didn't notice me. Or maybe it was because I'm Mexican, just like them. Ben told them he wanted out. I could hear they were planning a new shipment, but Ben said once that was over, he was done. They'd already given him the money to buy the drugs, and they were just waiting for the dead babies to get started."

From the look on her face, it was obvious that talking about it disgusted her.

"But Ben was planning to take off with his family and the money," Ilka said.

Fernanda nodded. Ilka's father leaned forward on the table.

"Where is San Antonio in relation to Mexico?" he asked.

"About a two-and-a-half-hour drive from the Mexican border. The drug deal was supposed to take place in Piedras Negras."

"And what about the papers in the crib—what were they?" he asked.

"They were records of all the shipments, with names of the people who had smuggled the babies across the border and detailed descriptions of where Ben was to pick up the dead babies. And then there were all the messages between him and the Rodriguez brothers. If Lydia had known she had all that information, she wouldn't have had to run. She could have given the police the names of all the men who had shot her family. But she didn't know the papers were under the mattress."

"But didn't she call the police?" Ilka asked.

Fernanda nodded. "She called and reported the shooting while we were driving away, but it was already too late."

"What do you mean, *too late*?"

"The official report was already different from what really happened."

Ilka turned to her father to see if he understood all this.

"The Rodriguez brothers have all sorts of contacts," Fernanda said. "But Lydia was lucky. She got hold of an officer who knew her brother, and that saved her. She reported the attack on the house, exactly how it happened. She told him we escaped, and we were on our way to the station to make our statements."

Fernanda's face was wooden as she spoke, except her eyes, which were wide with fear. She was clutching her upper arms, literally holding herself together. "Lydia told the policeman her brother had been working for the Rodriguez family, but he already knew that. Ben had contacted him and another policeman a week earlier; he told them he had information about the dead-baby smugglers. He'd agreed to inform on the Rodriguez brothers if the police gave him a new identity. But it never got that far, of course.

"The policeman told Lydia to get away from there as fast as possible, because one of the Rodriguez brothers had been killed at the house, and she'd never get a fair trial if the police caught her. The brothers had connections in the police department, all the way up to the top, and they'd already named her as the guilty party."

"How many brothers are there?" Ilka thought about the two men she'd left behind at the funeral home.

"Five, originally." Fernanda added that even though it was common knowledge in town that they were criminals, they were still powerful. "They owned several commercial buildings and businesses. And they'd just built a housing complex in one of the newer sections of San Antonio, so a lot of people were dependent on them. Carlos was the oldest brother; he was killed in a shootout long before all of this happened. Enrique was killed while I was in the car with Ethan—he was the one Lydia shot in self-defense. And Javi had been upstairs with a few of their gorillas. Ben shot one of them when they broke into the house, before they killed him and Cindy."

"Lydia said she was accused of killing eight people, but if I'm counting right, from what you've said, only seven died in the house that day," Ilka said.

Fernanda shook her head. "No, it was eight. They also accused her of killing Ethan, because they never found him. And right before we drove off, a neighbor came over. He was shot before he even got to the house, but we've heard that Javi Rodriguez was sentenced for that killing."

"When did he get out?"

"In August. I learned all this from Lydia when she came down here with your father. And now the only ones left are Miguel and Juan."

Ilka stood up. "Maybe we should go inside?"

It was chilly, and she could see her father was tired. He leaned on her arm as they walked over the gravel. Fernanda had already turned on the lights in the house. The single painting in the small kitchen depicted the view of Lake Michigan from Artie's porch; other than that, only wood carvings like those she'd seen in Artie's house hung from the walls.

They put water on to boil, and Fernanda rinsed and warmed a teapot. Ilka's father eased down on the sofa. He slumped over, his head almost falling onto his shoulder, but before Ilka could react Fernanda was at his side. She leaned over and put his arms on her shoulders, then spoke softly: "Okay, Paul, time for bed." She helped him into his bedroom beside the kitchen.

Ilka glanced around the living room. Another door to the right of the dining room table was closed, and it was quiet inside. *Ethan must be sleeping in there*, she thought as she sat on the sofa and grabbed her phone.

"You have reached a number that has been disconnected or is no longer in service," the mechanical voice said. She tried Lydia's phone one more time, but got the same message. Ilka set her phone aside. She hadn't even thought about where she would sleep, but she tucked her legs underneath her on the short sofa. *Looks like it'll be here*, she thought.

A few minutes later, Fernanda brought the teapot in. "You have to find Lydia," she said. "She's out there all alone, with no money and no place to go."

Ilka nodded and said she'd tried to call Lydia. "She's been disconnected."

"Your father says you two should leave early in the morning."

"No way! He's not going, it's way too dangerous and difficult. I'm going back alone."

Ilka thought about the travel bag Lydia had left at her feet when she climbed in the hearse and slipped into the coffin. Then she pictured the two Rodriguez brothers they'd left behind. Lydia shouldn't be alone when she picked up her bag; Ilka needed to get back before she did.

"I'm coming with you, and that's it."

Ilka turned her head. Her father stood in the doorway wearing his dark-blue pajamas.

"No, you are not!" she nearly shouted. "You're forgetting; everyone thinks you're dead. You can't just show up all of a sudden. And I'm going to have to drive back in one stretch, to get there before Lydia."

His forehead wrinkled into an angry frown. "If you don't take me with you, I'll rent a car and drive myself."

"Paul!" Fernanda said.

"I'm leaving early tomorrow morning. I can't just sit down here and hide while all these people I care about are in trouble. It doesn't make any sense that Lydia had me declared dead. I need to get home and sort all this out."

He turned and closed the door behind him.

Ilka shook her head as Fernanda stepped toward her.

"He needs a nap in the afternoon. He hides it pretty well, but he isn't so strong now, after being injured. And his one leg isn't good, he can't drive a car. You'll have to drive the whole way."

Ilka was already resigned to him coming. She nodded and promised to make sure he rested during the trip, despite how annoyed she was at his insistence. It meant they would be spending twenty-four hours together in a car, and honestly, she wasn't sure if she was ready for that.

Fernanda handed her a cup of tea. Ilka asked what happened after the policeman advised Lydia to get out of town.

"Lydia called a woman—Alice Payne—and told her everything that happened. They've known each other for years, and Lydia trusted her. Alice said to come over, they could trade cars. The police had to be looking for ours. And she told Lydia to get rid of her cell phone so it couldn't be tracked. That's when I realized it wasn't the police Alice was most worried about, it was the Rodriguez brothers. When we got there, she had her car all ready for us. Clothes, food, blankets, some money too, so we could buy anything Ethan needed. She told Lydia to not use her credit card since it could be traced. She said she'd hide Lydia's car and promised to look after her house until everything died down—until the police arrested the right men. She suggested we drive up to Oklahoma and stick to places where it was easy to hide. At the time we had no idea how much trouble we were in."

Fernanda hadn't touched her tea. She still wore the shawl over her shoulders, though the cool draft from the open window didn't seem to bother her. She was somewhere else, Ilka thought. Twelve years back in time, and far from the Key West gallery.

"We heard about the case on the radio while we drove.

First it was just a short announcement about a shooting in San Antonio, but around noon they reported that Enrique Rodriguez had been killed, and then everything seemed to explode. Just like the policeman said it would. At first, they called it a gangster war, and they started sending live updates from in front of Ben and Jenny's house. Suddenly they knew everything, who the kids played with, where their best friends lived. I couldn't understand how it could happen so fast."

Fernanda's cheeks grew taut as she pressed her lips together.

"The girls were three and five years old, they said, but nobody mentioned Ethan. Already that afternoon they were connecting Lydia with the shootings. The police had searched her house and dug up the graves of two babies in the backyard. A boy and a girl, both under a year old."

"The two they were going to use to smuggle drugs, right?" Ilka said.

"Those two, yes. We'd already stopped for gas once, but we had to fill up again that evening, plus Ethan needed some things. I had no baby clothes, baby food, diapers. Lydia walked up to pay and saw herself on the TV by the counter. MANHUNT, they'd written above her head. I was in the bathroom, and by the time I came out Lydia had already switched our license plate with an Oklahoma car in the parking lot. So we wouldn't be driving with Texas plates."

The expression on Fernanda's face changed while she

spoke. Ilka pictured the two of them driving away, terrified, with no idea they would be running and hiding the rest of their lives.

"The next few days the story was all over the world. Javi Rodriguez was in jail. He said he'd worked for Lydia and her brother, which was a laugh. Everybody knew the Rodriguez brothers would never work for anybody else. He gave the police all the details about how Lydia supplied the bodies of infants, and he had names and dates for every one of them. He also told them Ben was the only connection to the people smuggling the drug babies across the border, and that he planned the routes and took care of the money. Javi gave them all these details to make it look like Lydia really was involved. The media called her the brains behind the drug ring. They wrote all these terrible things about how she slaughtered babies, or robbed them from graves and cut them open. And later on, when I found Ben's papers in the crib, we saw that a lot of the details checked out. Except they were the ones behind it all, not her."

Ilka nodded. Now she understood what Lydia had lost when she discovered the bag was gone. "We'll leave as soon as my father is ready in the morning."

Fernanda nodded and asked if she could help bring Ilka's things back from the car.

Ilka shook her head. "No thanks, I'll take care of it myself. I need some air anyway."

And a cigarette. Though she didn't say that.

8

After sleeping for three hours with his head back against the headrest, her father opened his eyes and started talking about his will.

Ilka could feel his eyes on her; she gripped the leather-covered steering wheel harder.

"I wanted you to know I never stopped thinking about you," he said. "Even after I married Mary Ann. It was important to give it to you, because you always meant so very much to me. You were my story, the part of my life where I wasn't controlled by other people or my own mistakes."

They were following a mobile home on the inside lane of the interstate. Ilka looked over at him. Since leaving Key West the day before, she'd been trying to call Lydia, but there was still no connection. She was worried, tense, tight as a fist inside, but her father's disastrous attempt to take care of her was so absurd that she started laughing.

"Thanks a lot! Next time you want to show somebody how much they mean to you, take my advice: Don't give them a funeral home about to go bankrupt."

She turned back to the road and shook her head. A few moments later she dropped all pretense of humor. "I've never heard of anything so stupid. Or so thoughtless, so uncaring."

The deep well of anger she'd been holding down since leaving Artie's house began rising.

They'd spent the night at the same Atlanta motel she'd stayed in on the way to Florida, and the same night manager had checked them in. It had been awkward when the man asked if they wanted one or two rooms, but because she didn't really know her father that well anyway, she asked for two. Once again, she told him they would be leaving early the next morning, and once again he answered that he couldn't care less as long as she paid in advance.

While driving the first day, she'd told her father what had happened a few days earlier: how Leslie, her half sister, had killed her own grandfather Raymond Fletcher, and Mary Ann had taken the blame for it. She also filled him in on everything leading up to the shooting, and for a moment she thought her father was trying to hide a tear when he turned away. But when he looked back at her, it wasn't sorrow she saw in his eyes.

He wanted to know how Mary Ann was doing. He looked worried, but she couldn't say much, other than that his wife had been taken away by the police.

"I can't even begin to tell you how much I wish you'd never, ever come up with that idiotic idea of yours, that will," she muttered. But then it occurred to her that she didn't really mean it. Because it felt so right that she'd met Artie. And Sister Eileen. And for that matter, her father. The reason she'd come to Racine in the first place was to find out why he'd abandoned her, and she'd succeeded.

"I couldn't know how it would turn out," he said.

"No," she hissed. "But you knew I was the one who would have to take care of the mess you left behind!"

"But it wasn't supposed to be so soon that you would get involved."

"Well, guess what, we don't usually get to decide when our time is up. So even if you and Lydia hadn't created this situation, theoretically you still could have died, and all these problems would have been mine anyway."

Slowly she simmered down. She even felt sorry for him. He'd written letters to her—she'd found that bundle of them in his desk drawer. Thoughts he had wanted to share with her, even though he never could send them. And ultimately, that had been enough—more than enough—to make her feel she'd never been forgotten.

"Why did you let Raymond Fletcher come between us?" She had also told him briefly about meeting his father-in-law, and explained that she knew why he had abandoned her and her mother. But he didn't answer her.

For a long time, they drove in silence. Finally, as they were approaching Chicago, he said, "I was afraid of Fletcher back then, that's why I went along with him. Afraid something would happen to you and your mother if I stood up to him. It was like he took over my life. And I let him do it. My weakness and bad judgment put me in that horrible situation. I was afraid of myself, too. I was causing problems for everyone, and I thought the best thing to do was just let him take over. Or maybe it was more that I thought I could get away from the part of me I couldn't control."

After a moment he cleared his throat. "You could say he bought me. And I let him do it."

He was choking up, and Ilka felt sorry for him, but she kept her eyes glued on the road as he spoke.

"I wrote you into my will because I hoped you'd find out how my life had gone, and that you were never for-gotten. And I won't deny it, I've been waiting a long time for my father-in-law to die. The second he was gone, I would have contacted you. Way back then I promised him I would be a loyal husband and father, and said that wouldn't change even if I kept in touch with you, but he wouldn't budge. And I wasn't strong enough to stand up to him."

Ilka was seething again, yet she could hear how badly he had missed her, and that kept her from boiling over. They didn't really know each other, though he'd been in her thoughts as far back as she could remember. Sitting so close to each other in the hearse felt almost claustro-phobic.

They pulled into a gas station to fill up. Every time they'd stopped for gas, Ilka had tried again to call Lydia, but the same mechanical voice kept answering.

After paying for the gas, she bought two sandwiches and two cups of coffee and carried them out to the car. She settled into her seat and asked her father to try Lydia's number one more time.

"Have you tried the funeral home?" he asked. "If she did make it back, she might still be there."

Ilka had left without locking anything up, and of course she couldn't know if the Rodriguez brothers had still been there when the police arrived. In any case, any-one could have gone in and taken whatever they wanted. Including the travel bag with the leather handle, she thought. Ilka listened anxiously as he called the funeral home, but no one answered there either.

North of Chicago, signs for Racine began popping up. Ilka stayed in the right lane. She was tired of driving, and she asked her father if it would bother him if she rolled down her window. He shook his head.

A short while later, after she signaled to turn off at an exit, he said, "I loved your mother. She was the love of my life."

Ilka glanced over at him in surprise.

"The first time I saw her, she was surrounded by kids

at the zoo. The kids in the class she was teaching. I'd just eaten lunch in the cafeteria. This was not long after I took over the funeral home on Brønshøj Square."

Ilka kept an eye on the GPS and slowed down to make sure she didn't miss the Milwaukee exit.

"So, I was walking out of the cafeteria, and your mother was telling the kids about flamingos. Maybe it was the way they listened, but anyway it caught my attention. You don't often see a big group of kids stand still and listen to someone. Her hair was long back then, it curled down on her shoulders, and she'd tied it back with a red scarf. She was one hundred percent focused on her class, as if they were the only people in the zoo. I walked over and stood close enough to eavesdrop, and then when she noticed I'd joined her class, she asked me if I wanted to go along to see the birds. So I followed them around, and before we split up, I invited her out for coffee the next day."

What stuck out most to Ilka was the warmth in his voice. Her mother had never talked about how they had met, and she'd never mentioned the zoo. Ilka could easily imagine her mother with the class—she'd been a popular grade school teacher—though the notion of her inviting a strange man to walk around with the kids sounded odd to her.

"Did you ever talk to her after you left us?" Ilka was thinking now that her mother might simply not have told her. But her father shook his head.

"Our lawyers handled the divorce. I signed a statement saying I'd been unfaithful to her, and I let her have everything."

"Were you? I mean, unfaithful?"

He shook his head again. "I was only thinking of her. And you. But when the opportunity to get away came, I knew I had to grab it. More and more I was turning into my own father, and I hated that. I didn't like the person I was becoming. Everything was slipping away from me. I'd borrowed quite a bit of money with the business as collateral, without telling your mother about it. I didn't want her to find out I was getting in over my head."

Ilka turned off to Racine. He looked down at his hands.

"I was so ashamed of myself, and at the same time I was afraid of what I might do. I felt like two people, me and some stranger. I lied and cheated to get my hands on more money, and then I gambled it all away at the track. I tried to get help. I've never understood why it's so hard for me to control. It's like some force that grabs hold of me when I get out too far."

Ilka asked him to call the funeral home one more time, but again no one answered.

"I never did love Mary Ann," he said.

She felt claustrophobic again; this was way too intimate. But she reminded herself that these were answers to questions she'd carried around since the day he'd left.

"I've always cared about her, though, very much so. I hate thinking she might go to prison."

Ilka wondered why he didn't even mention the murder, which was the reason Mary Ann had been arrested, but she let that go. And when he said he wanted to visit his wife, she shook her head and reminded him he couldn't just show up.

"Everyone thinks you're dead. You can't even register for permission to visit her; you have to have an ID for that. Which you don't have because you don't exist. You're going to have to wait until you can convince the powers-that-be you're not dead, explain there's been a mistake."

She told him his death certificate had been sent in with Maggie Graham's forged signature on it, courtesy of Lydia. "But Maggie is dead, she can't tell anyone she didn't sign it."

"Dead?"

Ilka nodded, then said she knew Mary Ann, not him, had been driving when the car crashed and she was disabled. And Ilka also knew that Maggie had blackmailed him afterward.

"That woman was a true bitch," he said.

Ilka looked at him in surprise. "Why did you pay her?"

At first, he seemed annoyed that she knew about it, but then he looked out the window for a moment. "I got off cheap. It wasn't Mary Ann's fault. She got in that car because of me, even though she shouldn't have. I knew she wasn't well, that sometimes she took tranquilizers to get through the day. I should have stayed home with her. I should've been there for her, even though living with her wasn't easy at the time. She'd just told me she wanted to leave me, but instead of helping her stand up to her father, I turned my back on her."

He took a deep breath. "It would have been best for everyone if she'd been allowed to live with the man she loved, but I couldn't deal with the consequences. I didn't know what a divorce would mean for my future, except that I still couldn't go back to Denmark. My father-in-law would never let that happen. I was still the father of one of his grandchildren.

"I paid Maggie off. It was the least I could do, to spare my wife. At least that's how I saw it at the time. Though if I was brutally honest, most likely I was just trying to save my own skin. Raymond would never have forgiven me if what really happened at the wreck had come out. It was bad enough that she couldn't walk because of me."

Her father nodded off for a while on the final stretch.

The afternoon traffic picked up as they drove into Racine. When she turned into the parking lot, the first thing she noticed was the closed venetian blinds in Lydia's apartment. A jolt of fear cut through her chest as she woke her father and told him they'd arrived.

Ilka hurried up to the front door. The CLOSED sign still hung there, and fortunately the door was shut—she'd been worrying about it being left wide open. She hesitated; several days had passed since she'd left the Rodriguez brothers there, but could they still be inside, waiting for her? She'd heard nothing from the police, and she had no idea what had happened after she told them the men who had attacked Artie were at the funeral home.

She nudged the door open. The little bell above rang, and a single glance told her no one was around. The two coffee cups she had given to the brothers before she and Lydia had fled were still there, though they were now empty. She peeked out the window to see if anyone was keeping an eye on the funeral home, but the street was deserted, just like Racine always was in the middle of the day, something Ilka had gradually gotten used to. It was past four, so she assumed most people were off work.

She walked through the foyer, past the arrangement room and office. The house was dark and quiet. Her father's cane tapped the floor behind her. She turned on the hallway light. It took her two long strides to reach the door to the garage.

There it was. The leather straps hung loosely over the dark-blue canvas bag. Her father reached the door as she picked the bag up. He looked pale. Ilka realized that in her relief at finding the bag, she'd forgotten that it meant Lydia hadn't made it back.

"Call her again," he said.

"I called right before we got here." Even Ilka could hear the fear in her voice. She walked over to the dirty window in the garage and checked the parking lot, but her father's old Chevrolet and the hearse were the only vehicles in sight.

She pushed the button of the garage door opener, and moments later she backed the hearse in. Toward the end of the trip back, she'd noticed a growling sound in the engine, and she'd worried that it was about to overheat. But now they were home. She closed the garage door.

When she brought the bag inside the house, her father was standing in the foyer, looking around. "What in the world happened? What have you done to my funeral home?"

Ilka followed his eyes. The glass cases were empty. The big round table with the tall glass vase was gone, as were the paintings on the walls and the candelabras on the console. All of it had been sold at the flea market she and Lydia held, to scrape together enough money to pay her considerable debt.

Her father walked over to the wall where the paintings once hung and touched the wallpaper. "It can't look like this when customers arrive. It's like some abandoned old house. What happened? Artie was supposed to take care of things."

He sounded so indignant that Ilka stared at him in astonishment for a moment before exploding. "I'll tell you what happened! We thought you were dead, and we were trying to keep your funeral home afloat—I fought like hell for this place, and you are not going to criticize me for not being able to pull it off!"

Her father was sitting down now on the single chair left beside the door to the guest bathroom. He listened silently as she told about how she'd tried to plug the holes—she'd exhausted all her modest savings from Denmark, as well as most of Artie's savings. They never had enough time to plan what to do before the IRS was due to take over the entire business. However, she didn't mention botching the sale of the funeral home that Artie had arranged before she'd arrived in Racine. When she had seen her father's room upstairs, she'd been too overwhelmed by memories and longing to think straight.

"I did the best I could," she said.

His long, lanky frame looked feeble, surrounded by the remnants of his daily life for the past thirty years. He looked up at her. "Didn't anyone help you?"

"Artie and Lydia did, yes. We fought together."

"But not Amber or Leslie? Didn't they treat you well when you showed up?"

Ilka smiled at that, but he didn't notice; he was reaching around for his cane to stand up.

"It's only because Amber's in the hospital that I've been able to talk to her. And I've never had contact with Leslie. No, your family hasn't exactly welcomed me with open arms."

"What, Amber is in the hospital?"

"Oh God," she mumbled. It was all way too complicated. But she made her father sit down again, then she told him about the afternoon at the Fletcher ranch when her half sister had been trampled by several spooked horses.

It was difficult for her to talk about the atrocious way his family had treated her. Not because she felt the least bit guilty about making them look bad. But even though she was livid with her father because of the situation he'd put her in, she also understood that it was a lot for him to swallow.

"She's doing better now," she said, hoping that would comfort him.

But he was obviously shaken. "I have to get to the hospital. I need to see Artie too. You have to come with me and tell them I'm still alive, so I don't walk in and shock them to death."

Artie. She'd been thinking about him all the way down to Key West, but on the way back she'd been so preoccupied with Lydia and her all-important bag that she'd completely forgotten him.

Ilka carried the blue bag upstairs and into her father's room. If he was disturbed by what he had seen downstairs, he definitely would not be one bit happy to see the room he sometimes slept in. She'd been through everything in there and had tossed out what she didn't want to take back to Denmark. The wardrobe had also been sold at the flea market, and most of his clothes had been thrown away. She had been trying to clean up and get the place in shape to be sold.

Ilka had noticed a cabinet door leading to storage space behind the desk. She pulled the table away from the wall to hide the bag in there, but just before pushing it inside, she loosened the strap and opened the bag.

There was no sign of a toothbrush, nightgown, or anything resembling personal items. For several moments

Ilka stared down at the stacks of money, thick bundles lying side by side that almost filled the bag. She could barely believe her eyes. The eighty-seven thousand dollars taken out for Artie's hospital bill had barely made a dent in the fortune in front of her.

Ilka's hands shook as she closed the bag and refastened the strap. The money had been sitting there in an unlocked house since she and Lydia drove off four days ago. She grabbed a sheet of paper and wrote *Call*, along with her Danish cell phone number, though without the country code. She didn't want to reveal too much, and no one would realize they had to punch in 0045—no one except Lydia. Ilka knew she'd probably be even more paranoid from now on. She decided to put the paper in the garage, at the spot where the bag had stood, in case Lydia came back while they were at the hospital.

Ilka held her father's arm as they walked to the elevators in the towering lobby. Today she could waltz into Artie's ward with head held high, without being the target of disapproving looks. The bill was paid, and she'd returned as promised. She nodded at the woman in the office and headed for his room, but they were stopped by the head doctor she'd spoken to before leaving for Key West.

"Mr. Sorvino is conscious now," the doctor said. "We brought him out of the coma this morning, and it went well. He can speak, and he seems to be aware of where he is."

"Why didn't you call me?" Ilka said. "You promised to call if there were any changes in his condition. I would have come if I'd known. Someone he knew should have been here when he woke up, I thought we'd agreed on that."

She felt her father's hand on her arm, and she stopped. Her voice had become thick as she criticized the doctor; she just hated to think Artie had been alone, no one to tell him everything was going to be okay when he opened his eyes. She should have been there, holding his hand.

Ilka turned away and took a moment to get hold of herself.

"He's sleeping now," the doctor said. "And we had to move him to a new room. You can go in, but don't wake him up. He still needs as much rest as possible."

Ilka stopped at the doorway, appalled by the sight in front of her. There were eight beds in the room, and all the other patients had visitors except for one man watching the noisy crowd. Artie lay in the next-to-last bed, sleeping with his mouth open a crack. He looked like some sort of exhibit, lying there among all the strangers. A black stocking cap covered his head.

Without a single glance at the others, she walked over and pulled the curtains on both sides of his bed to give him some privacy. The head doctor followed along.

"Why does he have that stocking cap on?" Ilka asked. She glanced at her father, who was misty-eyed now. She lugged a chair from the foot to the head of the bed so he could sit down.

"He was very annoyed when he discovered we'd shaved his head, which we had to do, to insert the drain. He borrowed the cap from one of the porters."

Artie's hair had been long. A sort of statement, Ilka guessed. He usually tied it up in what twenty-somethings called a man bun, though to her it was just a plain bun. But now it was gone, without him having a say in the matter.

Her father reached out and carefully laid his hand on his friend's shoulder.

"He's still in a lot of pain, and we're giving him something for it," the head doctor said. "We'll be planning a course of treatment soon, but first we'll do a new scan, and also test his vision and hearing and brain responses to stimuli. It's going to take time for him to regain fine motor skills in his fingers, and the normal use of his arm. You should be prepared for a long rehab. It's going to require a lot of patience on his part, but the chances are good that his arm will be fine. We're more concerned about his head."

One of the other patients was having a birthday party, and his guests began singing. The doctor stuck her head through the curtain and asked them to keep it down.

"He has to have another room," her father said. "Lying here in the middle of all this noise is making him worse."

"There are no other rooms available."

Ilka thought that was rather abrupt. "He was in a private room when he arrived, so I know there are other rooms."

The doctor turned to her. "Those rooms are for patients who arrive in critical condition, before we assess
their chances of survival."

She merely nodded when Ilka added that he'd also
been in a room earlier with only two other patients,
where it had been quieter. "All the rooms are occupied.
Everyone in this room will be going through a course of
treatment."

Course of treatment! That phrase annoyed Ilka to no
end, but she tried to sound friendly. "When do you think
he'll wake up again?"

Her father laid his hand back on Artie's shoulder.
"Old buddy."

"Tomorrow," the doctor said. "We've given him
something to help him sleep. Again, it's important for
him to get lots of rest."

If rest were so important, Ilka thought, a quieter room
would help. "Can we take that as a good sign, that he
was awake earlier today? Does it mean he's recovering?
That he hasn't suffered brain damage?"

She knew those were leading questions, but surely it
meant something that Artie had been angry about his
hair. That gave her hope.

The doctor was blunt. "It's difficult for him to speak.
And it's still too early to say if his memory has been
damaged."

She'd retreated a bit, but now the doctor stepped close
to them. "Unfortunately, it's also too early to say if his
frontal lobes have been damaged, but hopefully we'll

find out from the next scan. If they have, it can affect his behavior and personality. The next several days are vitally important for his recovery. After that we'll be able to assess how serious the injuries are."

Ilka asked again to be kept informed should anything happen. She added that she would try to be there as much as possible the next few days.

She reached out and held Artie's hand. She wanted to stay until he woke up, but at the same time she hoped he would sleep through until tomorrow, as the doctor had said he would. The most important thing was for him to be himself again. She leaned over and kissed him, then she asked her father if he wanted to see Amber.

9

The private room of Ilka's half sister was in the section of the hospital where wealthy patients could buy much better service in more comfortable surroundings. The lower building was set back behind the rest of the hospital, and on the way there Ilka sensed her father was beginning to tire. She was exhausted herself, with a pounding headache on the rise. She felt stiff from the long drive, and she couldn't wait to lie down. Suddenly it seemed like years since she'd found him on the terrace behind the small bar.

It wasn't going to be easy to walk in and tell Amber that her father was right outside her room, but they might as well get it over with, she thought. Then she could leave the two of them alone.

A few moments after entering the building, a message beeped in on her phone from a number she didn't recognize.

Fuckdate? was all the person had written. Signed, Jeff.

She stared at the message in astonishment. How had he gotten her number? They'd met on Tinder, but back then she hadn't known he worked for Fletcher. And the next-to-last time she'd seen him, they practically got into a fight.

She ignored the message and stuck her phone back in her pocket. The conversation she'd soon be having bothered her more by the minute. Even though Amber was the person in her father's new family she'd talked to the most, it would be wrong to say she knew her well, or that they were close.

She decided to take a page from Lydia's book.

"It's a long story, and I think he's the one who should tell it."

Amber stared at her. "Dad's not dead?"

She'd been lying in bed, reading a book, when Ilka stepped in the room. Her half sister had more color in her cheeks, she noticed, and the metal frame around her hip was gone, as were her bandages. She simply looked much better, and Ilka assumed she'd be released in a matter of days.

"No. He's not dead. He's outside in the hall and wants to see you, very much."

"Isn't that great! My mother's in jail and my father isn't dead after all!"

Ilka looked at her in surprise. She hadn't thought about how Amber would react, but she definitely hadn't expected a fit of laughter.

"Does that mean I should tell him to come in?"

Amber held her tongue for a moment, then narrowed her eyes. "Are you really serious, Dad is alive?" She sat straight up in bed.

Ilka nodded. "A situation came up, and he had to make it look like he'd died." She decided not to say more; her father would have to explain it all.

"But did something happen to him?"

"He's fine."

"Did you know?" Amber said. "Know all along he was alive?"

Ilka shook her head in annoyance. "Of course not. If I'd had any idea at all he was alive, I would have gone back to Denmark a long time ago. Maybe I haven't been clear enough, so I'll say it now—all the stuff that's happened to me here, I wish I'd never gone through."

Amber's expression smoothed out as she nodded. "I know. I'm sorry! I just haven't been myself lately."

Ilka smiled. It suited Amber, actually, to flare up the way she did. "I'll tell him to come in." She felt Amber's eyes on her back as she walked to the door.

Her father was standing right outside the room and apparently had heard what she'd said about coming to Racine.

"I'm sorry you ended up in the middle of all this. It wasn't how I'd hoped you'd meet my family here."

Again, he made it sound as if he'd always counted on Ilka meeting them. And maybe he had, she thought. He'd been waiting for Raymond Fletcher to die so they could all be with him. And now it had happened. Only he wasn't the one who had brought them together—that was Ilka's doing.

She stayed in the background as he walked to the hospital bed and gave Amber a kiss. When he straightened up, she noticed the tears in his eyes. He caressed his daughter's cheek while whispering something to her Ilka couldn't hear. Amber took his hand.

Ilka carried a chair over to the bed for him to sit down, then she sat in an easy chair by the balcony door.

Her father kept swiping at his tears as Amber told him about being injured out at the stables. Ilka didn't listen. All the hours behind the wheel were catching up to her, and their voices were a murmur in the background until she heard something that made her sit up.

"I'm pregnant," her half sister said. "And I felt so bad I couldn't share my joy with you. At first, I spent some time sitting outside the funeral home, on the bench under the big tree, pretending you could see me and feel how happy I was. That's how you were there for me."

"Oh sweetheart!" Her father was so moved that Ilka couldn't breathe for a moment. She rose and stood by the balcony door.

The father was Tom, the stable manager, Amber said. They had kept their relationship a secret because they didn't want anyone interfering. Soon Ilka understood that Amber's pregnancy was why she hadn't been released. The doctors wanted her to stay in bed until they were sure she could carry the baby to full term, after all that had happened.

"Mom doesn't know yet. I don't know how she's going to take it, but I've decided to go away. To move. It just felt so lonesome, starting a new life you were never going to be a part of."

"What does Leslie think?" he said. "You told her, right?"

Amber shook her head. "I haven't talked to Leslie since all this happened. I can't get hold of her."

"What do you mean?" Ilka said. "She hasn't visited you?"

Ilka frowned. Just before the police took her away, Mary Ann had told Leslie to come in and tell her sister what had happened, so she wouldn't hear about it from someone else.

"No, I haven't seen her at all. Tom told me Grandpa was dead. And of course, it was in the paper, even though there was only an obituary."

"But they must have written that he'd been shot," Ilka said, thinking that the murder of a wealthy man, one of the city's most public figures, had to be a major story.

"No. Even dead he's somehow above being dragged into that sort of scandal."

Ilka hadn't heard her half sister speak contemptuously about her grandfather before. She'd thought the two of them were very close.

"Is Leslie staying out at the ranch?" Ilka hadn't given a single thought to Amber's older sister since leaving Fletcher's ranch four days ago.

"I don't know where she is," Amber said. "Mom

called from jail, but she only mentioned that the practical stuff with my stay in the hospital was taken care
of. Insurance covers my rehab and R-and-R at a place
in California somebody recommended to her. But I'm
not going anywhere without Tom, and, like I said, Mom
doesn't know about the baby."

"Your mother hasn't heard from Leslie either?" Ilka
already had picked her bag up off the floor.

Amber shook her head. "Nobody's been able to get
hold of her."

"I'm going out to the ranch," Ilka said. She turned to
her father. "Can you take a taxi home? I have to find her.
The last time I saw her, she was in no shape to be alone."

10

Leslie wasn't Ilka's cup of tea, and as she neared the ranch, she realized this was the first time she'd been the least bit concerned about her. She felt a bond, a family tie. Not that that made her think any better of Leslie, but she felt obligated to do something. Also, there was no one else she could ask to step in.

Leslie had looked and sounded apathetic when she promised to go to the hospital and tell Amber about their grandfather's death. She'd buried herself up in her room when she was told she'd been lied to, that Paul Jensen wasn't her biological father.

An endless row of pastures lined both sides of the twisting road as she neared the ranch. The gate at the end of the driveway was open, just as it had been when she'd left. She noticed a car in front of one of the stables, so she drove over and parked beside it.

"Hello," she called out. A few horses stomped around when she stepped inside the stable. "Hello!"

She noticed a man's back at the end of the stable, and she called out again.

"Need some help?" he said as he walked toward her.

Ilka introduced herself and said she was Amber's and Leslie's half sister.

"You're the one from Denmark." He looked her over.

This had to be Tom, she thought. "Have you seen Leslie?"

He shook his head. "When are you talking about, though? I mean, I saw her when she and Mary Ann moved out here."

"After that. Now. Or recently. The last few days. Do you know where she is?"

She noticed a glint of annoyance in his eyes. "They'd barely hauled Raymond Fletcher's body away when everybody disappeared. There's no one left to take care of the horses or run the place. Twenty-four valuable trotters we have here, and every one of them needs special attention, then there's Amber's prized horses *I* had to track down and bring home again. I haven't slept more than four hours straight since Fletcher died. So no, I haven't been keeping an eye on Leslie's whereabouts."

His voice was flinty, but Ilka knew his frustration wasn't with her. The stable was filled to overflowing with horses, and he was clearly exhausted.

"But she still lives out here, right?"

The look in his eyes shifted again; it was as if Ilka had

accused him of not taking care of Amber's sister. "I have no idea."

Ilka trotted over to the front door, which to her surprise was unlocked. There were signs all over the cavernous hallway that the police had been there. Muddy footprints on the wooden floor, strips of barrier tape. She headed for the office where Raymond Fletcher had been shot.

The rug where Fletcher had died still lay there; his body had been traced, and his blood had dried. The room was pin-drop quiet, and Ilka shivered and slowly retreated. It was the only room in the spacious house she'd been in, but now she walked over to the door on the other side of the hallway. The walls looked thick and massive to her, thanks to the high, dark-stained wood paneling and framed paintings. She stepped out into a small side hall, then into an enormous kitchen with a rectangular table that could easily seat twelve people. Ilka doubted it was ever used, but there were cupboards from floor to ceiling, and the tableware was neatly stacked in large display cabinets.

She walked back to the hallway and glanced inside the rooms flanking the office. Mary Ann had slept in one of them. Two heavy sofas had been pushed to the side to make room for her, and her belongings were still there—toiletries, underwear, things too personal to just be lying around. Ilka closed the door.

The dining room was taken up by a long, polished table with high-backed upholstered chairs. A double door opened into a room with an elegant sofa group and heavy curtains. Ilka quickly moved on to the last door next to the staircase, the den, but no luck there either. A fireplace, but no sign of Leslie.

She stood for a moment listening to the silence before venturing a few steps up the stairs and calling out Leslie's name. Her voice sounded loud and distant, though she might only have whispered, she couldn't tell. She continued up and stopped on the landing for a look at the framed family photographs. The largest one was of Fletcher. Ilka recognized Leslie and Amber together with a woman who resembled Mary Ann—obviously their grandmother. But there were no photographs of Mary Ann in her wheelchair, and no pictures of Ilka's father.

She climbed the steps reluctantly, unsure of what she would find. Leslie had practically been petrified with shock when Ilka had seen her last, and since no one had been helping her, Ilka feared the worst.

On the second floor, she called out again and stared down the hall. All the doors appeared to be closed.

"Hello?" she said. She noticed she was holding her phone; she must have grabbed it without thinking.

The first door she opened was a bathroom the size of the den below. The next room was obviously Raymond Fletcher's bedroom. The bed had been made with military precision. Quickly Ilka closed the door and moved on to an unoccupied guest room with two folded towels on the bed. The door to the last room was open a crack, and from the hall Ilka noticed the unmade bed. She called out Leslie's name again, but no one answered. She inched over to the door and pushed it open.

Leslie lay fully clothed on the bed. The pillows were mashed together, and her blond hair lay in a tangled mess. The blanket had slid off onto the floor. Her back was turned to Ilka, and she was staring straight into the wall.

"Leslie," she said, her voice barely above a whisper.

Was her half sister breathing? She wasn't moving, anyway. A sweater covered her shoulders, and she'd put on a bulky jogging set that looked all too big on her.

"Leslie." She walked over to the bed.

Leslie's eyes were wide open. Her face looked pale against the pillows, and her cheeks were sunken. Ilka had never seen her like this; her usual meticulously groomed, perfectionist look was long gone. But at least she was alive.

She blinked slowly, but her eyes were focused straight ahead. Ilka wasn't at all sure what they saw.

"Leslie." Carefully she sat down on the bed, then reached over and laid a hand on her half sister's shoulder.

"Go away." Leslie's voice was hoarse.

"No."

"Go away."

"Absolutely not!"

"I don't want to talk to you."

"You don't have to," Ilka said. "Are you thirsty?"

Leslie pressed her lips together, but after a moment she nodded.

"Have you had anything at all to eat?"

Again a few moments passed before she shook her head.

Four days had passed since the killing, and it looked as if her half sister had been lying there all that time. Alone. An empty water glass stood on the night table, along with an empty cracker package. Parts of a sandwich lay on a table over by the window; the bread was dry and curled up at the corners.

Ilka filled the water glass up in the bathroom. She lifted Leslie's head and held it up to her lips. After she'd taken several small sips, Ilka went out into the kitchen to look for something her half sister could eat.

"I don't want anything," Leslie whispered, her voice still hoarse, when Ilka handed her a plate of crackers with butter and jelly. She'd also made a cup of tea, and now she lifted the tea bag out. "Just go away."

"Stop acting so stupid! No one's heard from you for several days, and your mother and sister are upset and worried, they think you've killed yourself! They think you're lying around dead somewhere and they didn't even have a chance to help you."

Ilka was startled by her own outburst of anger. "I don't know if you even realize it, but they're not here because they *can't* be, not because they don't want to be."

She took hold of Leslie and sat her up. Her little speech had gone in one ear and out the other, it looked like. As if Leslie wasn't even listening.

She held out a cracker, and her half sister took it reluctantly. She also drank a bit of the tea. She was weak, and she seemed distracted, so much so that Ilka feared she was affected mentally as well as physically. She hadn't had anyone to talk to since the dramatic events several days earlier, and she seemed unable to deal with them on her own.

Ilka knew all about what loneliness could do to you. After Flemming's death she had buried herself in their apartment and refused to speak to anyone, even though her mother showed up every day to check on her. Her thoughts spiraled down into darkness. Then came the day her mother and Jette marched in and went through the entire apartment, cleaning every last inch of it. They stuck tulips into vases and dragged Ilka out of bed, gave her a bath, dressed her in clothes she normally wore. They simply took over. And it had helped. Now Ilka had to try to do the same for Leslie.

She opened the window and let the cold air stream in. She glanced around the room, then began packing Leslie's clothes in the suitcase on the floor. "Are your toothbrush and toothpaste and toiletry things out in the bathroom?"

Leslie nodded listlessly. Her eyes seemed way too large, foreign in her sunken face. But she obeyed when Ilka ordered her out of bed and said she was taking her back to the funeral home. An iPad and phone lay on the night table, and Ilka stuck them in her bag before texting Amber.

"Is there anything else we need to take along?" she asked.

Leslie shook her head. Ilka packed her into a large coat hanging from a hook behind the door, then stuck her bare feet in a pair of winter boots. She held her half sister's arm as they walked down the steps. Ilka felt ashamed; she should have taken her back to the funeral home the day of the shooting, but she'd completely forgotten about her. It was bad enough that she'd been lying there all alone, but that no one had even thought about looking in on her seemed even worse to Ilka.

On the way back Ilka told her their father was alive and back in town. Leslie was in shock to begin with, and Ilka wasn't sure how to help her deal with the news, but her half sister simply gazed out the window and nodded and said, "Hmm!"

11

Ilka wondered how many times Leslie had set foot inside their father's funeral home. Amber had told her that Leslie didn't want anything to do with the dead, that she preferred to stay away. Now she looked unhappy as they approached the back door. Ilka was relieved to see that all the windows were dark, because it meant their father was still at the hospital.

It was almost eight o'clock, and Ilka was practically starving. Why hadn't she brought along the package of crackers she'd found in Fletcher's kitchen! She was nearly nauseous from exhaustion as she unlocked the door and punched in the code on the alarm. She turned on the lights, dragged Leslie's suitcase over the doorstep, and held the door for her.

"This way." She pointed toward the arrangement room; she planned on parking Leslie on the sofa until she'd gotten her half sister back to the land of the living. Or at least close enough to talk about her future.

She was about to follow Leslie when the door behind her opened. She whirled; to her horror, Miguel Rodriguez stepped inside, followed by his younger brother. Before she could react, he grabbed her arm and jerked her back, then sneered and said they'd come to have a little talk with her. Out of the corner of her eye she saw Leslie slowly turn her head and stare at the two men.

Ilka struggled noisily and finally broke loose from his grip, but she straightened herself and kept her wits about her. "What can I do for you two this time?"

She stepped in front of her half sister, who then backed up against the doorframe.

"Lydia Rogers," Miguel said.

Ilka nodded. "What about her?"

She told them to follow her into the reception, but once more he grabbed her arm.

"You're not pulling that stunt on us again!" It hurt when his fingers dug into her skin.

"I can't help you." Finally, he let go, and she stepped back. "I don't know where she is."

The diamond in his left ear glinted, and he made a fist, squeezing so hard that the skin on the back of his hand turned white.

"Lydia Rogers stole our money," the younger brother said. "Four million dollars. We're here to get it back."

Ilka was totally exhausted, and on some level she simply didn't care. She stared right back at him. So what if they were mad at her for outsmarting them, escaping with Lydia? If they planned on beating her up as they had Artie and her father, so be it. It surprised her that nothing in their manner scared her, even though she knew what they were capable of. She just wanted to get this over with before her father showed up.

"And we want to know what happened to our brother," Miguel said. He was still in charge. His younger brother with the tattoos stayed in the background, but Ilka had noticed the butt of a gun sticking up from the waist of his pants. She kept an eye on him.

"We know Javi found the Rogers woman, and nobody's seen or heard from him since. And we found out she was the nun who worked here. Like my brother said, she's got something that belongs to us, and we're here to get it back. And to find out about our brother."

"It's true, he came here looking for her."

She retreated a step and glanced back and forth between the two men. "She told me your brother showed up late one night. He broke into her apartment and threatened her and made her give him a bag. And if there was so much money involved, like you say, then it makes sense."

It was her exhaustion talking, she thought. The way she was handling this situation. "Think about it. Why would he share the money with you two?"

She shook her head at them. "Like they say here, he headed for the hills. With the money."

She sat down and looked up at them. "But then you

came along, and that was dumb. You should have left Lydia alone, because really, I don't think she'd have made anything more of it."

Leslie was still standing in the doorway, staring silently at all of them. Ilka ignored her.

"There were documents in the bag too," Ilka said. "Were, until Lydia took them out. Her brother wrote down all the details of your smuggling ring. Names and dates. Messages, addresses. More than enough to convince the police that they'd been wrong back then."

She spoke quietly, and they leaned forward to catch everything she said. "The papers are on the way to Texas now, she'll hand them over to the police and give her statement. Nobody will accuse her anymore of being behind what happened back then. But you could try to catch up to her and see if you can make a deal."

"When did she leave?" Miguel asked.

He believed her! She'd won. She flashed back to the day the older brother had showed up during a memorial service and asked for her father. Lydia had been out in the reception when he pushed his way inside, and later she'd seemed terrified. Ilka should have known something was very wrong. If she'd been on her toes, she would have sent Lydia away. Everyone would have been okay.

She glanced up at the clock. "A few hours ago. If you leave now, maybe you can catch up to her."

The brothers looked at each other.

"What was she driving?" the younger one said.

Ilka shrugged. "It's a light-colored car. Silver-gray, I think. But probably your best bet is to wait outside the police station for her."

"Which police station?" Miguel asked, as if he were testing her. But again, Ilka shrugged.

"I've heard you have good connections, surely you can find out. I'd think the one in San Antonio is a good bet."

"Why should we believe you?" Juan said.

"That's entirely up to you." She stood up. "The question is, can you afford not to believe me. Lydia isn't here. She left a few hours ago, and I've just told you what she told me."

"And why should we believe Javi would run off with the money?"

She shrugged once more. "That's what she told me." Suddenly she couldn't remember if she'd pushed the desk upstairs back in place, to hide the space where the bag was hidden.

The two brothers looked at each other again and spoke in Spanish, which Ilka didn't understand. Miguel scowled at her, but then they nodded and walked out the back door, slamming it shut behind them.

Ilka turned to Leslie. "Okay, let's make the sofa up for you," she said, trying to sound cheery. Her half sister nodded, as if nothing had happened. For a moment Ilka wondered if Leslie was even aware of where she was, what was going on.

She locked the back door and checked to make sure

the front door was locked too, then went upstairs to find bedding for Leslie. A folded-up rollaway bed stood in the storage room across from her father's room; she planned on sleeping on it now that her father was back. She grabbed the pile of sheets on the bed and stuck it under her arm. Her father: She hadn't thought about him since the Rodriguez brothers left. Maybe she should call Amber and ask if he'd left. Suddenly she didn't like the idea of him out there alone after what had just happened.

She rejoined Leslie and showed her the bathroom, then she offered to make something to eat while her half sister took a bath. She found cup noodles in the back of a cupboard, so she turned on the electric kettle. She also picked up two tea bags.

When she heard water draining out of the bathtub, she carried the tea and noodles into the arrangement room and waited. Leslie came out in a bathrobe—the one Ilka normally used—and a towel wrapped around her head.

"Is there Wi-Fi here?" Leslie sounded as if that were more important than food.

Ilka nodded and gave her the code, then sat in a chair and watched Leslie eat. "Do you think you can fall asleep?"

Her half sister nodded. "Our doctor gave me some pills. I've been taking them since they arrested Mom."

Maybe the doctor should have made sure she had someone to talk to instead, Ilka thought.

They sat in silence until Leslie had finished the noodles. Ilka said good night and shut the door. She was holding her phone, about to try Lydia one last time before going to bed, when she heard her father out in the reception.

"Has she been here?" he asked as she walked up to him.

She shook her head, then she told him the Rodriguez brothers had stopped by. And no matter how stupid, idiotic, and irresponsible her father might have thought her lies were, he smiled when Ilka said she'd sent them back to Texas.

It was not until she was stretched out on the rollaway bed that she realized she hadn't told him that Leslie was there. He'd been so focused on talking about Amber that when they finally said good night, they were both all talked out. Which is why she hadn't mentioned all the money in the storage space in his room either.

12

Her father was still asleep when Ilka tiptoed in the next morning to get the bag. As quietly as possible she lifted the desk, moved it away from the wall, and opened the door to the storage space. A few moments later, after pushing the desk back, she scribbled a note to tell him she was going in to see Artie. She stood a moment with the bag in hand, looking him over.

Leslie is sleeping in the arrangement room, she added in the note. *Call if Lydia shows up. See you later.*

On the way to the car, she stopped by Lydia's apartment, but the door was locked. It looked deserted, just like the last time she'd checked. The thought of the nun somewhere out there on her own worried her; she cursed herself for telling the Rodriguez brothers about the papers. Essentially, she'd given them another reason to look for her, and Ilka knew they would do everything in their power to stop her from getting to the San Antonio police headquarters. Mostly, though, she hoped they were so intent on stopping her that they'd left Racine immediately.

It was just past ten when she stepped out of the elevator and headed for Artie's room. The ward smelled of coffee, and the nurses were moving briskly between beds. Her mother had texted her, asking her to call back, but Ilka decided that would have to wait. She stepped aside for a porter pushing a patient in a hospital bed. She thought it might be Artie, and she glanced down as they passed, but a woman with short blond hair stared up at her. She looked frightened.

A voice called her name from the office where she earlier had paid for Artie's room. She turned and saw a woman waving at her. Her stomach sank; were there more problems, bad news? Slowly she walked back to the office.

"We still don't have a copy of Artie Sorvino's insurance policy." The woman sounded anything but patient. Which was odd, Ilka thought, given the large sum of money she'd already paid into his hospital account. Ilka sounded more annoyed than she would have wished when she repeated that they were still in the process of finding the policy.

"The papers have to go through administration, they have to be in our database, it's standard procedure."

"I thought we'd already informed you, we're trying to find his insurance policy," Ilka spat out. She offered to put more money in his account, if that was the problem.

The woman shook her head. "In cases when a patient's treatment extends over a longer period of time, we need to confirm that the patient is insured."

"I'll talk to Artie about it," she said. They hadn't even bothered to call when they brought him out of his coma, she thought. And they knew very well that she hadn't yet had the opportunity to ask him about it.

The wall between Artie's eight-bed room and the hallway was lined with tall metal lockers, the kind she'd seen in dressing rooms. Ilka asked a nurse which of them was Artie's, and how the digital locks worked. His was second to the left, and Ilka was told she could choose a four-number code. The nurse asked her to write the code down and give it to the office, in case hospital personnel needed to get something out of the locker. Ilka stuffed the bag in the locker and punched in her mother's birth date on the lock's black buttons.

Several of the other male patients in the room were napping. Coffee cups and small containers of yogurt lay around on their bed tables—obviously they'd been awake—but the buzz of visiting friends and family the day before was gone, and the room was quiet and lifeless. Some were receiving oxygen or hooked up to a drip, and tubes and monitors were connected to machines foreign to her. A medical assistant was taking blood samples, filling up one glass tube after another while the patient lay with eyes closed.

Artie was asleep, and there were no cups or any signs of his having eaten breakfast on his table. Ilka carried a chair over to his bed, and she was about to sit down when a nurse appeared in the doorway. Ilka expected to be told that she wasn't allowed to be there before visiting hours later that morning, but the woman said hello and pulled the curtain around Artie's bed.

"I'm guessing you don't want to watch the other patients being washed." The nurse winked at a grateful Ilka.

Artie's hand lay on the blanket, and she held it, caressed it with one finger.

She was lost in thought when suddenly he whispered, "Hi."

His voice was feeble, but he looked at her in his familiar Artie way.

"Hi," she whispered back, very much aware of the tears filling her eyes. She stood up and leaned over, put her cheek to his. "Hi."

She didn't dare hug him, not knowing how much pain he was in, but she didn't move away, either. It felt so nice, the warmth of his cheek. Her tears dampened the pillowcase.

She straightened up and wiped away her tears. "How are you?" she asked, her voice husky. She glanced around, then turned and pulled out a few tissues from the box on his table to blow her nose. She stalled for time to get a grip on herself.

He didn't answer, but he followed her with his eyes. For a moment she was afraid he didn't recognize her, or that he was mixing her up with someone else and was wondering why she'd bent over him like that.

She folded the tissue and dried her face off one last

time. "Are you in pain?" she finally asked; the silence between them suddenly felt awkward, as if she'd barged in on him.

He raised his hand off the blanket. "Come here."

She turned back to him and took his hand. He lightly pulled her toward him, and she leaned over again, thinking he wanted to tell her something, but instead he kissed her cheek.

"Thanks," he whispered in her ear.

Now she was sure he thought she was someone else, that the blow to his head had affected his short-term memory. She was about to explain that she was Paul's daughter from Denmark when he began talking again, in a whisper. It made her think his voice had lost its strength.

"They told me you've been here since I came."

Ilka was about to say that wasn't true, though she'd wanted to stay with him, but really, there was no reason to start explaining about why she'd had to leave. Anyway, not until she could bring it up more casually.

"Thanks," he repeated.

She stroked his cheek and asked again if he was in pain. There was something about his face when he spoke. As if some part of it wasn't moving when he changed expressions.

"Have you seen what they did to my hair?"

He was still wearing the stocking cap, but she nodded. "They had to do it, to insert the tube and drain the pool of blood in your head."

"I'll probably never have hair that long again."

Ilka smiled but didn't say how pleased she would be if that were the case.

She cupped her hand against his cheek. "There's something I have to tell you."

His eyes grew dark, as if alarm bells were ringing inside his head.

"No, no," she hurried to say, "it's nothing bad. On the contrary, it's good news."

Artie relaxed, though he still looked wary. Ilka slid her hand away from his face and sat down. "My father isn't dead. It was just a story Sister Eileen made up, to protect him from the people who also attacked you. He got off a lot easier than you did, because she was there."

Artie's eyes began darting around. She explained that her father had been hiding in Key West, staying in his house. "He had no choice."

She heard the certainty in her own voice, how convinced she suddenly sounded. She really *did* understand; Lydia had *had* to get her father out of there. She also knew how much Artie blamed himself for not being there the night he thought her father had been killed. And how badly he'd felt at not being able to help with all the practical matters that followed.

"They did it to save him. But I think it's best that he tell you just what happened."

"How is he?"

She told him that he'd been at the hospital the day before, and that he was planning on coming again later that day.

As weak as he was, Artie was clearly moved by this news.

"He felt so terrible seeing you lying here. We all feel terrible about it."

"What about Sister Eileen?" It was as if he could sense she was keeping something from him.

"We were here with you after they brought you in. She sat with you the first night while I slept."

"Where is she now?"

He was watching her closely, and she looked away to avoid his eye.

One of his eyes was still swollen, though now it was a yellowish brown instead of black. He had a large purple bruise above his left temple. Speaking was obviously difficult for him, but his eyes were focused and clear.

She leaned forward, and in a voice low enough that no one else in the room could hear, she told him about Lydia Rogers. The whole story, from start to finish. Including how they had parted, the automatic weapon, everything that had been said. Then she told him what Fernanda had said.

"Of course, I didn't know anything about that when I left Sister Eileen. I was practically in shock when I read the articles about her in the newspapers. I was scared."

She paused. Artie had closed his eyes when she'd started talking about the sister, though once in a while he'd peeked out, but now he looked at her.

"Lydia Rogers," he said, as if he were tasting the name. "I found out about Fernanda and the kid. But not until several months after they moved in. I figured out Sister Eileen wasn't living in that little apartment by herself. At first it was the food she took over. Then I started seeing these clothes on her line that didn't look like hers."

Ilka realized he was ignoring what she'd told him about the shooting in San Antonio. He closed his eyes again. "I had a girlfriend once, the first great love of my life. But it didn't take long to find out, she was on the run from a man who thought he owned her. That's why I recognized the pattern. I hid her myself back then, until her ex found us and took her away."

"I'm scared that something's happened to Lydia," Ilka whispered. "And it's all my fault."

Artie raised his hand again and gestured for her to take it. "It can never be your fault. She should have told you the truth, told *all* of us the truth, instead of thinking that stupid idea of Paul being dead would make everything go away. I'm just sorry she didn't dare trust us."

He sounded reproachful, but not bitter about how her lack of trust had ended up so disastrously for him.

"She was trying to protect us," she said. "She thought she could handle it all."

Ilka hadn't told him about all the money in the bag. Only about the papers that could prove Lydia's innocence.

He squeezed her hand. "Lydia will be okay. She's smarter than they are, and she's already saved her nephew and his nanny."

Ilka felt tears welling up again. From relief that he was alive, she thought. Though it could just as well have been from the worry on his face as he spoke. Also, she noticed him wincing when his mouth moved; obviously he *was* in pain. Ilka had been so happy to see him alive that she hadn't really picked up on how badly he'd been hurt. He looked like an older, weaker version of himself. He had a long way to go before he was the man he had been. If he ever got that far.

"I offered to help Sister Eileen," he said. "And I told her I'd keep everything under my hat. She trusted me, and she brought out Fernanda and her nephew. At first, I figured it was the sister's kid, but then she said she knew him through her brother. I never asked if her brother was the one Fernanda and the boy were running from, it was none of my business. Anyway, I knew from my own experience that it's hard to talk about stuff like that. I thought I could help my girlfriend back then, but no. She was always on the run, and finally we lost contact. I gave Lydia the keys to my house and told her Fernanda and the boy were welcome to stay, if they'd look after the gallery, sell some of my things once in a while."

He smiled, though it looked more like a twitch.

"And they're very happy you let them stay." Ilka told about meeting them at the house when she picked up her father. "They've made a good life for themselves down there. They're safe."

Two nurses had begun talking and bustling about at the bed nearest the door. One of them pulled back the curtain from around Artie's bed, and a cart with cleaning supplies was rolled into the room.

"I'd better go." She smiled at him while searching for words, to make him see how much it meant to her that he was conscious now, back to life.

"Have you talked about it?" A nurse in the doorway was staring at Ilka.

"About what?" Artie was back on alert, as if he'd been expecting all this time that the worst still hadn't happened to him.

"They've asked about your insurance, and I've been holding them off until we could talk," Ilka explained.

"Yeah, of course." He told her he was insured through the funeral home, and that the policy was probably in a file folder in the office. "Paul knows where it is. And if you can't find it, I have copies of old receipts at home."

Ilka promised to find it. "Is there anything I can get you from the house?"

His eyelids were half closed now. At first, he shook his head, but then he told her he wouldn't mind having his iPhone pods. So he didn't have to listen to all the yakking going on around him. He thought he had a pair in the preparation room. His phone lay on the bed table.

She could imagine him lying there, listening to the Beach Boys. It would definitely be good for his spirits, she thought. She leaned over to kiss him goodbye. For the first time since returning from Key West, she felt at ease, knowing Artie was going to make it.

On the way out, she stopped at the office and

promised to find his policy number when she got back to the funeral home. They didn't ask about the locker, and she didn't give them the code.

Back at her car, she noticed that her mother had called again. Three messages on her answering service and a text asking her to call back.

Suddenly she longed to hear her mother's voice, but that would have to wait. Not until she knew what to tell her, she thought. She stuck the phone back in her pocket.

13

Ilka let herself in the funeral home and stood for a moment listening; all was quiet. The door to the arrangement room was closed, but when she put her ear to the door, she knew that Leslie must be in there. On the way back from the hospital, Ilka had bought groceries with a few of the bills she'd snatched out of Lydia's bag before stashing it in the locker. She went out into the kitchen to put coffee on and make a few sandwiches.

Her father had called as she was paying in the supermarket. He was on his way to see Amber. She was getting the results of some tests taken the day before, and he wanted to be there; he was concerned about his youngest daughter. That stung Ilka. Which was childishly jealous, she realized at once. She was ashamed of herself. Before hanging up, she'd promised to help him find out how to have a death certificate annulled.

Ilka balanced the food tray on one hand and knocked on the door before entering the room. Leslie lay fully clothed on the sofa when she stepped in. At least her half sister had gotten up, though so far that was about it. Her head was resting on a stack of pillows, and her earbuds were hooked up to the iPad on her lap. Ilka set the tray down on the table and turned to her.

"How about if I open the curtains?" She walked over to the window.

Leslie nodded listlessly, as if she hadn't really noticed the room was still dark even though it was long past noon. She was watching a movie or TV series on the iPad—someone was kissing—but Ilka didn't recognize any of the actors.

"And maybe I could open the window, to get a little fresh air in here?" She was trying to fight off the annoyance creeping into her voice. The last thing she needed was an adult zombie lying around all day like this. But she held herself back and shifted into a friendlier voice.

"Dad took the bus in to see Amber. I'll drive you over if you want to visit her. She's been asking about you."

Leslie still hadn't reacted to the news that their father was alive, and she hadn't asked any questions either. She simply stared at the screen, as if she'd checked out mentally.

Ilka patiently held the plate out to her again. Leslie hesitated but finally accepted a sandwich and sat up just enough to drink her coffee without spilling.

For several moments Ilka stood watching her, not knowing what to do. Leslie hadn't even mentioned the clash with the Rodriguez brothers, nor had she asked a single question about Lydia. Did Leslie even know the nun had been working for her father the past twelve years? Ilka wasn't sure. She seemed lost in her own world; maybe she'd simply decided it didn't concern her.

Someone stuck a key in the back door of the home. Leslie stiffened and watched wide-eyed as Ilka walked out of the room and closed the door behind her.

"How did it go?" Ilka asked.

Her father took off his coat. "Fine. Everything looks good, very good. Tom came while I was there. They seem very happy together."

Ilka sensed his relief; it truly looked as if a weight had been lifted from his shoulders.

"I stopped by to see Artie too." His face fell. "He doesn't seem to remember much, short-term. And several major nerves in his arm were severed. It looks like he has a tough road ahead of him...I'm afraid he'll never be the same."

Ilka stared at him in astonishment. "He seemed to be just fine this morning. He remembered things, like how he found out Lydia had been hiding Fernanda and the boy, that he'd told them they could stay at his gallery."

Without answering, Paul looked over at the door to the arrangement room. "Is she still in there?" He said he'd looked in on Leslie before leaving for the hospital, but she'd been asleep. "How is she?"

Ilka shrugged. "Nothing seems to really get through to her." She walked over and rapped on the door, then opened it.

"Leslie? Our father is back. He wants to see you."

Leslie slowly raised her eyes from the screen, but when he walked in, she looked back down without a word and focused on the iPad. Her face was a blank slate.

A heavy, awkward silence filled the room as Ilka and her father stood in the doorway.

Finally, without looking up, Leslie said, "I thought it was her coming back."

"Coming back?" Ilka didn't understand. She'd checked the front and back doors, which were both locked, before she'd left for the hospital, and she was sure her father had been every bit as cautious since she'd told him about the Rodriguez brothers returning.

"The nun. She came when I was on my way to the bathroom. She let herself in the reception."

Ilka glanced quickly at her father.

"She's been here?" he cried out. "When?"

Leslie shrugged. "Not long after I woke up."

"You just let her leave again?"

Leslie looked bewildered at Ilka's question. "What is it I should have done?"

Their father took a step into the room. "Did she say anything?"

Leslie thought that over a moment then shook her head. "Most of the time she was out in the garage, but when she came inside it was like she was looking for something. She came in here too and went through all my things."

Suddenly Ilka realized this was the first time she'd

heard Leslie speak coherently since she'd picked her up at the ranch. "Did she leave a message?"

Leslie shook her head.

"Did you notice if she had a cell phone?" he asked.

Leslie shook her head another time as they peppered her with more questions.

"Did she take anything with her?" Ilka asked.

She shrugged. "I didn't really notice. I don't even know the woman."

"But she just left?" her father said. "She didn't say anything about where she was going?"

He looked ashen as he stared at Leslie. Again, she just shook her head, and it went without saying that she hadn't thought to ask Lydia.

While her father tried to squeeze more details out of Leslie, Ilka walked out to the garage, but she saw no sign of Lydia. She hurried back into the reception to see if she'd left a message.

No messages. No trace of her. Nothing that pointed to her having been there at all. Then Ilka remembered the small silver necklaces, the only things she could think of that might be worth something—and easy to sell when you were on the run. The funeral home used to sell cremation jewelry, which family members would fill with the ashes of their deceased loved one. Ilka had planned to get rid of the necklaces at the flea market they'd set up, but then they shut the whole thing down early, so Lydia had packed them back into their velour-lined boxes.

When Ilka opened the cupboard, the small boxes tumbled out. Lydia had emptied them all. Ilka didn't blame her. She imagined her searching for any valuables she could find after discovering her bag was gone. And she'd have wanted to get out of the funeral home as quickly as possible to avoid the Rodriguez brothers. Ilka felt terrible; Lydia didn't know she'd sent the brothers back to Texas.

She ran across the parking lot to Lydia's apartment. The last time she'd tried the door it had been locked, but seconds later she stood in the entryway, half expecting to be met by the barrel of Lydia's gun.

The apartment was empty. An open cabinet door and a pulled-out drawer in the bedroom were the only signs that anyone had been there. None of her things had been touched, and it didn't look as if anything had been taken from the living room either. Ilka guessed that Lydia had simply grabbed some clothes and taken off.

Ilka hung her head as she walked back. If only she'd been there when Lydia had arrived, she could have told her where she'd hidden the bag.

But wait: Lydia might have been keeping an eye on Ilka and her father; she might have known they were out. Maybe she hadn't wanted to see them. Or to answer their questions.

Ilka regretted taking the bag to the hospital. It had been a spur-of-the-moment decision, and it made things that much more difficult for Lydia.

Then she remembered about the insurance. She'd promised the nurse on Artie's ward that she'd call when she found the policy number.

* * *

The arrangement room door was closed when she returned, and her father had gone upstairs. She rushed into the office and began looking through the stacks of file folders on the shelves, then knelt down and started going through all the files. In the left lower cabinet she found a ring binder with all the prepaid funeral agreements and another one filled with receipts. In the middle cabinet she found copies of death certificates, and finally, in the cabinet closest to the window, she took out a ring binder with EMPLOYEES written on its spine.

She laid it on the desk and quickly flipped to the section labeled ARTIE, where she found his insurance papers. GOLD STAR INSURANCE was printed in one corner, and farther below she read that Mr. Arthur Sorvino was insured under the Platinum plan.

Ilka sighed in relief. She slipped the most recent payment receipt out of the folder to copy the policy number. Then she noticed the date; it was a year old. She flipped through the rest of the payments to check if they were out of order, but all the others were older. For a long while she sat and stared at the policy. Finally, though she was barely able to breathe, she stood up and went out into the reception to look for a bill from the insurance company.

One by one, she pulled out all the drawers in Lydia's desk, and finally she found the stack of unpaid bills, but none of them were from the insurance company. Then Ilka remembered the mail and advertisements she'd set aside the day she discovered the threatening letter from Maggie.

Ilka had only been interested in the handwritten envelope; everything else she'd tossed into a pile and forgotten about. Now she found the pile, and there it was. The bill from Gold Star Insurance. She hadn't even opened it.

She did so now and pulled the bill out. The expiration date for the insurance was printed clearly in the middle of the page. It had passed long ago.

"There's been a mistake," Ilka repeated to the Gold Star agent. "It must be some electronic error. The money was deposited in the wrong account or something." No, she didn't have a receipt for the transfer of funds. They didn't use a payment service. And she didn't remember the exact date the payment had been made.

"He's insured on the Platinum plan," she added. "If you look him up, you'll see that you've been covering him for many years."

The agent confirmed that Arthur Sorvino's policy had been active for fifteen years, without any claims having been made during that time.

"You see? And we didn't cancel the policy. It's still active. This is simply a mistake."

She accused their bank of screwing things up, and it sounded as if the woman on the phone was inclined to agree with her. When she said she would check to see how quickly they could activate the policy again, Ilka thanked her so profusely that an awkward silence followed. Finally, the woman cleared her throat before adding that, naturally, Arthur Sorvino would have to take another physical examination, and when they received proof that he was in good physical health, that he had no chronic illnesses or disabilities, she would send his application on to be evaluated.

Ilka called six other insurance agencies before giving up. She begged, exaggerated, even lied to some extent to convince them to insure Artie. Initially, they were more than willing, ready to promise the world and all its gold, but as soon as they heard he was in the hospital, with a long course of treatment in front of him, the conversation was over. They wouldn't budge an inch.

She sat and stared into space. She would have to suck it up and admit to Artie that it was her fault if they sent him home without the treatment he needed. But she couldn't, she just *couldn't* do that. She was going to have to figure something out before the hospital demanded to see the insurance policy again. Ilka assumed there was still money in his hospital account; otherwise they would have contacted her already.

"Damn you, Lydia Rogers," she mumbled to herself.

Suddenly she longed for home. Everyone in Denmark had the right to hospital care, insurance or no insurance. Maybe not every inch of hospital floor was spick-and-span, and the food could be better, but no one was turned away if they needed a doctor.

Ilka stood up slowly. She was determined to find a solution. If she couldn't get Artie covered, she would at least be prepared when they demanded cash instead.

14

The bag! Ilka had to get back to the hospital and use the money from the bag to pay them. By the time she grabbed her coat and was on her way to the car, she was already concocting a cover story. She simply couldn't tell Artie she hadn't paid his insurance, that she'd laid the bill aside after finding the letter from Maggie. That she'd neglected the responsibilities of running the funeral home she'd inherited.

But really, though, she told herself as she headed for the hospital, who could have imagined running into characters like the Rodriguez brothers? Who could have foreseen all these dangerous things happening?

In fact, she wasn't even sure of her own insurance status. At some point her mother had told her that she was covered by travel insurance for sixty days. But did that include being assaulted by drug dealers from Texas?

The incessant monologue in Ilka's head continued all the way to the hospital and up the elevator to Artie's ward. She would dump so much money on them that their counting machine would burn up. By the time she walked into his room, she was so anxious that she could barely breathe.

Artie lay with eyes closed. A large bouquet on his bed table blocked most of his face from sight. She knew she would have to explain what had happened with the insurance at some point—just not now. Not until she could promise it wouldn't affect his treatment. But that would also mean she would have to tell him about Lydia's money.

The man in the bed beside Artie gazed at her with eyes half shut. He was the only other patient in the room. Two beds had been removed, and the four other beds were empty.

Ilka said hello, and he nodded weakly at her. She draped her coat on the chair beside Artie's bed so the man would know she was a visitor, then she walked over to the locker. She was about to punch in her mother's birth date when she noticed the door wasn't completely closed. She flung it open; the lock had been broken, and the locker was empty.

For several moments Ilka stared at the bottom of the locker while trying to wrap her head around the situation she would soon be dealing with. She turned slowly and glanced over at Artie's battered face. He was watching her now, and she realized her father was right. She'd been thrilled to know he was still alive, and maybe that's what had affected her judgment, made her believe everything would be fine. Her relief from his regaining consciousness had blinded her, but now, as he lay there with the black stocking cap on his head, she saw how badly injured and weakened he really was. Or perhaps his condition was just more obvious, now that her ability to help him had vanished along with the bag.

She tried to smile as she walked over to him. "Has someone been in and moved your things?" She sat down on the chair.

Artie raised his eyebrows in puzzlement.

"When I was here earlier, I stuck a bag in your locker and locked it up, but now it's open." She didn't mention the lock had been broken.

Artie shook his head and mumbled that he didn't even know he had a locker. "Lydia was here. She came just after Paul left."

His words were slurred and weak, as if he had to struggle to find them. Ilka wondered if they'd given him an extra dose of painkillers. He seemed dazed, a bit confused; it was almost as if he were talking to himself.

"I could sort of feel her, sitting beside the bed here, but we didn't talk." Now he was looking at Ilka, though his voice was still fuzzy. "She brought the flowers."

Ilka slid over and reached for his hand. "Did she say anything?" She was relieved Lydia had figured out what she, Ilka, had done with the bag, but she knew the money that could help Artie might be long gone. It was not a pleasant thought. "Did she leave a message?"

Artie stared into space somewhere over her left shoulder for several moments before shaking his head. "We didn't talk." His voice sounded sturdier now, as if he was concentrating on making sense. He managed to sit up in bed before Ilka could help him.

"I need to ask you a favor." His chest seemed thin inside the hospital shirt, and his stocking cap was pushed up further now. Ilka noticed the bandage on the back of his head.

She leaned forward to hear him better.

Artie wet his lips and began speaking slowly. "I sent my bank a power of attorney, so you can withdraw money from my account and pay my bills while I'm in here. I didn't know Paul was back, or I would have assigned it to him."

Immediately Ilka grabbed his hand. "That's no problem. Of course I'll help. I'll stop by the bank and make sure everything gets paid."

It warmed her heart that he would include her in something so private as his financial affairs. Maybe it was because he looked so feeble lying there, she thought, but his trust was touching. Though now it would be even more impossible to explain that she'd screwed up his insurance payments.

She gave it another shot. "Did Lydia say where she was going?"

"I think I sort of nodded off. First I thought I'd dreamed she showed up, but then there's the flowers. She *was* here."

He nodded at the small card on the table. *Get well soon* had been written on it in Lydia's stiff handwriting.

Ilka laid the card back on the table and tried to hide her desperation. Artie was in free fall, and she couldn't grab him. She blinked away a few tears and stroked the back of his hand. His eyelids were growing heavy again.

She sat there until he fell asleep. Then she stood up and pulled the flowers out of the vase, but there were no more cards. No hidden messages, no sign that Lydia wanted them to know where she was headed. She was gone. She and the bag.

"Unfortunately, I'm not the one who makes the rules." The woman in the office had stopped Ilka again as she was leaving the ward. "We need to see his policy now, or else we will have to stop treatment."

"But I've already paid!" Ilka stepped back; suddenly she was literally up against the wall. "Eighty-seven thousand dollars. You ran them through your counter yourself."

The woman pushed her glasses up on her forehead and nodded. She must have launched herself out of her chair the second she spotted Ilka walking by, but now she eased up a bit. "I know all of you involved have much to think about. His condition is still serious, and I certainly sympathize with the difficult situation you're in. The money in his account is enough to cover three more days of hospital care, but his treatments will be canceled until his insurance company confirms that he is entitled to inpatient treatment, or until further funds are deposited in his patient account. Our system has canceled a scan scheduled for today, and the next three days he will receive only standard hospital care."

"But you can't cancel his treatment," Ilka stammered.

"He will then be discharged."

"But you can't send him home in his condition!"

"I'm sorry."

"He hasn't even been out of bed yet! We don't even know if he can stand up. This just isn't right."

"Home care is a possibility," the woman suggested.

"Who's responsible for taking care of that?"

"You, his family," she said, as if that was obvious.

"But he isn't at all ready to be discharged. We don't know if all the blood trapped in the back of his head is gone."

The woman nodded. "Yes, I saw in his records that it was one of the reasons for a new scan. But as the situation stands, he's going to be discharged."

Ilka gasped. "But he *has* insurance," she said, without thinking. She took a deep breath and focused. "I realize that yes, you're not the one who makes the rules. And I understand the hospital system here is different from Denmark. But because I'm Danish, and because Artie and I aren't married, it's been a bit complicated for me to get confirmation from the insurance company. But it's coming, and of course I'll make sure more money is deposited in his account, so that won't influence his treatment."

The woman nodded again. She seemed relieved that Ilka finally understood the gravity of the situation.

"Please, reschedule the treatments that were canceled! And I'll make sure everything is taken care of before the system automatically discharges him."

The woman promised she would do so.

When Ilka finally got into the car, she sat for a long while before backing out of her parking space. People were on their way home from work, daylight was fading. Ilka drove over to Lake Michigan and parked at a small lookout spot. She zipped her coat up to her neck, and for over an hour she walked gloomily along the water, her hair whipping in the wind.

Darkness had fallen by the time she returned to her car. It was clear to her now: She needed help finding Lydia.

15

Ilka grabbed her phone and found the message from Jeff: Fuckdate?

She texted him back. Where are you?

After waiting a few minutes, she called his number, but got his answering service. "Hi," she said. "Call me."

She didn't give any hint that she was calling for a different reason but also didn't say a word about screwing him. She turned up the heat in the car and waited patiently at the lookout site for him to return her call. Ten minutes later she gave up and decided to look for him.

She parked in front of the bar where they'd first met, on an awkward Tinder date. The woman behind the bar had known what was going on. The place had been deserted, and Ilka had nearly dragged Jeff out, even though he'd just bought beer for both of them. If the same woman was behind the bar now, she'd definitely know which Jeff Ilka was looking for.

"Nope." The woman rubbed her bare tattooed arms as she shook her head. "Haven't seen Jeff today. He dropped in for a beer a few days ago, but maybe he's on his boat. Losing his job wasn't the greatest thing for him. If you know what I mean."

Ilka didn't, not exactly. She shook her head.

"He's no good at not working."

Ilka still didn't get it.

"I've seen him with some guys you don't want to hang around with, if you got a job to get up for the next morning."

"Okay." Ilka nodded. The only thing she really cared about was that he didn't have a new job, which meant he had time to help her. "I'll check the boat."

She felt the woman's eyes on her back as she walked out, but really, the tattooed lady could think whatever she wanted. Ilka couldn't care less; she had more important things to worry about than her reputation. She slid into the car and drove down to the marina.

The streetlamps along the wharf painted a narrow strip of light on the water. Jeff's boat was moored down at the end of the pier, and even from a distance Ilka could hear music and loud voices. As she neared the boat, she noticed a dark-haired man bowed over a table; though the boat's lights were dim, she saw him jerk up straight and throw his head back. Snorting coke, she thought.

She stopped. More than anything in the world, Ilka wanted to turn and walk away, but she needed Jeff. And as she stood wondering what to do, Jeff spotted her and headed across the deck. She stepped closer. Several eyes on the boat locked onto her as she stood towering above them in the dark. The small gangway swayed gently with every wave.

Jeff stepped onto the pier. "You should've called." The look he gave her was clear enough; he assumed she'd come because she regretted not taking him up on the fuckdate.

"I did, and I also left a message."

Something in the men's voices told her they'd been drinking—either that, or the whole gang was doing coke. She turned back to Jeff. His pupils were dilated, but he didn't seem as high as the others. In the short time they'd known each other they'd had a few serious run-ins, and hearing from him out of the blue had surprised her. But okay, he must be bored now that he'd lost his job as Raymond Fletcher's bodyguard. Screwing her was probably as good a diversion as any for him.

"I need your help. What I mean is, I have a job for you. You told me you're good at shadowing people. Are you just as good at finding them?"

Jeff had led her away from the boat. She felt his hand on her ass; she couldn't really slap it away, seeing that she needed his help, but she turned to face him.

"Of course I can track down people," he said.

"Do you know Sister Eileen? The nun who worked at my father's funeral home?"

Jeff nodded. "I know who she is."

"I want you to find her. Someone else is looking for her, and I need to get to her first. She's gone underground, so it won't be easy. She was at the hospital earlier today, but I'm pretty sure she's planning on leaving town."

Ilka kept eye contact with him to emphasize she needed help now—*right* now. Not tomorrow.

"Nobody goes so far underground that I can't dig them up." He sounded convincing. "But what's in it for me?"

"Money. I promise you'll get a substantial reward when you've tracked her down. But don't bring her back to the funeral home. These people looking for her are the same ones who shadowed me—you know them, you're the one who sniffed them out. They're keeping an eye on us, and it's extremely important you find her before they do."

"Is that an order?"

He's getting huffy, she thought. "No, no, it's a job. A well-paid job I'm offering *you*, before I look for somebody else who can handle it for me."

He lifted his palm in surrender.

Ilka described what Lydia had been wearing a few days earlier, the sweater and jeans. "I'm sure she's changed clothes since then, of course." It occurred to her that she didn't even know what kind of clothes the woman might be wearing. "She could have taken her nun's habit with her."

It wouldn't do any good to fill Jeff in on how the sister wasn't really a nun, so she settled for telling him that she would most likely be in civilian clothes. She started explaining how Lydia had left the hospital that afternoon, but even she could hear she was repeating herself in her eagerness to provide Jeff with what leads she had.

He laid his hands on her shoulders. His pupils were still big, but he seemed calm enough. "I'll find her, don't worry. Then I'll set up a place you can meet without anyone seeing you."

She stood staring at him long enough to feel the warmth from his hands, the peace of mind it gave her. Then a gleam appeared in his eye and pushed aside all seriousness. He stepped closer to her.

Ilka backed off. "You'll be paid in cash. And you get a bonus if you can get us together tomorrow."

"Yeah, my fee. It'll cost you five thousand a day."

"I'll double that if you find her tomorrow. But the daily rate goes down the longer it takes you to find her."

"So, I get ten thousand dollars if I can hook you up with her tomorrow?"

Ilka nodded. "The quicker you find her, the more you get paid."

At the moment she was ready to promise him anything. It looked as if he'd taken the bait. Ilka watched the wheels spinning in his head, perhaps calculating what was in it for him in the long run, if it turned out she had access to the Fletcher fortune. She'd almost mentioned the bag, but then she realized that would make Lydia too vulnerable. If he thought the ten thousand was the Fletcher family's money, that was fine with her.

"I'll find her for you," he promised again.

Ilka told him he could call her anytime, day or night. She said it in the most business-like manner she could, to stop Jeff from hitting on her, but he seemed to have already gotten the hint. Before she turned to leave, he clapped his hands and yelled to his buddies on the boat that it was time to move the party.

It wasn't only his promise to find Lydia that eased Ilka's mind; clearly, he would do practically anything for a day's pay of ten thousand dollars. And she was certain he had a broad network to shake the bushes. He'd understood the message: If anyone else found her first, there would be nothing for him.

16

Leslie's window was dark when Ilka parked the car and got out, but the office and the foyer were still lit, as well as her father's room upstairs. She found him in the office's plush leather chair, engrossed in a book. The remains of a sandwich lay on a plate beside him.

"Leslie's asleep," he said, and Ilka nodded. "Have you eaten anything?"

He laid down his book and pointed at his plate. "There's another sandwich if you're hungry."

He looked tired. Ilka had the feeling he'd stayed up waiting for her. On her way to the kitchen she asked him if he wanted a cup of tea, but he merely grunted. She realized she didn't know her father well enough to know what he liked. They had only eaten together a few times, and she'd seen him drinking coffee, but otherwise she had no idea what he usually drank. She dropped a tea bag in the boiling water. Her fingers got smeared with curry mayonnaise when she unwrapped the chicken sandwich and laid it on a plate.

Back in the office she pulled out the desk chair and looked at him expectantly, but he held his tongue. Suddenly she was nervous: Had the hospital informed him of the situation with Artie? Or maybe the insurance company had called him. She squirmed in her chair; she had to say something.

"They're going to scan him again tomorrow. So the doctors can see if the pool of blood in the back of his head is gone."

"It's not easy for Leslie," he said, as if he hadn't heard Ilka. "She's so mad at her mother that she won't visit her. I tried to tell her that she'd feel better if she talked to her. Both about what happened back then, and also about that day out at the ranch. It would help Leslie understand why Mary Ann broke off contact with Leslie's biological father without telling him she was expecting his baby."

He leaned forward and massaged his temples, as if he were squeezing some old sorrow out of his head. "But she won't listen to me. She won't even talk about it, she just lies in there on the sofa, and I can't even tell if she's listening."

He stroked his chin and looked up at Ilka in resignation. Clearly, he had no idea what to do. It was as if Leslie's despair were a tool someone had placed in front of him that he didn't know how to use.

All her life, Leslie surely must have thought of herself as the daughter of a funeral director. Half Danish, half American. Presumably she had been told more than once that she looked like her father. People always said that; sometimes it wasn't so much a physical resemblance as a similarity of movement, language, manner. The things that rub off from living in a close-knit family. Everything you absorb and mirror because you've seen and heard your parents do it. Inherited traits aren't only genetic, Ilka thought. She hadn't had the opportunity to copy her father's movements and expressions, she hadn't assimilated his language and favorite expressions, but the look in their eyes was the same. Their height, their slightly angular physique. It had been the opposite for Leslie.

It didn't surprise her that their father had no idea how to help Leslie. Had he asked Ilka one single time in the past few days about how she'd handled his abandonment, how she felt?

A pair of headlights out in the parking lot swept across the window; then a car door slammed, then another, right outside the back door. It was nine thirty. She glanced up at her father; he was sitting straight in his chair, staring through the window. They heard voices outside.

Ilka rose slowly as her father leaned over and opened a drawer. He brought out a thick wooden bat and rested it in his hands. The trunk of a car slammed shut, and two figures out in the darkness approached, their voices clearer now. Ilka stepped away from the window and over to the door. She froze when she heard a female voice cut through.

She couldn't believe her ears! She turned to her father, who sat ready for battle, his eyes glued to the hallway door. "It's Mom. And Jette."

Slowly he stood up, staring at her in bewilderment. "Your mother?"

Ilka nodded and headed for the hall as they began banging on the back door.

Before Ilka could react, he stepped past her with the bat in his hand and hurried up the stairs.

The banging continued. "This has to be the place," she heard her mother say. Jette suggested they walk around to the front door.

Ilka didn't budge when they hammered on the door once more, nor when her phone in her coat pocket began ringing. It was as if signals from her brain had been disconnected from her feet. She couldn't visualize, couldn't imagine how she could plunge her mother into the middle of all this chaos. And what if the Rodriguez brothers came back? It would be much too dangerous.

It was quiet upstairs. Her father had closed the door to his room.

Ilka straightened up and pulled back her shoulders, then walked out into the hall and turned on the outside light. She focused on the door a moment before opening it.

Her mother clapped her hands a single time when she saw Ilka in front of her. "What an impressive place!"

She glanced up at the white wooden funeral home, illu-
minated now by the porch light. It *was* a beautiful old
building; it had had the same effect on Ilka the first time
she'd seen it. "I just said to Jette, this had to be the right
address, I was sure of it. We saw the sign out front too,
of course."

"What are you doing here?" It was the only thing Ilka
could think of to say.

Her mother lifted her suitcase and looked at her
daughter in puzzlement. "We're here to help you."

"Help," Ilka repeated. "How did you find your way
here?"

"We met your friend down at the square when we got
off the bus. He drove us the rest of the way. What people say about Americans being friendly and helpful, it's
absolutely true. He carried our suitcases and wouldn't
allow us to pay him for his trouble."

"Friend?"

Ilka peered out at the parking lot; it was empty except
for her father's car, the one she'd parked there minutes
ago. But when her mother explained he was an older
man, and he'd also been a funeral director, Ilka guessed
that they'd been lucky enough to run into Gregg.

"Come in."

Ilka stepped aside and ushered them in, then quickly
shut the door behind them. She remembered Leslie and
worried that all the noise might have woken her up, and
for a split second she was angry at her father for leaving
her alone to handle all this. Yet she knew she absolutely

had to keep him and her mother apart. Who could tell what would happen if her mother found out he wasn't dead after all?

"You two must be exhausted," she said. Could she get away with taking them to the hotel right now, or did she have to ask them if they'd like something to eat or drink? Suddenly she realized she hadn't said one single word of welcome. She locked the back door and led them into the foyer. Her mother stopped and gazed at the empty glass cases where the cremation jewelry had been displayed. Ilka grabbed the suitcase out of her hand and offered to take the weekend bag Jette was carrying over her shoulder.

"Is there something I can get you? I could make tea."

"We ate on the plane, and we had wine too," her mother said. "And I watched a few wonderful movies." As if that in itself were a memorable experience. This was the farthest her mother had traveled, her first trip across the Atlantic. She and Jette had flown to Malta and Sardinia, but normally she was a homebody.

Ilka smiled at her.

Jette glanced at her watch. "I can feel it's five in the morning back home. I did set my watch while we were on the plane. They say it helps with jet lag." She yawned.

"Did you book a hotel room?" Ilka said, thinking that if she could get them settled and into bed, she would have time to clear her head.

Neither of them reacted.

"I'll call down to the hotel and rent one for you." She headed to the office for her phone.

"No, don't," her mother called out. "We'll sleep here, we'll be fine. We came to be with you."

Ilka turned to her. "It'll be a lot comfier for you down at the hotel, it's right outside the marina, a great view."

"Nonsense. We'll find a place to sleep here. We've thought about it, there must be lots of space in the room where you hold the services you told me about. All the sofas where the families sit. And we've seen it in the photos you've sent. We'll be fine there."

Her tone of voice at the end settled it. If Ilka made any more of an issue of it, they would think she was throwing them out. "So, what about some tea?"

They both nodded.

Slowly, it was sinking in that her mother really and truly had shown up, that she was standing just a few feet away. Her thick gray hair lay flat against her neck from all the time on the plane and bus. She was wearing her favorite shawl and a colorful blouse, and her eyes were warm and sparkling as she talked and pointed around the high-ceilinged foyer. Ilka felt the warmth in her chest growing, until finally she rushed over and buried her nose in her mother's hair, and for several moments Ilka hugged her, this woman who had traveled all this way to be with her. When she finally let go, her mother ran her hand through Ilka's hair and told her everything was going to be fine. Ilka merely nodded, then she smiled at Jette and gave her a big hug too.

"It's good to see you," her mother's partner murmured, and again Ilka felt a surge of warmth.

Ilka showed them the bathroom before putting water on to boil and taking down crackers and teacups from the cupboards. She hadn't felt this way since arriving in Racine. The mere scent of her mother was enough; even though she was the last person Ilka wanted to drag into this enormous mess, Ilka felt a familiar sense of security.

She led them into the reception and closed the curtains. "You should have told me you two were coming." She set her steaming teacup down.

"But I did! I wrote to you before we packed, I asked you if it was cold here."

"Cold?"

Ilka remembered the message she'd received back when she was sitting in the hearse as Lydia walked out of sight on the highway. Back then she thought her mother was asking if she was keeping warm enough. "I'm sorry, I misunderstood you."

"It's not easy to get hold of you, you know." Her mother explained that she'd also called from the airport before leaving Copenhagen, to ask Ilka to find out where the bus left from. "But we managed ourselves. The bus trip wasn't really so bad."

Ilka glanced over at Jette, who was obviously exhausted.

The two women were the same age but very different in temperament. Her mother was full of life, sensitive, with an explosive temper. Outgoing and creative. Down-to-earth Jette took care of all the practical details, made sure things went the way they should. Ilka had always felt that nothing could really go wrong when Jette was around. She was compact but strong, energetic, and Ilka loved the woman for being there for her mother and keeping their lives on an even keel. They made a good pair. Her mother tossed up balls and Jette juggled them.

Ilka studied the two of them. That's how the trip had gone, she surmised: her mother full of enthusiasm, Jette taking care of the tickets, finding out which bus to take after landing in Chicago.

Her mother blew on her tea. "We are so excited to meet Artie and the nun you've talked about." She glanced around the reception. "It's a nice place to greet people here, but it would help so much if it was more personal. Cozy. Something to make it look inviting. And it certainly wouldn't hurt to have some indication of the Danish connection."

She sounded as if she'd come all this way just to inspect the funeral home. Ilka merely nodded. Her mother was actually right; the place wasn't all that cozy and appealing after they'd taken away the large mirror and all the lamps, but anyway, what difference did it make now? The funeral home was out of business.

"You can stay over in Sister Eileen's apartment. She's away, and it would definitely be more comfortable than the sofas in the memorial room. And you'll have your own bathroom."

Her mother nodded. "Perfect."

"I should warn you, though, Leslie is staying here for the time being. She's the older of my half sisters."

Her mother tilted her head. "They treated you so horribly at first. Wasn't she the worst of them?"

Ilka nodded vaguely.

"Well, it's wonderful that you're getting along now."

Jette hadn't touched her tea, and had in fact fallen asleep sitting up.

"Come." Ilka stood up and helped Jette to her feet.

"Why in the world are you so sleepy?" her mother grumbled. "We slept on the bus!"

"*You* slept," Jette mumbled. She let Ilka take her suitcase and followed slowly, cautiously, as if she were afraid of dozing off on the way.

Ilka let them in the nun's apartment and pointed out the drawers Lydia had emptied. "I'll bring over some comforters."

They also kept extra bedding in the washroom, and Ilka was on her way to fetch everything when her mother called out after her.

"There's a rollaway in here behind the wardrobe, and comforters and bedding in the dresser."

A rollaway. For guests. Lydia had been living a secret life, Ilka knew that, but the notion that she'd had people staying there overnight after Fernanda and Ethan moved out surprised her.

"Do you think she'll mind us using her bedding?"

"No, not at all. Go ahead, put it on."

Her mother had opened her suitcase, and the first

thing she brought out looked like a black suit, which wasn't at all what she usually wore. Her mother loved deep colors such as green, purple, Bordeaux, rust, but Ilka had seldom seen her in black. Or anything that resembled a suit, for that matter. She knitted most of her clothes herself.

"What do you think?" She waved the black skirt around and said it was the type of thing she wore back when she was struggling to keep the funeral home on Brønshøj Square afloat. "We found it in a Red Cross shop. Jette has one too."

Ilka stared at her. "You're going to wear that?"

Her mother hung the skirt up. "Only here at the funeral home. It's just a uniform. An undertaker's uniform."

"But the funeral home is closed. I tried to sell it, but I couldn't, and we had to close it down. Everything went exactly as you said it would. I ended up with an enormous debt."

Her mother had advised her not to go to Racine, fearing that even after his death Ilka's father would pull her down into a bottomless pit. And she'd been right. It hadn't been easy for Ilka to call and tell her mother that she was coming home with a debt of several million kroner, if they even let her out of the country.

She looked away. Now that her father wasn't dead after all, she assumed his will would be nullified and the worst of her financial problems would disappear, but right then she couldn't start explaining everything to her mother. Once again, Lydia and the bag with all that money crossed her mind. The money could easily have covered what her father owed the IRS, but instead she'd let Artie use his entire savings to buy Ilka some time. Now Artie was in a situation where he desperately needed his money. Her anger with Lydia flared up again.

Suddenly she was aware of her mother speaking to her. "Sorry, what did you say?"

"I just said that we'll get this business on its feet so we can sell it for a reasonable price. I've done it before, and I can do it again. Even though I swore I was through with carrying coffins."

Her mother sounded enthusiastic as she stuffed the comforter into its cover. It seemed as if thinking about the project ahead of them was energizing her.

"I thought you hated the funeral home business," Ilka said.

Her mother nodded. "But we're always here to help you, you know that. And I won't have your father ruining your life like he did mine."

Oh boy, Ilka thought. "I don't think it's going to be so easy," she mumbled.

"My idea is to give the business a Danish feel, make it cozy, emphasize Danish history. Because that's what *we* can do that others can't. And anyway, Danish *hygge* is so popular nowadays. You have to stand out in some way to attract customers. Our driver agreed with me."

"Gregg." Ilka nodded.

"Yes, Gregg. He knew Paul, and he also offered to help if we needed an extra hand. In fact, it sounded as if he wouldn't mind having something to do again. I think he needs to be around people and feel useful."

Ilka wondered how they possibly could have covered all that during the relatively short drive from the square downtown to the funeral home, but that was typical of her mother. People opened up the minute they met her.

"But Mom, the funeral home is closed."

Her mother had finished hanging all her clothes up, and she turned to Ilka now. "It never pays to sell a business that's been shut down. When we get it up and going, it will be a much more attractive investment, and we'll get a good price for it. I've googled the other funeral homes in town, and honestly, they all look depressing. Just wait, we'll get those customers back."

Ilka gave up.

Her mother pushed her own suitcase under the bed and started unpacking Jette's things. "It was so lucky for us that Gregg came by just as the bus left. Getting a taxi in this town isn't easy, it seems. And we don't have that Uber thing installed on our phones, but Jette says it's probably a good idea to figure out how it works."

Ilka could hear that her mother was running out of gas, and she took the opportunity to say good night when Jette came out of the bathroom in her nightgown.

Jette nodded at Ilka then climbed into bed and rolled over to the side close to the wall. She pulled the comforter up and covered her head.

"We'll have to find something to liven up the walls in the reception," her mother continued.

Ilka stepped over and gave her a kiss. "We'll look at it in the morning. Call me when you wake up, I'll come down and let you in."

"You can just leave the door unlocked, so we don't need to disturb you."

"This is America," Ilka said, trying not to sound harsh. "We lock the doors, and you need to over here too."

Her mother nodded and followed Ilka to the door. She was clearly exhausted now; it was six in the morning in Denmark, and she wasn't used to traveling.

"I hope you both get a good, long night's sleep." Suddenly Ilka wished she was staying there with them. She shut the door behind her and waited until she heard the door lock click. Moments later the light in the small living room vanished.

She walked across the parking lot and let herself in. Her mother showing up had brought out that old familiar feeling in Ilka of being safe and warm, but it also terrified her. As if she somehow was more vulnerable simply because her mother and Jette were there. She trudged up to the second floor, stopping for a moment outside her father's room to put her ear to the door, but it was quiet inside. She would have to smuggle him out before her mother and Jette got up.

17

The rain pounding against the window woke Ilka. For a moment she lay listening in a daze until everything came rushing back to her. Her mother and Jette had flown over. They were here. In Racine.

Ilka rolled out of bed and slipped into her pants, which she'd left on the floor the night before. She felt listless. Her dreams had kept shifting scenes; one moment she stood in panic in an empty office in the hospital, trying to convince the administrators that accidents could happen, the next she was watching Lydia disappear down a long, straight stretch of highway, carrying her bag. Her back had grown smaller and smaller, until at last the light swallowed it up.

She jerked a thick sweater down over her head, flung the storage room door open, took one step out onto the landing, and froze: Her father's door was open. She stuck her head in and noticed the curtains were open and the bed made. She glanced at the portable alarm clock on the windowsill. It was almost nine thirty.

She cursed herself under her breath—why hadn't she set her alarm? Her mother and Jette had been up for hours, no doubt about that. Her palms turned sweaty as she headed down the stairs. At the bottom step she ran into the smell of fresh-brewed coffee. But she couldn't hear any voices. Only the coffeemaker bubbling out in the kitchen.

She strode in and noticed the thermos was gone. Empty bakery sacks rested on the table, and that made her nervous. She walked past the arrangement room, to the doorway leading to the reception, where once more she stopped in surprise. Lydia's desk had been converted into a sort of breakfast table. Her father had laid out plates of kringles and rolls, peanut butter, and several jars of jam, and set the table for five. He sat at the end of the table and smiled at Ilka from behind the morning paper.

She remembered asking her mother to call when they woke up so she could let them inside, but now she noticed her phone was on mute. Fortunately, no messages or calls had come in. She turned off the mute. "This is a surprise! So, you've decided to be here when they come in." She glanced around the table.

Her father nodded, but she saw the doubt in his eyes. She clearly wasn't the only one worried about how this would go.

"I should have given your mother an explanation years ago. I owed her that. But I'm a coward and a scaredy-cat. And the way things turned out, well, suddenly it became too difficult. I'm not going to run away today. Last night was just so overwhelming, hearing her voice again. I heard all of you talking down here, but I just needed time to get myself settled."

Ilka noticed that, though he hadn't forgotten how to speak Danish, many of his words sounded odd.

"I'm so ashamed at the way I treated both of you. And it's time for me to face up to it."

She nodded. He had the same expression on his face as when he had spoken about Leslie earlier: dejected, but also resolute. As if he was determined to do what was demanded of him.

"Honesty," he said. "You're better off being honest."

A spike of anger shot up through Ilka, but she pressed her lips together and kept it down with a shake of her head. "I think I'd better prepare them for this, that you're not dead. So you don't scare *them* to death."

But it was too late. She heard her mother yelling out a hello.

"How did they get in?" Ilka asked. She glanced at the table, wishing she could make the food, the plates, the coffee, everything disappear.

"I left the back door open when I got back from the bakery."

"For God's sake! Lucky for us it's not the Rodriguez brothers standing out in the hall yelling!"

Jette walked in first, followed by Ilka's mother, who wore a turquoise sweater, a gold-colored necklace, comfortable shoes, and an enormous smile. "We thought about walking into town to get a sense of the atmosphere, talk to people."

She spread her arms to give Ilka a big hug. "I've seen there's a café that's also a secondhand store. We'll have a look. Maybe we can find something nice for out here. Would you like to go with us?"

Jette had stopped in the doorway and was staring at Ilka's father and the table set for breakfast.

Her mother was still walking over to Ilka when she caught sight of her ex-husband, who had folded up and set aside his newspaper and was standing up.

"Who's this?" Her mother's arms fell.

"It's Dad," Ilka said.

Her mother stared at him and began backing up slowly, with tiny steps, until she was out of the reception.

The three of them stood frozen; Ilka had never experienced a silence as loud as that moment. Then her mother walked back in.

"Why aren't you dead?" she said. It was an accusation.

Jette's fingers dug into Ilka's arm as she drew her off to the side. "How long have you known?"

"Only a few days," Ilka answered quietly.

Jette turned and stepped toward him. "Do you have any idea what you've caused?" she said in a dark, distorted voice Ilka barely recognized. "Do you know what it cost Karin, you abandoning her the way you did? Do you have any idea how much pain is involved with a betrayal like that? No, obviously you don't, otherwise you would never have put someone in that situation, and certainly not the mother of your child."

All the while she was waving her arms in the air in disgust and indignation. "And anger. It is so self-centered to force such anger on another person. Karin isn't an angry person, but you forced it on her. You *made* her angry. And she nearly strangled in that anger for so many years. You not only destroyed her love, you destroyed her trust in life. You are to blame for her becoming bitter, for living in sorrow. That's all on you. You—"

Ilka's mother stepped over and laid a hand on Jette's shoulder. "Jette. Let's give Paul a chance to speak."

Jette was quivering with rage underneath her blue, round-necked sweatshirt. Ilka knew her mother's partner would never forgive her father for Karin's suffering. She felt sorry for Jette. She was the one who had listened patiently with loving care every time her mother had unloaded another bitter story about her ex. She was the one who had picked up the pieces that were Karin and slowly put them together again. In fact, she was the one who had defended her father to a degree over the years, claiming there might be a side to the story they weren't aware of.

Ilka walked around the table and pulled out a chair for

Jette, then gestured to her mother to have a seat while she went out for the coffee. On her way back, she heard Jette, at it again.

"I just cannot understand how you could do this. To a person who loved you so much."

Ilka's mother shushed her again. "This is Jette," she explained. "We live together."

Ilka's father was back in his chair. She handed him a cup of coffee. He set it down and rolled his sleeves up, as if he needed to get himself ready for action in the midst of Jette's barrage. But he hadn't looked away. Several times he'd nodded, seemingly agreeing with every word she belted him with.

Her mother, on the other hand, sat with her hands folded in her lap as she studied her ex-husband. She looked shaken, so much so that Ilka wondered if she was going into shock.

Suddenly she said to him, "My God, you look just like your father."

Her father frowned as he ran his hand over his head. "I sincerely hope not." His white hair lay like a wreath, circling his head above his ears. He was suntanned, and his blue eyes looked light against his dark face.

"But it's true. You've aged just like him. You have the same wrinkles in your forehead. Like ocean waves."

She drew waves in the air with her finger. "And around your eyes."

"There's no one in the world I'd hate to look like more than him. Would anyone like something to eat?"

Suddenly her mother seemed to be enjoying herself. She followed his movements, absorbing them, while Jette sat with her arms crossed, staring down at the table. At her father's words, Jette straightened up, reached for a roll, and buttered it, focusing on her plate. She took a few sips of coffee.

Several times her father's lips moved, as if he was about to say something more, but not a single word came out. Finally, though, he succeeded.

"It was Annegrethe." He turned to Ilka's mother. "Back when my sister died, something happened to me. All my long life I've talked to people who were grieving, and of course I know how you can easily blame yourself when a loved one dies. I often think if I'd been the one who fell out the window that night, my sister would still be alive. Or if I just could have stopped my father from getting so worked up, she wouldn't have had to hide behind the curtains, on the windowsill. If I could've kept my father away from my mother, he wouldn't have beat her those nights he came home after losing at the track. My sister wouldn't have been so afraid of him. There are so many things I wish I could have prevented."

"You were just a big kid when your sister died," her mother said. "And you did what you could to get between them. Your mother told me those stories so many times, it started to feel like I'd been there."

Ilka sat watching her parents. It was so strange, unreal to her, seeing them both in one room, so very different from all the dreams she'd once had of them getting back together.

Her mother still hadn't touched her coffee or the roll Jette had buttered for her.

"It was blowing up a storm that day out at the track," her father said. "They were talking about canceling the races, and maybe that was why I gambled the way I did. I put all my money on a bunch of losers to win, place, and show. I was out there alone, sitting by myself in a box seat. Ilka had just come home from a school trip, they'd spent Friday night in a cabin up in the Hare Forest. I picked her up that day while you were out visiting your folks. Do you remember?"

After a moment her mother nodded.

"We watched TV that evening," he continued. "Ilka fell asleep on the sofa with her clothes on, and you asked me if I was going to the track the next day."

Ilka caught herself holding her breath. It was the details, the way he was speaking. That he could remember that evening, an overnight trip with her school, her lying on the sofa asleep. He hadn't forgotten; it was still etched in his memory.

"I told you I wasn't, I said I had a funeral in Vangede, and I'd have to drive the coffin out to the crematorium. I promised to do some shopping on the way home. You were going to bake those cumin kringles I liked so much. But there was no funeral, I knew that of course. The funeral home was failing, there wasn't much to do, and it was all my fault. I was neglecting the business, and I'd also lost Verner. He was the one who'd been keeping it afloat, but I couldn't afford his salary, and he finally quit. He just couldn't keep going home to his wife and telling her I hadn't paid him."

Her father took a sip of coffee. "Several days earlier, I'd brought in some money by driving a corpse to Sweden for another undertaker whose hearse was in the garage. And I made a deal with myself: If I bet the money and won, I would take you all out for a weekend in Malmö. We would sail over on Friday evening and come home Sunday."

Ilka's mother's birthday was the weekend after her father had disappeared. She'd constantly reminded everyone about that over the years. *It was a birthday present I could have done without*, was how she usually put it. It was also the reason why she always went all-out on birthdays in general. There had to be a celebration, and everyone had to be happy when a birthday came along. Those were the rules.

"So, the funeral was a lie too." Her mother nodded to herself.

Jette had finished off a large piece of kringle, even though she wasn't much for sweets. Having something to do with her hands seemed to calm her down. She began buttering another roll.

"I lied," her father said. "I was going to surprise you both."

First her mother shook her head, then her father.

"They didn't cancel the races, and I was the only

one who picked right on win, place, and show, all three horses. My winnings were a record, and it still stands as the largest amount paid out for a single race."

"But you didn't take us to Malmö," her mother said after a few moments of silence.

He shook his head. "They came to me when I was standing in the winner's circle. I'd seen them out there a few times, I knew they were American scouts. Everybody's on their toes when Americans show up, because usually it means a lot of money for trainers or owners. Now all of a sudden it was me they were interested in. My cousin introduced us."

Ilka already knew this, but it startled her mother. His cousin had kept in touch with them after her father was gone, and he had helped her mother when they moved from their house to a small apartment. He'd remained a part of the family throughout the years.

"They gave me a good offer, and I knew you wouldn't go along. I wanted to prove to you, and to myself, maybe mostly myself, that I could be a success. That's why I left. I wanted to show I could be something other than a loser, and I didn't want to end up like my father. I could feel it, I was losing control, and I didn't want to put you through what happened to me. I saw it as my chance to make a new start."

He barely took time to breathe between sentences.

"Why in the world did you believe I wouldn't go with you?" her mother said.

He looked at her in surprise.

She persisted. "What made you think that?"

"Would you have?"

She leaned over and took his hand. Jette slammed her coffee cup down on the table.

Ilka was standing at the window now, looking out at the rain-covered street, the school on the other side. A car drove slowly up alongside the curb in front of the funeral home, and she jerked back away from the window when she noticed the car's front plate: Texas.

From behind she heard her mother say, "Ilka had just started school back then, we could easily have taken her. And I'm sure I could have gotten a leave of absence."

The car kept driving and turned into the funeral home's parking lot. Ilka was about to run out when suddenly Leslie appeared in the doorway.

"What's going on here?" She looked back and forth between Jette and Karin.

"This is my mother," Ilka said. "And Jette."

"And this is my daughter Leslie," her father said. He pulled out a chair for her.

Before Leslie had time to react, Ilka's mother stood up and gave her a long hug. "It's so very nice to meet you," she said. She sounded like she meant it, even though she'd heard about how rude Ilka's half sister had been.

While Leslie sat down and greeted Jette, Ilka eased out into the hall and hurried down to the memorial room with its large windows looking out onto the parking lot. The car had parked in front of Lydia's apartment, and her throat tightened with fear when she recognized the man in the long, black coat knocking on her door. He'd barged in asking about Lydia Rogers on the day the sister realized she'd been outed. Now he knocked several times before finally giving up. It looked as though he left something at the door before climbing back behind the wheel and driving away.

Ilka ran through the rain across the parking lot and picked up the card he'd stuck between the door and frame. *Please call, I can help you.* A name was printed on the back of the card: *Calvin Jennings, Texas.*

She trotted back and stood under the carport. Her hands shook as she reached for the pack of cigarettes and lighter in her pocket.

"Could I have one too?"

She whirled and found herself facing Jette. Ilka hadn't heard the door open.

"You smoke?"

Jette shrugged. "I don't know, I've never tried. Right now feels like a good time to find out if I do or not."

Ilka smiled at her and offered Jette a drag of hers, but she shook her head and said she wanted one of her own. She lit it and drew the smoke deep into her lungs, staring at Ilka while waiting to see what happened. She didn't cough, she simply watched the smoke seep out of her mouth in a column until she took another drag.

"I don't get it," she said. "How can she take all this so calmly? They're sitting in there talking like they've known each other all these years. She seems to have forgotten all her anger."

"Are you jealous?"

"You're fucking right I'm jealous." She let out a laugh. "Jealous of an old man we all thought was dead. Jealous and mad."

Ilka laughed along with her, mostly to loosen up the knot in her chest. "It is strange, damn strange." She'd also felt a stab of jealousy when her mother had hugged Leslie.

They put out their cigarettes and went back inside. Jette said the best part of smoking was when the smoke hit her lungs. "The aftertaste isn't anything to write home about." Ilka agreed; the only reason she smoked was for the dizzy feeling, not because she enjoyed it otherwise.

Leslie was cutting off a piece of kringle when they returned.

"How about you two, would you like some?" her father asked.

Ilka accepted a piece. After she took a bite, her phone rang: Artie. She stood up and walked out into the foyer.

"They canceled the scan today," he said. "The one that was supposed to show if the blood in my head is gone. And they told me I'm probably going to be discharged from the hospital tomorrow."

Ilka was having trouble understanding him. "You're not being discharged tomorrow. The office told me the money in your account covers three more days."

"They said they haven't seen my insurance policy and they can't continue treatment."

"No one's sending you home! There must be some mistake, a misunderstanding. I'll talk to them." She simply had to get her hands on more money, somehow.

She wished she could console him, assure him everything was fine, but nothing came to her. She flashed on herself standing and screaming in an empty office on the ward.

"I'll take care of it right away," she finally said.

Lydia! If she were there right now, Ilka would roll her up in barbed wire and bury her alive! She was the reason Artie was in the hospital in the first place, and now she'd run off with the money that could have helped him. There was still no word from Jeff, and she hoped, she *prayed* he was out there looking. She texted him, asked him how it was going, then she jammed her phone back in her pocket and rejoined the others to tell them she had to run an errand.

Leslie was talking about the big library in town, the reading groups and lectures that took place there, which was news to Ilka. She also hadn't known about the monthly Danish evening in the Scandinavian Club. Apparently, Leslie was breaking out of her stupor, and her mother and Jette were lapping up everything she said.

"Surely we can use that to our advantage," her mother said.

She and Jette had both taught school, and Jette was interested in history in particular. She arranged walking tours around Copenhagen, pointing out small unusual spots that few Copenhageners were aware of. Now they were both jotting down addresses of places they wanted to visit in Racine.

"And that coffee bar," her mother continued. "That's probably a place where creative people meet. Let's stop by there and put up a notice, an open invitation to a Danish evening here at the funeral home. We'll serve kringles and talk about Denmark."

"Why?" Ilka said, bewildered by their conversation.

"To bring people in," Jette said. She seemed to have forgotten her anger and was now just as enthusiastic as Ilka's mother.

"Bring people in for what?"

"To the funeral home," her father explained.

Apparently, a lot had happened while Ilka had been preoccupied with the man from Texas.

"I think your mother's right," he said, "it's probably best to open up as soon as possible, before the prepaid customers start wanting their money back. If we do it right now, nobody will even know we've been closed."

Ilka took this to mean they thought she'd made a mistake by closing the funeral home. And that stung. "But you don't have Artie. Who's going to do the embalming?"

"Gregg can!" her mother said. "He's an undertaker, and he handled everything at his funeral home. And your father can too."

"But you're dead, for God's sake!" Even Ilka could hear how screechy she sounded. She looked around the room; she had the feeling they were all suffering from some sort of mass psychosis. Even Leslie, who now had some color in her cheeks, added that she could keep the books, besides being a registered nurse. It wouldn't be hard at all for her to be certified as an undertaker.

Ilka shook her head. "You can't just all of a sudden start welcoming people in," she said to her father. "They'll have a heart attack when they see you. I know, it would be good for business, but you don't have a license anymore, you don't have a Social Security number. You don't have anything, because you don't exist."

"Easy," her mother said. "Let's not make this sound harder than it really is. Leslie and Paul have already started taking care of it. And today I'm going in with them to confirm your father is still alive, and that he and I have a child. We'll tell them there's been a mistake. Does anyone know when the nun is coming back?"

Her father shook his head.

"Until she's back, I can handle the reception work, answer the phone. I just need to know what to do when someone needs our services. And can people just walk in off the street?"

Ilka glanced around at them. "There's something I have to take care of." She turned to her father. "I'll take your car."

"When will you be back?" Leslie said. "We have to get going too."

"You can take the hearse. Everyone might as well get used to driving it."

18

Ilka still had the twenty thousand dollars she'd taken from Fletcher's desk drawer, money that could have helped her get back on her feet when she returned to Denmark. But now she hoped it was enough to cover the scan and Artie's hospital room for the next several days. She knew his care would require much more, given how fast the bills were mounting up, which was why she brought along the envelope with the power of attorney Artie had given her, along with her passport. She was nervous, and that annoyed her. Ideally, she could waltz right in to the bank and empty his account, but what if they asked about her relationship to him? Or if they wanted information she couldn't provide?

She shook off her thoughts and drove into the long, narrow parking lot in front of the bank.

"Yes," she answered, "he asked me to withdraw all the money in his account."

A young, black-haired man with steel-rimmed glasses sat behind the glass counter. With no more than a cursory glance up at her, he began counting out bills and informed her he'd need a signature. Ilka had no idea how much Artie had in his account, but she nodded when he asked if she preferred large denominations.

He tucked eleven thousand dollars in an envelope and asked if she wanted to close the account.

"No." She stared down at the money she'd been handed; it wasn't much compared with the bundle of bills Lydia had given her. Her bad conscience from emptying his account made her weak in the knees. Once more it hit her that Artie had used most of his savings to help her—sixty thousand dollars to buy time for her to think about what to do with the business she'd inherited. Not once had he criticized Ilka for being unable to sell it and pay him back; on the contrary, he'd suggested she keep the money as a down payment on the house, which he wanted to buy. And now when he needed it most, there was hardly any money left.

Ilka got in behind the wheel. A sense of loss overwhelmed her, crushed her; she doubted she could even make it up to Artie's ward. Reluctantly, she started the car, but by the time she parked in front of the hospital ten minutes later, she had a plan.

"I have had it up to *here*," she yelled. Several people in the ward's hall turned and stared at Ilka standing in the office's doorway. "I'm holding this hospital responsible if canceling Artie Sorvino's scan—which is supposed to happen *today*—affects his progress and harms his chances for recovery."

The woman she'd spoken to the day before stood up, but she couldn't get a single word in before Ilka cut her off. "I get it, I understand your hospital needs information on the health insurance policies of their patients, and I apologize for not being able to provide it yet. I've spoken with the insurance company again today, but the reason I can't get the information is that I'm not officially the owner of the funeral home that took out the policy. Several months ago, I inherited the Paul Jensen Funeral Home from my father, but the appropriate government agency hasn't registered that yet."

Ilka handed her the old insurance policy. "The agency is working on it, but I still don't have a Social Security number, which means they can't register me as the owner. And officially I'm also blocked until my work permit comes through and my visa has been approved. We all know these things take too much time, and all we can do about it is be patient. But if you'd bothered to contact Artie Sorvino's family before canceling the scan, which by the way worried him, a *lot*, you'd know his treatment will still be paid for in cash."

All this was total bullshit on her part, yet she'd worked herself up into an indignant rage. "I don't know if you can imagine how he feels, being put through your cancellations, threatening to send him home. We're not going to take this lying down, our lawyers will step in if this continues, these irresponsible and unethical decisions."

"Really, I'm very sorry about all this," the woman said. "I didn't know you were a recent immigrant. My husband is from Greece, we've been through all this green card business, all the waiting. But as I said earlier, our database automatically registers if treatments can be carried out."

"I must insist that all communication concerning his further treatment go through me," Ilka said. "So he won't have to worry unnecessarily and can focus on his recovery."

She pulled the money out of her bag and asked the woman to reschedule Artie's canceled scan. "I understand why intensive care was so expensive, when so much was done to save his life. But I'm assuming this will be enough to cover the next several days, so he doesn't have to fear being thrown out."

Thirty-one thousand dollars. Suddenly she remembered how much she'd promised Jeff for finding Lydia. She tried to appear as casual as possible as she peeled ten thousand off the pile, then she told the woman to keep her up to date with the expenses so she would know when the money was about to run out. "We don't want to run into this situation again, do we."

The woman nodded and seemed reassured, now that there was a substantial sum of money in Artie's account again. "I'll make a note of this in his journal, that cash has been deposited." She sat down in front of her computer.

Ilka thanked her and reminded her about scheduling a new scan. "Will he have to wait?"

She watched impatiently as the woman's fingers flew over the keys, then finally she leaned forward and mumbled something about rearranging the schedule. She turned to Ilka. "We can get him in this evening."

Ilka felt like hugging her.

"We just have to have this approved by the doctor," the woman added.

"Is there a problem?"

She shook her head. "I'll use the authorization we already have, and I'll note that there's been a delay in the system."

Ilka smiled at her; they were on the same team now. The team that doesn't shy away from bending a few rules when necessary. "Thanks."

She suspected the woman had seen through her, but cash spoke its own language. Now it was simply a matter of coming up with more of it to keep feeding the hungry hospital monster.

She headed down to Artie's room. It had been hard to understand him on the phone. He'd had good reason to be afraid; the mere idea of being discharged from the hospital in his condition was absurd. Whatever the case, she was sure he was still nervous about what would happen, because he'd figured out she was lying when she told him things were going smoothly.

She peeked at him through the narrow glass window in the door. His black stocking cap was gone, and he lay on his back, though she couldn't tell if he was asleep.

She stepped aside. Suddenly she realized she couldn't go in there, not until she could look him straight in the eye and promise him everything would be fine.

She turned and walked back to the elevator.

19

Ilka slowed down when she drove past the funeral home and noticed the front door standing wide open. A ladder blocked the doorway, but her mother and Jette stood just inside, busy doing something. Ilka parked, and when she got out, the hearse rounded the corner. It startled her to see Leslie behind the wheel, with her father in the passenger seat. Leslie jumped out of the car and ran to the house, sobbing all the way. Ilka reached the hearse just as her father stepped out. He looked like he was about to cry too.

"What happened?" she asked.

He explained that they'd just visited Mary Ann at the jail. His lower lip was quivering as they walked to the back door. His steps were short and slow, as if he lacked the energy to move his feet.

"Wasn't she happy to see you and Leslie?"

He nodded as they reached the door. He leaned up against the doorframe and finally looked her in the eye. "It's horrible. They don't have the resources to take care of a prisoner with her handicap."

Ilka stepped over to help him with his coat, but he shook his head.

"I have to get back. They don't have the right kind of ostomy bags. Mary Ann uses a single bag, it's easier for her to change and takes up less space. The jail's infirmary says all they have is two-piece bags, and now she has an infection around the opening. Mary Ann empties the bags herself, but she needs to be washed off—she needs proper care, and they can't provide it."

His voice broke. Ilka could tell that he blamed himself, that he was thinking that none of this would have happened had it not been for his disappearing act. Then Leslie would still be taking care of her mother. Ilka wanted to tell him he was wrong, that the real reason was the clash between Mary Ann and Fletcher, her father. A result of secrets resurrected after so many years of lies.

Instead she said, "Can't we get hold of the right bags and have them delivered to her?"

Her father nodded. "I have a whole box of them, it's in the trunk. Along with bandages and everything she uses to wash herself with. We always kept extra supplies in the car, in case something came up and she needed to change."

He shook his head; all their routines had been wiped

out. "Even changing to a different kind of bag, with a different adhesive, is enough to irritate the skin."

Ilka nodded. She hadn't even thought that Mary Ann might have had a colostomy after her accident. "Is there anything I can do?"

Her father stared into space for a moment. "If you don't have any other plans, you could deliver the bags for us." He added that it had been very difficult for Leslie to see her mother in jail. "She broke down after we left. But I think it was good for them to see each other, even though they didn't talk much."

He explained that prisoners were permitted only one weekly twenty-minute visit. Leslie and her mother had sat across from each other, separated by a glass wall, and spoke by telephone. Most of the time had been spent talking about the problem with the ostomy bags.

"Didn't you talk to her?"

He shook his head and said that he'd waited outside, because an ID was required to get in, and he didn't have one.

"Your mother and Leslie went with me to get an ID and license. But they won't come for several days, even though the mistake was corrected in their database. And anyway, the important thing was for Leslie and Mary Ann to speak together."

"But she knows you're back?"

He smiled a bit wearily and nodded. "Amber called her and explained."

"I'll drive over and deliver the bags," Ilka said. "If they'll let me in!"

He looked at her, obviously grateful for the offer. "They said that family and friends can deliver medicine in the lobby of the jail, twenty-four hours a day. Prescription medicine has to be approved by the jail's doctor, but that's not necessary with the bags."

"How do I find it?"

Her father wasn't sure what she meant.

"The jail. Where is it, is it far away?"

He smiled. "It's right downtown, across from the library. On the same side of the street as Oh Dennis! The Racine County Jail takes up half the block, you can't miss it."

Ilka was surprised. What a place, she thought. Jails and crematoria, right in the middle of town. Not something you'd see on the Kongens Nytorv, in the center of Copenhagen.

She heard her mother and Jette chattering out in the foyer. They were picking up and rearranging things, she saw when she stuck her head in the room. They'd pushed the large glass cases up against a wall. Ilka asked if they needed anything from town, or if they wanted to go along.

"We have a meeting with Gregg," her mother said. "He's stopping by for a cup of coffee."

Ilka nodded and said she'd be back soon. The door to the arrangement room was closed. She thought about checking on Leslie, but she decided her half sister probably needed time alone after the trip to the jail. She pulled on her coat and followed her father to the car. He opened the trunk, grabbed a brown cardboard box, and handed it to her.

"It's all in here," he said. "Just go in and say it's to be delivered to the prisoner Mary Ann Fletcher Jensen, so they get it registered in their database."

Ilka stood out on the sidewalk holding the box as she looked over the enormous red-brick building. Should she just stroll on in, or was there a place to check in first? She walked over to a double door that slid open when she approached. Straight ahead sat two uniformed men behind the front desk. One of them tilted his head up and looked at her expectantly.

"Mary Ann Fletcher Jensen." Her palms felt sweaty. "I'm here to deliver her ostomy bags, they're waiting for them."

The officer didn't seem to be listening, but he leaned forward, his eyes glued to the screen in front of him, and apparently typed in her name.

"The prisoner was transferred this afternoon to health services." His voice sounded mechanical over the speakers in front of her.

She explained about the ostomy bags and bandages that needed to be changed, which was why it was important to deliver the box to Mary Ann. She still wasn't sure the officer was listening, but she stood at the front desk and waited. Nearly five minutes later a door to the left of the desk opened noisily, and an older man in a white coat stepped into the foyer.

Before he reached Ilka, he said, "Is your mother allergic to penicillin?"

"My mother?" Her mind raced; her father and Leslie had probably said they would be coming back with the supplies, and she ran the risk of being thrown out if she set them straight. "Sorry, I don't know."

The doctor turned and headed for the door. Ilka followed him, not sure if she was breaking the rules. Holding on to the box bolstered her confidence. But just inside the door, she was blocked by a counter and a long enclosed glass booth with more officers in uniform. Farther on she saw a brightly lit hallway that was mostly a row of white doors. All of them closed. Cells, obviously, she thought.

She was told to sign a form, stating she was the one who had delivered the box.

"And we'll need an ID," the officer said. He opened a small door to the right of the booth and motioned for her to place the box in the shallow chute.

Ilka fumbled around in her bag to find her billfold and her Danish driver's license. She hoped they wouldn't refuse to take the box when they discovered she wasn't Leslie. The chute door closed, and the officer studied her license closely. She took a step back and waited; no doubt she was being checked up on, but there was precious little they would find on her.

The doctor had vanished, but one of the white doors opened and a nurse walked out. At once she closed the door behind her and checked to make sure it was locked.

Ilka tried to imagine the lives being led behind those doors.

Another door farther down opened, a broader door, with indentations around it. At first, she didn't recognize the person coming out, but—although the officer frowned at her—she stepped close to the glass wall when she noticed the wheelchair.

Mary Ann's long blond hair hung down over her body. It was thin and parted in the middle. She wore an orange prison jumpsuit and sat crumpled in the chair, staring straight ahead as a uniformed woman pushed her down the hallway. Even at a distance it was obvious she was in pain. Her skin was pale, translucent even, and the elegance Ilka had once seen in her father's wife had disappeared. Her eyes were empty, and when the woman behind spoke to her, she didn't react.

"All right, thank you, ma'am!" The officer handed Ilka's license back to her. The door behind her opened.

Mary Ann was wheeled into a room right behind the glass booth, and the woman shut the door. Ilka stared at it.

"Thank you, ma'am," the officer repeated. Slowly, she turned and walked out.

20

It's about Raymond Fletcher," Ilka said, after entering the police station. "I'm here to make a witness statement."

She chose to call it a family tragedy, not a murder, when she asked to talk to Stan Thomas. He'd been the first one to enter Fletcher's office after the dramatic shooting. Mary Ann had immediately confessed to killing her father, adding that no one else had been in the room. Leslie had sat motionless and stared straight ahead, while Ilka had stood in the doorway. Twenty minutes earlier Ilka had seen Mary Ann calmly remove the rifle from her daughter's hands.

Officer Thomas told her to take a seat.

"It's not true that Mary Ann was alone when she shot Raymond Fletcher," she began. "Leslie and I were both there when it happened. Of course, I should have given a statement right then, but I assumed Mary Ann would tell you what happened before the shooting. And I've been out of town for several days. Maybe you've heard about my father?"

He nodded without commenting on the undertaker's surprising return.

"That's why I just found out that Mary Ann didn't tell you that her father threatened Leslie."

Thomas leaned back in his seat and listened.

"Fletcher was crazy mad. He'd just returned from the police station after his release, and he accused Leslie of riling her mother up and getting her to report him for fraud and false accusations. He claimed that Leslie had made everything up, that she was out for revenge after discovering the truth about her real father. Fletcher threatened to kill all three of us! And you know he wasn't the type who made empty threats. He kept a gun in his desk drawer—but surely you found it."

Ilka had noticed the gun when she opened the drawer and took out the envelope containing twenty thousand dollars. From the look on Thomas's face, she could see they hadn't searched the office. Mary Ann's confession had been enough for them.

"Mary Ann shot her father in self-defense. She saved our lives, all three of us."

Thomas scooted his chair in to his desk, and for a moment they sat in silence. Then he looked her straight in the eye. "And Leslie will confirm this?"

"Yes, of course. She was there."

The officer leaned forward and typed something in on his computer, Ilka couldn't see what.

"I'm absolutely sure Mary Ann is trying to protect her daughter, so all this private family stuff doesn't come out. That's why she didn't tell you about her father threatening Leslie."

Even though she didn't particularly like her father's wife, the image of her in jail kept coming back to Ilka. And she couldn't imagine how humiliating it must be for Mary Ann to have her personal hygiene become a problem. Ilka felt that Mary Ann had already been punished enough by having to live most of her life under the thumb of her father.

Thomas rubbed his nose and turned back to Ilka. "What you're saying is, we should reopen this case?"

"What I'm saying is, Mary Ann shouldn't be in jail. She acted in self-defense, and she saved two lives, besides her own."

Ilka nearly added that Mary Ann had been moved to the jail's infirmary, and it was vital that she be released as soon as possible, but she held back. She didn't want to make Thomas suspicious. She did say, however, that if Mary Ann didn't have a lawyer, she would contact one immediately.

Thomas checked on his computer and shook his head. "No, no lawyer. The case is being treated as a voluntary confession. But from what you tell me, we need to bring her back in for questioning."

Ilka couldn't stop herself. "How soon could she be released?"

"That depends on how soon you can get her a lawyer.

And then it's up to the lawyer to find out if she really wants to change her statement. If she doesn't want to tell us what really happened, we can't make her do it."

"Leslie will confirm it," Ilka said. "And I'm sure she can convince her mother to tell the truth, even though there's so much private family stuff involved."

Ilka could see how annoyed Thomas was that all this hadn't come out when they arrested Mary Ann, but she also caught a glimpse of understanding and goodwill on his face.

She thought it was possible Thomas had been at the police station when Raymond Fletcher was brought in, after Mary Ann had reported him for fraud, corruption, and making false accusations against one of his employees. But they'd only been able to hold him for less than an hour. Ilka imagined it had been hard for Thomas to see Fletcher wriggle out of the charges made against him—and who knew what threats Fletcher had made to get the police to release him.

In addition to being a powerful man, Raymond Fletcher had been generous to the town of Racine, in a manner that many would describe as blatant graft: an indoor swimming center, new mosaics in a church, a marina. He'd been a man who expected—and demanded—something in return, so the police looked the other way when he and his men were involved in certain corrupt activities. And now that he was dead, it wouldn't be difficult to find people willing to turn against him. Mary Ann hadn't been the only one living under his thumb.

Fletcher had been over eighty when he died. The

lives of so many people would have been different had someone killed him much earlier, Ilka thought. She had absolutely no scruples about lying to get her father's wife out of prison. She stood up when Thomas called in an officer to take her statement and enter it into their records. She already knew which lawyer to contact: the one who had defended her father's friend, Frank Conaway, against Fletcher's false accusations.

"So, let's see if we can't help her," Thomas said.

It only took an hour. By signing her witness statement, Ilka officially swore she was telling the truth. The officer made a copy. Outside in the police station parking lot, she called the lawyer and told him exactly the same thing she'd said to Stan Thomas. It was self-defense. Mary Ann had saved their lives.

Ilka also told him that Leslie was still in shock. *She's very fragile right now*, she said. But it didn't sound as if the lawyer believed it would be necessary to bring up Leslie's family history in the case, and it definitely wouldn't be part of the public record. He promised to contact the jail immediately and set up a meeting with his new client.

Before hanging up, Ilka told him that Mary Ann would probably cling to her version of events to protect her daughter. "She thinks Leslie has already gone through too much."

The lawyer understood. He knew about Leslie's situation; he'd worked for her biological father's family, so they would all be on the same page in this case.

21

We have a customer," Jette said when Ilka returned to the funeral home. She was in the kitchen, looking for coffee filters. "Leslie drove over to the bakery for milk and kringle."

It seemed her half sister had taken the hearse for her grocery run, which annoyed Ilka.

A man was sitting in the reception area with her mother. The ladder still stood in front of the door, and Ilka noticed the buckets and rags scattered around the room, the large gold-framed mirror back on the wall. They'd begun cleaning.

Her father came downstairs and greeted the man.

"Eric's wife is dying," her mother said, "and he needs our assistance."

Ilka stood in the doorway, hoping that Leslie would get back soon so they could speak before the police and the lawyer contacted her.

She noticed that the man was older than her father. Quite a bit older, probably in his eighties. The skin on his hands was paper-thin, and the color in his eyes seemed faded. His hand shook faintly when he reached out for her father.

"I can't understand what my wife says anymore. The last five years she's been suffering from dementia, but now she's dying and she can barely talk."

"Would you like a cup of coffee?" Ilka said.

Slowly, he turned toward her. "Just a glass of water, thanks." He nodded in gratitude. "My wife has forgotten her second language, we can't talk anymore."

His voice was feeble. He pressed the bridge of his nose with two fingers and closed his eyes a moment. Ilka held out a glass of water to him when he opened them again.

"Eric's wife is Danish," her mother explained. "She came here with her parents when she was fourteen, and now she can only speak Danish."

The man nodded.

"Their daughter works at the library, and she saw the notice that Jette and I put up about our Danish evening. She's the one who suggested Eric contact us. They need someone to be with his wife, someone who speaks Danish."

Jette appeared in the doorway. "A night nurse," she said, in Danish. "They need a night nurse who can talk to her so she doesn't feel alone."

Eric looked down at his folded hands as she spoke.

Ilka had never considered that someone could forget a language in their old age. That it could disappear the same way as the memory of a loved one. That was about as lonely a situation as Ilka could imagine.

"I want so much to understand what she's saying," Eric said. "I just don't think she knows she's talking to us in Danish. And I think she's scared."

Tears welled up in his eyes.

"I'm sorry, but regretfully we don't provide a night nurse service," her father said. He suggested contacting a home care provider.

Immediately her mother piped up. "Of course we'll sit with your wife." She took Eric's hand. "We'll help, of course we will."

"And what about when it's over?" he said, his voice barely audible.

She patted his hand. "We will help with that too. But at the moment, we must ensure that you and your wife can talk to each other while she's still alive."

Ilka's mother had once taught English, and she spoke distinctly in a pleasant British accent.

The man appeared so relieved and grateful that Ilka discreetly wiped a tear from her cheek. He explained that they lived only two blocks away. "I walked over here."

He wobbled a bit as he stood up.

"Why don't we walk back with you and meet your wife; then we can see if she would like us to be there."

Ilka's father asked if he should go along, but the two newly arrived Danish women clearly had the situation under control. Her mother offered the man her arm, and Jette grabbed his cane.

Ilka followed them out and watched them cross the street. As she turned to go back inside, a car pulled out of their parking lot. She noticed the Lone Star license plate, and when the car turned onto the street, she glimpsed the tense face of Miguel Rodriguez and a shadowy figure beside him, presumably his brother.

She had the feeling they'd noticed her, and she rushed back to the house, but they either weren't interested in her or had something urgent to take care of. Miguel floored it, and the car quickly vanished.

Her heart pounded so hard that her chest hurt as she ran through the house, flung open the back door, and sprinted across the parking lot. Even before she reached Lydia's apartment, she saw the door standing open. They'd made no attempt to hide how they'd kicked the door in and splintered the doorframe, exposing bare wood around the lock.

For a moment she stood in the doorway and listened, despite having seen the brothers drive away. When she stepped inside, at once she realized what they'd done. Clothes had been ripped off hangers, the chest of drawers under the mirror emptied, everything flung onto the floor. The living room had been turned upside down, and her mother's and Jette's things lay scattered all over the bedroom. Ilka looked around in shock. They'd searched every square inch of the apartment, in broad daylight, while she, her mother, her father, and everyone else had been just next door in the funeral home. She shivered, shaken by how callous and unconcerned they were.

She hurried back to the funeral home and called out for her father. "You have to come over here and see this."

She held the back door for him. It was as if he already knew what had happened; he strode over to the apartment and barely stopped to glance at the broken door, the splinters of wood lying on the ground.

"We'll have to get your mother and Jette out," he said, after inspecting the apartment. "Do you know where their suitcases are?"

Ilka pointed; they'd been ransacked and shoved underneath the bed.

"Call the hotel and reserve a room, then we'll pack their things."

He'd leaned his cane against the wall and was standing now, arms at his sides, surveying the chaos. Fear was written all over his face, and he looked feeble again. "They're still after her."

Ilka nodded. That much was obvious. They must have found out she'd lied to them about Lydia being in Texas. What scared her most, though, was how they'd taken off like a bat out of hell. Obviously, something was going on—but did it have to do with Lydia? Ilka was afraid they knew where to find her.

She grabbed her phone and texted Jeff. You need to find her now. They're closing in.

"You and Leslie can't stay here either," her father said. "Did you get hold of the hotel?"

Ilka ignored him and googled the hotel's number.

* * *

"A double room," she repeated. She began packing the two suitcases and Jette's weekend bag. Toiletries, clothes, shoes. After finishing, she set the suitcases outside and went back in to pick up the worst of the incredible mess. They'd even emptied the upper kitchen cupboards; flour and pasta nearly covered the floor.

"I'll pick up here. Just take their things over to the funeral home so they don't see this."

Ilka whirled at the sound of Leslie's voice. She hadn't heard her come in and didn't know how long she'd been standing in the doorway. Her father had gone back to the funeral home, and now she noticed that he'd forgotten his cane. The break-in had shocked him after all, she thought, and it also must have been a grim reminder of the night he'd been attacked just outside.

"Thanks." She smiled, or at least tried to; she was trembling all over.

She called Jeff and got his answering service. She left a message, offering him five thousand dollars extra if he could find a way to get Lydia to safety immediately. Not that she had any idea where the money would come from, but at the moment there were fifty-one women sitting on death row in American prisons, and soon there would be one more if Jeff didn't step up.

She thumbed a final desperate text: Call. Then she stuck her phone back into her pocket and turned to Leslie.

"There's something I need to talk to you about."

22

An hour later her mother and Jette returned from Eric's house and were told they would have to move. Her father said they'd booked a room at the hotel, and Ilka held up the car keys.

"I'll drive you down there."

"No," the two women said, nearly simultaneously.

"Sorry," her father said. "Sister Eileen came back and needs the apartment, so unfortunately you can't stay."

Ilka looked away, thinking about the day Lydia had packed Ilka's suitcase without a word and moved her things down to the hotel. Back then she'd thought the nun wanted to get rid of her, when in fact she was trying to protect her.

"It's a good hotel, and it'll be easier to walk around town if you stay down there," Ilka said.

"But we'll be going over to Elly's. We promised to

stop by again." Her mother obviously was taking this personally.

"But you'll only be sleeping there," Leslie said. "You can be here the rest of the time."

Earlier Ilka had explained to Leslie what she'd told Officer Thomas, adding that she should expect a visit from the police. Ilka's half sister had taken it surprisingly well; in fact, she'd even offered to call the lawyer. It was as if Leslie had renewed her membership in the human race, and it suited her well.

"But did the police swallow the story?" she'd asked.

Ilka assured her that they had, and that all Leslie had to do was act convincing when she told the policeman that her grandfather had threatened to kill all three of them.

Leslie nodded and asked if the police would want to know where she was standing when the shooting occurred.

"Tell them you were so shaken up that you don't really remember. And say that if your mother hadn't grabbed the rifle out of the gun cabinet, he would have shot us with the pistol in his desk drawer."

Leslie had nodded.

Now her father spoke up. "This is just how it has to be."

All five of them stood awkwardly, looking in five different directions, until Jette nodded and took Ilka's mother's arm. They didn't at all understand what was going on, but they seemed to accept that it was none of their business.

"Then I guess we'll get to see the harbor," she said, her face blank. She grabbed the two suitcases. "If it's because we're not welcome..." Her mother gave her father a look.

Ilka stepped over and put her arm around her mother's shoulder. "No, no, you *are* welcome; absolutely. It's just that when I said you could stay in the apartment, I didn't know Sister Eileen would be back so soon. I'm so sorry. Whenever you're ready to come over, just call me and I'll come get you. Or you could also take the car."

She knew very well why her father wanted them gone. It wasn't a problem when everyone was at the funeral home, but the Rodriguez brothers might decide to come back. Letting them sleep over there by themselves simply wasn't an option.

"Hello! Anybody here?"

Ilka recognized the deep voice coming from the reception: Jeff. She rushed out to meet him.

"Have you found her?"

The others had followed along, and he smiled at them. "Just need to borrow Beautiful here for a sec." He placed his arm on the small of her back and winked at them. Ilka glimpsed her mother smiling at Jeff as he led her out the door.

"Where is she? Is she all right?"

He opened the door of his BMW for her, and Ilka got in. Her mother stood in the doorway and watched. Ilka knew what she was thinking; her mother longed for Ilka to move on from losing Flemming. *You should be looking around for another man*, she'd said—several times.

"I got your message about the extra bonus," Jeff said. Ilka nodded, assuming this wasn't the time to tell him she didn't actually have the money. That would have to wait until they found Lydia.

"But I want an evening with you too," he added.

"An evening?"

He looked away. "Yeah, like back on the boat."

Their erotic encounter on the table in the close quarters of his cabin hadn't exactly been memorable. What it had been was quick—a physical release, and that was it. No talk, no affection. No emotions. It seemed he now wanted a repeat performance. Fat chance of that happening. Did he think he could have anything he wanted from her just because he'd found Lydia?

The idea angered her.

He seemed nervous. Or maybe he was just excited.

Ilka recalled the line of coke his friend had snorted on the boat, and had the feeling Jeff had already begun celebrating his success, which meant he would soon be fifteen thousand dollars richer. She tried to check his pupils, but they were hidden behind his sunglasses. Then again, he seemed more hyper than high; he kept a steady, rapid beat with his thumbs on the steering wheel as they sped through town.

"Where are we going?" she said. The marina flashed by on her right, and soon they'd driven past the last stoplight and were out of Racine.

Jeff ignored her and kept tapping his thumbs, as if in time to loud music in his head. Ilka turned and stared at the landscape of open fields. Moments later they turned off in the direction of the lake.

"Has she been hiding in Artie's house?" A jolt of fear rocked her; the Rodriguez brothers knew this place. It angered Ilka to think that Lydia would hide somewhere they could find her so easily.

She was out of the car before Jeff could shut the engine off. He hopped out and caught up to her. "She could be armed, you don't know," he hissed as he grabbed her arm. "Use your head. If you scare her bad enough, she might shoot before she sees it's you."

Ilka stopped. "But are you sure she's in there?"

He nodded and nudged her toward the door, but Ilka wrenched free of his grip. The windows that had been broken during the attack on Artie now had sheets of plywood covering them, but the one beside the door had escaped damage. She walked over to it, cupped her hands against the pane, and peered into the living room. Then she tapped on the glass and waited, hoping Lydia would spot her and come out when she saw who it was.

"Hello in there," she yelled.

Jeff pushed the door open and waved her over.

"When did you see her?" Ilka whispered.

"She was here this morning."

Ilka stepped in the doorway. "Hello! It's me!"

She walked inside and stood a moment listening, even though she already knew the house was deserted. She wiped her shoes off on the mat and entered the living room. Glass still lay on the floor, but the first thing she noticed was the bag on the coffee table, its soft leather strap hanging over the edge of the polished wood surface. The bag was empty. Ilka felt a cold gust of wind, and she ran through the room and to the wide-open back door. But there was no one in sight.

Ilka walked back to the living room. "Where is she? Did you take the money?"

When Jeff didn't answer, she stepped over and grabbed his jacket and pushed him up against the wall, all in one movement, too quickly for him to react. "What have you done with her?" she yelled.

He had pushed his sunglasses up on his forehead, and now they flew off onto the floor. He stared at her in surprise. She glimpsed something vulnerable in his eyes, but a second later they were dark with anger. He wrested free and pushed her back, hard.

"What the hell are you talking about, you bitch!"

His sudden rage frightened her; had he brought her out here to get rid of her, after discovering what was in the bag? He could easily push her over the cliff and watch her disappear in Lake Michigan. Killing her was all he needed to do if he really had taken the money. She had felt his gun holster under his jacket.

"She was here," he snarled, though he seemed to be trying to hold himself back. "She's been staying in the house at least since yesterday. I don't know when she came, but I know somebody a few houses down from here, he saw a woman fitting her description yesterday afternoon. I've been keeping an eye on the house ever since, I just wanted to be sure it was her before I got back to you."

"Where's the money?"

Jeff stared at her.

"You took it, all of it," she continued. "The temptation was too great, and now you think I can't figure out what happened."

He shook his head. "I didn't take any money, but you owe me, a lot. And I want it, right now. We had a deal, and I held up my end."

Ilka shook her head. "I don't owe you a thing. You were supposed to find her for me, but she's not here, and how do I know she's even been here? You should've stayed and kept her in sight until I showed up."

His lips were clamped together from rage, and for a split second she thought he might shoot her, but without a word he turned and stomped out of the house and onto the sidewalk. She ran out after him.

"Where is she?" she yelled.

When he reached his BMW, she noticed the ruts behind Artie's black pickup. Two broad, deep tire tracks in the rain-soaked ground. Someone had driven in and backed out again, so fast that the tires had dug into the mud. Jeff's car was on a paved portion of the driveway, and there was no dirt or mud splatter on his shiny black car.

Standing by his car door, he turned back to her. His icy voice felt like a slap to her face. "She was here. I did what you wanted me to do. You're going to pay what you owe me."

He got in the car and slammed the door shut, and moments later he was gone.

Ilka stood in the driveway, shaken by his anger. Up on the road, a white Toyota with HAPPY HOMES written on the door slowed and turned in. The driver approached slowly, as if he wasn't sure it was the right address.

She stood her ground as he parked and shut the car off. A chubby man holding a briefcase under his arm got out and walked toward her. His coat was unzipped even though it was starting to rain.

"Good afternoon. Are you Mrs. Sorvino?"

All Ilka wanted to do was sleep. To turn her back on him and walk inside and jump into Artie's bed under the blankets.

She shook her head but asked if there were anything she could help him with. A strange blend of numbness and fear overtook her. His voice sounded distant; Ilka barely understood the words coming out of his mouth.

"I'm here to assess Mr. Sorvino's house. He contacted us earlier today and said he's interested in selling."

"Selling? The house?"

The real estate agent smiled politely. No doubt he was thinking she must be a relative with limited intellectual abilities, someone to humor so he could pull off the deal.

"He contacted you today because he wants to sell his house?" Ilka said.

He nodded and showed her a key. "I've just been by the hospital; I picked up the key and written permission to go inside, since he's unable to let me in himself."

He reached to open his briefcase and show her the paper, but she simply nodded and told him the house was open.

Artie had seen through her, had found out she couldn't be trusted. Couldn't be counted on. She flashed on him lying in his hospital bed, calling the insurance company because he'd sensed something was wrong, that she was lying when she assured him everything was fine. He knew the hospital would be sending him bills from now until he died if he didn't do something about it himself.

Ilka turned her back on the real estate agent and slowly walked up to the highway. She headed for Racine in a fog of tears and rain, crushed that she couldn't find a way to help Artie. And scared stiff that the Rodriguez brothers had found Lydia.

23

Ilka yelled and cursed all the way back to town. The sorrow she'd felt had given way to fury; she didn't feel cold, even though her clothes were soaked and her legs almost too weak to carry her. She built up a wall of anger against her father. This was his fault—that they had landed in a situation where a calamity of this magnitude could happen. That the fucking insurance policy had disappeared in the pile of blackmail letters and advertisements. Who the hell was so stupid and irresponsible that they didn't use a bill payment service to automatically handle important bills? Ilka's cheeks stung with rage as she sped down the highway, screaming her lungs out. It was his fault for going underground. It wasn't one bit fair that she was solely responsible for the consequences. Or that Artie now had to sell his house.

When she finally reached the funeral home and kicked

her wet shoes off in the hallway, she was ready to tear into her father, the stream of bitter words dammed up right behind her lips, ready to gush out. She made a quick search of the house, but to her annoyance she couldn't find him.

Leslie wasn't in her room either, but when Ilka neared the reception area, she heard her mother and Jette taking off their coats as they talked about the caustic odor from the prep room. It had been a long time since Artie had worked in there, but the smell still hung in the hallway.

Ilka couldn't hold back her rage; she erupted at the two women, words gushing out of her in waves as she tried to make them understand, how it was not her fault Artie was lying in the hospital without insurance and might not ever fully recover.

"I tried to help," she said, over and over again. "But now he knows I couldn't, I let him down, and he's not even sure he'll ever be able to work again."

The words kept coming, and she barely noticed when her mother helped take off her wet sweatshirt and wrapped her in a blanket before settling her in an easy chair in the reception. Suddenly Ilka noticed how badly she was shaking, and she clutched the blanket and pulled it close around her.

"You need to eat, something nourishing," Jette said. "Let's go to the hotel, we'll have dinner together down there."

They ordered her up to her room to change into dry clothes, as they debated whether or not to turn out the lights in the funeral home. The hotel was the last place Ilka wanted to go. She tried to wall off her fear, but images kept running through her head: the Rodriguez brothers and Lydia, the empty bag, men throwing the nun into Lake Michigan with a cement block tied around her. Or maybe she was in the trunk of their car, screaming for help.

Later, when they sat down at a table in the hotel restaurant overlooking the harbor, she finally surrendered her worries. Her mother insisted she order a decent meal, something other than burgers and fries. As the waiter was picking up the three bowls of soup they'd decided on as a starter, Jette walked out of the restaurant. A few minutes later she returned and told them she'd asked the reception to add a single bed to their room.

"So you can stay with us tonight," she said. The waiter brought their chicken and a large bowl of steamed vegetables.

Ilka looked at her in surprise, but instead of protesting, she nodded. Right now, she couldn't care less where she collapsed for the night, as long as she could get a break from all the thoughts dragging her down.

"But remember," her mother said, leaning toward her, "it's only money we're talking about here. No one has died. Surely we can figure it out."

"But we don't *have* any money, we can't help him," Ilka said. "And over here if you don't have insurance, you need to show them cash."

"There must be some way," her mother insisted.

"When the hospital finds out he can't pay for the

treatment he's already been given, they'll do everything they can to get their money. That's why he's putting his house up for sale."

Ilka explained that they would send out a debt collector. "And because he owns a house, he'll be forced to sell it to pay his debt. He'll have to liquidate all his assets."

"What about that lovely place in Key West?" her mother asked.

"They'll take that too, if they have to." She'd shown her mother a few photographs from the gallery and the main street of the town. "If you have anything of worth that can be sold, they'll do anything to get their hands on it."

"But not everyone owns something so valuable," Jette said.

"Hospitals get rid of those people as soon as they can."

"But Artie does own property, so everything will be okay," her mother said. For a second, she looked relieved, even though she'd never met the man.

Ilka shook her head. "No, everything *won't* be okay. He might be able to pay for the treatment he needs, but when he gets out, he won't have a home to go back to."

Ilka was about to embark on a long harangue about the American system, but her mother interrupted by clapping once and announcing it was time to go to bed.

It was hard to say which of the two women snored the loudest: Jette, who had stood on her head for several minutes as part of her evening yoga ritual, or her mother, who had fallen asleep with a book in her hands.

Ilka's rollaway bed had been shoved in under the window, where narrow shards of light from outside tattooed the blanket in the dark room. The sounds from Lake Michigan felt like heavy waves lapping over her as she tried to fall asleep.

She thought about the time Flemming had left her. She'd known he was going to; she'd certainly given him reason enough. Back then she'd thought she would never be able to get control over her dark side. Find the strength to fight off the urge to let go. To disappear.

It was the racetrack, again. About a year after she'd lost all the money Flemming had saved up for his son's confirmation. Late that summer they had planned on vacationing in Nice. They'd been looking forward to it; they'd rented a car and a room in a boardinghouse up in the mountains, at Bargemon. The sun had been shining all day at the racetrack, and it was about to go down when Flemming found her, just as he had back when they'd first met. She'd lost on that day too, and her fragility had attracted him.

But it didn't the second time. What hurt the most was that he didn't even really get mad. Only sad, very sad. So much so that Ilka immediately believed their relationship was broken beyond repair.

Fortunately, she'd been wrong. And she had her mother to thank for that. She'd come by to care for Ilka in the days that followed. The first day with food, fresh tulips, milk. The next day she simply sat with Ilka, who refused to get out of bed or even eat. That might have been the day she'd begun reading out loud; Ilka wasn't sure anymore. It could have been later on. Anyway, her mother had read for her as if she were a small child. The days flowed by as she listened to her mother's stories, and the intimacy that grew between them during their daily routine had the same effect on her as a poultice, applied at the moment of greatest need. Slowly, Ilka began to heal, and to this day she was convinced that her mother had gone to Flemming and persuaded him to give Ilka one more chance, even though the two of them both insisted it wasn't true.

The important thing, though, was that Flemming came back to her, and it had been the very last time Ilka had set foot on a racetrack. But lying there in the hotel, with ribbons of light shining in from the marina, remembering how absolutely horrible she'd felt, Ilka realized she was willing to risk that pain and sense of loss if it could somehow free Artie and Lydia.

24

Ilka hadn't fallen asleep until late that night. Her thoughts had grown darker as the hours passed, until finally she was sure there was no way out for Lydia, plus Artie would end up disabled and never forgive her. When she woke up the next morning, she felt woozy. She gazed around the room. Her mother and Jette were gone, their bed neatly made.

Her lanky body ached as she slowly crawled out of bed. It was nine thirty. Her mother had left a note in the bathroom, informing her that they'd left for the funeral home and that the hotel served breakfast until ten.

Only a few guests were still sitting in the breakfast section of the hotel's foyer. Starbucks coffee stood on a counter, with cornflakes, milk, and a toaster for the white bread. She poured herself a cup of coffee and toasted a slice of bread. She turned to look for a table, and there he was, standing with a cup in his hand, eyeing her. The man from Texas.

Ilka whirled around to drop everything and run, but she caught herself. Maybe she was safer here than anywhere else. She took a moment to gather herself, then she walked over to sit at a table close to the hotel's reception desk.

"I don't know where she is," she said, when the man approached her.

"May I have a seat?" He nodded at the chair across from her.

"I'd rather you didn't. I know you're looking for Lydia Rogers, but you're too late. Your friends have already found her."

He studied her for a moment, then he shook his head and pulled the chair out to sit down. "You're wrong, the Rodriguez brothers are no friends of mine. I'm guessing that's who you're talking about."

Ilka nodded.

He held his hand out to her. "My name is Calvin Jennings. I'm here to help Miss Rogers."

She shook his hand reluctantly. Something about his face reminded her of an actor. Ed Harris. Maybe it was his eyes, his high forehead.

"I'm a Texas policeman. I took part in the investigation, back when Lydia's brother was killed. I never pegged her as the Baby-Butcher."

Ilka hadn't touched her toast, and now a young woman was clearing the tables.

"We already knew back then that the Rodriguez brothers headed up a drug cartel—in fact, we were zeroing in on them when Lydia's brother showed up. He wanted to go into the Witness Protection Program in exchange for telling us everything he knew. He had records of every delivery he'd been a part of."

Ilka was starting to believe this man. She sipped her coffee and listened.

"Then Ben Rogers was killed, and in no time flat all the evidence was pointing to his sister. It was my job to dig around in her past, and I found out she'd been a member of a religious cult—God's Will, they call themselves. A man named Isiah Burnes has been leading it for forty-two years. It started in Utah then expanded to a little town in West Texas, where Lydia and her brother happened to live. The members of the cult are completely shut off from the outside world, but because they're Christian, and their financial situation is solid, they have the support of the locals. Unfortunately, that includes the police and local authorities. Right off the bat I knew this story about Lydia Rogers being behind these brutal crimes—the mutilated corpses of babies—came from the Rodriguez family. They happen to have close ties with God's Will. Lydia left the cult, which they don't allow, and up pops this chance for them to punish her. And they took it."

Ilka caught herself staring at him, holding her coffee cup way too high in the air.

"But we searched for her anyway, put out an APB, went to the press," he said, disgusted by the memory. "It ended up being a regular manhunt. We found evidence that the Rodriguez family planted two baby corpses in her backyard to tie her to the case, which made me even more interested in her."

"But if the police knew it wasn't her, why didn't they stop searching for her? The last twelve years she's been living underground with a death sentence hanging over her. How could all of you let this happen?"

"She did shoot three men. And back then it was a big relief for everybody when we identified a guilty party that very afternoon. People were terrified; it was all anybody talked about, these little corpses of babies. We needed somebody we could point to. Lydia got caught between her brother and the Rodriguez family, and we had strong evidence against her."

"But still!"

He hesitated for a moment. "I talked to her the day she fled from Texas."

"You were the one she called, to report that her family had been killed?"

Jennings nodded.

"You let her get away."

He nodded again. "We'd just heard that Enrique Rodriguez was among those killed, and that his brother Javi had been in the house. She'd never have had a fair chance in Texas. And I felt bad about not getting there in time to help her brother—I felt guilty as hell about that. He and his family were wiped out, right after he'd come to us asking for help. We didn't take it serious enough."

He looked away for a moment. "I just wanted to get her out of there. That way I figured there was a chance we could still bring the guilty ones to justice, the Rodriguez family. She'd been in the house, she was a main witness, but I needed time to gather evidence and make the case. And that wasn't going to happen if Lydia was in custody. Then I found out about the cult, and I realized they're the ones who wanted to pin this on her. It made me even happier she'd managed to get away."

"But you knew it wasn't her! Surely you could have put her someplace safe and helped her?"

"We had a different sheriff back then. It was more important to him that we had *a* guilty party than *the* guilty party. And for years he benefited from the protection the cult gave him."

"Protection?"

"The cult has a peace force they call the God Squad. Isiah Burnes's private army, is what it boils down to. They keep folks in line, and they deal with the people who either get thrown out or leave the cult. Lydia and her brother were born into God's Will, and children of parents who have devoted their lives to the cult automatically belong to the cult. They become the cult's children, you could say. I don't know how much you know about these things."

Ilka shook her head. "Nothing." Of course she'd heard stories of Jehovah's Witnesses, members who were expelled or chose to leave, but she didn't think they actually had their own militia, with the power that Jennings described.

He folded his arms on the table and leaned forward. "There's been serious accusations leveled against Burnes. Polygamy, sexual intercourse with minors, abuse. It's a religious cult with its own rules and laws. According to God's Will, a man has to have at least three wives to pass through the gates of heaven. But it's common for the older men to have a lot more than that. Girls born into the cult are given a number at birth. They don't have a name until the day they turn twelve, when they get baptized and declared ready for marriage. Nobody's interested in the boys, though. When they grow up, they're competition to the older men, who aren't about to share their girls and women. When a male baby is weak, they throw him away. I'm talking literally here. They take him out in a meadow and leave him. I've heard some mighty gruesome stories about women who don't get to nurse or take care of their baby boys; the children grow up with no physical contact with their mothers. The ones who survive are sent out to work when they turn five or six. And a lot of them get thrown out and have to fend for themselves the day they turn fifteen."

"Where do they go?" Ilka said.

"They drive them out of state and just dump them somewhere, and they don't know anybody, they don't have any money. Boys who've never lived outside the cult. A lot of them kill themselves or become criminals, it's just so hard for them to make their way in life."

Jennings folded his hands, a funny look in his eyes.

"Lydia's brother was one of the boys who were thrown out."

"But Lydia stayed." Ilka pushed her cup aside. The coffee was cold.

He nodded. "She stayed, yes. Until her brother managed to get her out. There's a kind of underground railroad that helps women and children escape from the cult. A woman by the name of Alice Payne runs it. She's the one who helped Lydia and her brother back then, and now Lydia helps her. Lydia managed to live in freedom for four years, until her brother and his family were murdered."

"Why did she stay after he was thrown out, back when he was young?"

"Like I said, the cult doesn't let people walk out." He stared into space for a moment. "But you have to remember, it's the only life these people know. I've talked to several women who escaped, and almost every one of them said they felt bound to Isiah Burnes, despite the incest and abuse. It's impossible for us on the outside to understand."

"They're brainwashed."

He nodded. "And the God Squad keeps an eye on everybody. Burnes calls it a peace force, but it's nothing more than a bunch of goons, a gang, and they'll kill without batting an eye. And not only the people in the cult. They come down hard on anybody who sets up against them. Against the family. The brotherhood. Prisons can be many things. The God Squad are executioners, but the most terrifying part of it all is that most of the members stay loyal to their guru. I talked to one woman who believes that all the good Burnes has done outweighs the misery he's caused. Misery to the children of the cult, is what she meant."

Ilka squirmed in her chair. This was beyond anything she'd ever imagined. "Where does the money come from to keep the cult going?"

"The leaders make sure new cult members give up everything they own. They put on revivals, *free-spirit seminars*. And once they get their claws into people, the new members give it all up gladly."

The more Ilka asked questions, the more she got answers she really didn't want to hear.

"Another cult leader was arrested in Utah not so long ago. He has sixty wives and they say he's fathered several hundred children. He's been charged with murder, kidnapping, rape, and statutory rape. The police in Texas will drop the charges against Lydia if she'll come in and testify against Isiah Burnes. It's estimated that God's Will has between four and five thousand members, but it could be more, lots more."

"I don't know where she is," Ilka said. "I'm afraid the Rodriguez brothers found her."

Jennings raised his eyebrows. "What makes you think that?"

Ilka told him about Lydia hiding in Artie's house. "But when I got there, all I found was her empty bag. They had taken the money and her brother's records."

He nodded. "The money. There was a rumor going around that she got away with quite a bit of the drug money."

"It was a mistake. She didn't know what was in the bag when they threw it in the car, and the records were hidden in her nephew's baby carrier. She didn't find them until later on, after she'd gotten away. And she couldn't go back and return them, could she."

"The nephew." He leaned forward. "We never found Ben's son. The Rodriguez boys claimed that Lydia killed him and used his corpse to smuggle drugs."

Ilka shook her head. "Ethan's alive." She told him how Lydia had rescued the boy and the nanny from her brother's house and taken them with her.

Jennings looked surprised. "Are you sure about this?"

Ilka nodded. "I met him," she said, but didn't tell him where. "How could you let her take the blame? Why didn't you do anything to help her?"

"I *am* doing something, I'm here now. And the last time I saw you, you weren't much for helping me find her."

"I didn't know you were asking about Lydia. And now she's gone."

He glanced out the window, and for a moment he gazed out at the tall masts of the yachts in the harbor. His eyes sank deeper into his face as he frowned. "I don't think the Rodriguez boys took her," he finally said, in a slow drawl. "They're not interested in the reward. They just want their money back, without drawing any attention to the old case. Javi Rodriguez got off easy, twelve years in the pen, and the only reason they didn't try to get him out before he finished his sentence was all the money he was making inside. The prison drug business was too good. Besides, back then they had this verbal agreement with the sheriff: He gave them free rein and they did the same with him. It's not like that nowadays."

"But still, I don't know where she is," Ilka said. She wasn't sure if she should be relieved or not.

"If anyone's got Lydia, I'm thinking it's the God Squad, and that's not good. It might mean they've tracked down the underground railroad."

"And?"

"And that means we might never see her again. Promise me you'll contact me the second you get any sign she's alive."

He pulled a card out of his pocket and gave it to Ilka. It was the same one he'd left in the doorway of Lydia's apartment. "We need to find her; it's important."

She watched as he left, then kept staring after he was gone. Now she understood; Lydia knew it wasn't only the Rodriguez brothers looking for her. Ilka had seen the fear in her eyes. All this time she'd known she had more to lose than the bag, more to be afraid of than ending up on death row.

She tossed her crumpled-up napkin aside. Her fingers hurt from squeezing it.

25

The moment Ilka stepped into the funeral home, she knew; she saw it on everyone's faces. Her mother and Jette had told her father that she hadn't paid Artie's health insurance, and that Artie now had very serious money problems because of her.

He turned to Ilka in anger. "How could this happen? Why in the world did you go through my mail? Something as important as—"

"Hold on just a minute, Paul!" Jette said. "You were dead. Somebody had to take care of things. And it's also true, like Ilka says, that you should have used a payment service to make sure important bills like that were taken care of. What if the postal service had lost the letter? It happens all the time in Denmark. And we consider ourselves lucky if a bill reaches us before it's due. You can't count on anything with the mail, and you certainly can't blame your daughter."

"If she hadn't interfered, Sister Eileen would have taken care of it. And this wouldn't have happened."

Ilka knew her father felt helpless, and that he was deeply unhappy about Artie's situation. But she whirled around to face him and exploded.

"I have heard enough out of you! I tried to take care of your business while you've been gone, and I could have done better, I admit it. But don't fucking stand there and accuse me of interfering, because believe me, I did *not* want to interfere, it's the last thing I wanted to do."

Tufts of the white hair surrounding his head seemed to bristle as her father rose furiously from the table to shout back at her, but Ilka cut him off.

"If we'd found Lydia, all these problems would have been solved. She has enough money to cover Artie's hospital expenses, and I'm absolutely sure she would do it. But I don't know where she is. And us standing here yelling at each other isn't going to help."

"But I thought she was here," her mother said. "Wasn't that why you had us move to the hotel?"

The four of them stood looking at each other, but Ilka didn't at all feel like explaining. All she could think about was what Jennings had said about the God Squad, how he was scared they'd never see Lydia again.

She started to turn and walk away, but her father cleared his throat and calmly said, "I know where she is."

It took only one second, one step for Ilka to be in his face. "Where?"

"I'll take you there."

Ilka summarized what Calvin Jennings had told her while they drove. Her father shook his head at Isiah Burnes and the "peace force" he sent after people who broke the rules of his religious regime.

"Did you ever have the feeling she was hiding people in the apartment?" Ilka was thinking about the rollaway bed folded up under the window. "Or did she borrow your car, maybe?"

Her father stared out the passenger window a few seconds. "Once in a while she wanted to borrow the hearse, and of course I let her if we weren't using it. I assumed it had something to do with her parish. And you always want to help if you can."

"But she didn't belong to any parish."

"No, she didn't, as it turns out."

Quite a while went by before the towering chimney came into sight and Ilka realized where her father was taking her. She glanced at him. They hadn't spoken about his relationship to Dorothy, though Ilka had the feeling the two of them had been in contact after he'd returned from Key West.

She turned into the driveway leading to the old farm and crematorium. "How long has Lydia been here?"

"Since yesterday. She called me and said she'd asked Dorothy to come get her at Artie's house."

"Called? So you knew Lydia was around? Why didn't you say something about it?"

"Because you'd already left. And I haven't seen you until now."

"So that was where you and Leslie were last night?"

She parked in front of Dorothy's front door, and he turned to her. "Do you think Lydia can help Artie?" he said, ignoring her question.

Ilka nodded, but before he could ask anything else, she stepped out of the car.

Dorothy came out of the old crematorium and walked their way.

"Ilka wants to talk to Lydia," her father said. "They parted under difficult circumstances, I think you could say, back when she drove down to Key West to get me."

That's putting it diplomatically, Ilka thought. She could still hear Lydia spitting words in her face, saying she hoped for Ilka's sake that they'd never see each other again. As they walked to the door, Dorothy reached over and put her arm around Ilka. A type of intimacy had formed between them on the evening Ilka sat on Dorothy's sofa and listened to her explain how Fletcher had forced her father to not contact Ilka. That night convinced her that Dorothy loved her father, which was a comfort to know; by then she'd realized how lonely her father had been in Racine.

On the front doorstep, she stopped; she could see Lydia in the living room window. An indescribable sense of relief washed over her, knowing the tiny woman was safe inside the house, yet at the same time Ilka was angry to find out she'd been so close by. The feeling vanished, though, when Lydia opened the door and stepped aside to let them in. Ilka saw none of the woman's desperation and rage that had frightened her at the rest stop, where the bleeding man lay on the ground.

"You found the bag," Ilka said. She explained that she'd left it at the hospital with Artie because she'd been afraid the Rodriguez brothers would return.

"I guessed as much," Lydia said.

There was a look in her eye Ilka had never seen before, a determination. She'd made up her mind.

"Thank you," she said, so quietly that only Ilka heard her. "For helping me."

Ilka nodded at her, silently accepting that the way they'd last parted was history, something they wouldn't ever discuss.

Lydia stood by the coffee table as Ilka sat on the sofa. "Someone wanted me to tell you hello—Calvin Jennings. He's the one who came around asking for Lydia Rogers, that day you found out you'd been recognized."

Lydia nodded. "I know who he is."

"He can help you." Ilka shivered, even though the door to the back room and stairway was closed.

She described how Jennings had sought her out at the hotel. "He was the one you talked to when you called in about the shooting at your brother's house, is how I understand it."

Something shifted in Lydia's eyes.

"Fernanda told us what happened that day," Ilka said.

Lydia nodded again and waited.

"He wants you to go back to Texas with him, to act as a witness against Isiah Burnes."

That clearly startled Lydia, but still she said nothing.

"He can get the charges against you dropped. He can prove the cult planted the evidence."

"They did it?" Lydia slowly walked over to the easy chair and sat down with her hands folded in her lap.

Ilka told her how Jennings had left the police and was now a private investigator. "But he still has connections to the police in San Antonio. I think he's determined to stop God's Will and clear your name. A great injustice against you, is how he put it. He also told me you and Alice Payne work with the underground railroad that helps women and children get away from the cult."

Lydia looked up, her face pale now.

Quickly Ilka reached out across the table to her. "He's on your side."

"How can we be sure of that?"

Her father's voice startled her, and Ilka turned and saw him standing in the kitchen doorway.

"Why should we trust him? He could just as well be working for the Rodriguez brothers."

Lydia shook her head and looked down at her hands. "I think he's here to help. When I saw him out in front of the funeral home, I got scared. I thought he'd come to tell me something had happened to Alice. Or that she'd sent him to warn me. That's why I wanted to just get out of there."

Her voice was husky, and Ilka realized that Lydia was touched, even relieved. Or maybe it was from knowing she was no longer alone, that someone believed her and wanted to help.

Her father wouldn't let it go. "But can we trust him?"

Lydia nodded. "His own daughter joined God's Will when she was seventeen or eighteen. She fell in love with a guy in the cult, but a year later she committed suicide. I didn't know Jennings back then, or his daughter. She was several years older than me. But he was the one my brother contacted for help, back when he was planning on getting his family out of there. That's why I called him. I wasn't aware he knew Alice Payne, that she was helping women who wanted out. Alice and my brother helped me escape, and she supported me later on, too. It takes a long time to change your head when you've been raised a certain way all your life. Back then I lived with Alice and her husband."

Ilka glanced into the kitchen.

"Dorothy knows all about this," Lydia said.

"Jennings told me your parents were members of the cult," Ilka said. "Are they still alive?"

Lydia shrugged. "I don't know which one of the men was my father. Nobody cared about that, we were all children of Isiah Burnes. He could be the one—my mother claimed he was. But it could just as well have been any one of the others. I haven't seen my mother since she sent Ben and me to Texas. She stayed in Utah with my two younger sisters. I was thirteen, my brother was fourteen. It was the year before he was excluded. He tried to find her once when he was in his mid-twenties, he wanted to get back at her for what she'd done to us. Ben had this enormous need for revenge and justice. We both wanted her to pay for the childhood she gave her children."

Dorothy came in with coffee.

"Ben may have been thrown out of the cult, but he was never really free of it, of what it had done to him. It's hard to understand, I realize that. And most of us don't like talking about it. Boys were raped, just like the girls. It was just that we were worth more, because we were fruitful and could multiply, all that. I had a self-induced abortion when I was fourteen, and after that I couldn't get pregnant. Now I think it saved me, even though I nearly died back then. The day after my brother turned fifteen, they took him away, to New Jersey. It's a long drive from Texas, with two armed men in the car. I wasn't told anything about it; one day he was just gone, and nobody would say anything when I asked."

Lydia looked at Ilka's father. "That's when I first tried to run away, but they caught me, and after that they kept a close eye on me. I heard about Alice Payne when I was twenty-two, and I finally managed to escape—my brother had contacted her and asked her to help. He knew he wouldn't be able to get in with a message for me, Burnes's security people would find out."

"The God Squad."

Lydia looked at Ilka in surprise.

"Jennings told me about them," Ilka explained.

"Nobody gets in without their approval. Alice is a gynecologist, and she gets called in when there are complications. Otherwise the cult has their own doctors and midwives, so it's only when something goes wrong that they get help from outside."

"So you think Jennings can be trusted?" her father said.

Lydia nodded. "Definitely. Because of what happened with his daughter, he might be the person willing to go the farthest to stop Burnes. And if what happened down in Texas was their revenge on me for running away, if that's true, well..."

Lydia was clearly shaken, as if that new piece of information had finally soaked in and sounded plausible to her. "I'd like to talk to him, but he'll have to come out here. It's too risky for me to go into town if the Rodriguez brothers are still looking for me."

"I agree," Ilka said. She handed Lydia her phone and the card Jennings had given her.

They all waited in silence as she made the call. Lydia stared down at the coffee table while she spoke with Jennings. From her short answers, Ilka concluded she was prepared to give testimony against Burnes, if the police managed to arrest him.

"And you're sure the police will listen to me?" she asked for the second time.

Ilka pieced together that Jennings had told her about the new police chief in San Antonio, that things were much different now. And it sounded as if Jennings had the same records of drug deliveries as those that had been in the bag, including a list of people the drug ring had paid to cross the border with the dead babies.

Ilka thought about Javi Rodriguez. She realized that her own sense of justice had changed since learning what had happened earlier; she was much more willing now to accept that her father and Lydia had gotten rid of him.

"I can't leave right at the moment," Lydia told Jennings, her eyes still locked onto the table. "There's something I have to take care of first."

Dorothy looked uneasy, but Lydia hung up after promising to call again as soon as she was ready to meet him.

Ilka was worried too. What if the San Antonio police weren't as willing to work out a deal with Lydia as Jennings believed they were? The minute she stepped into police headquarters, she risked being arrested and ending her days in one of the country's most isolated prisons. Ilka had googled sentencing in Texas, and she knew how brave Lydia was to trust Jennings.

"What is it you have to do?" Ilka's father looked at Lydia as if he already knew he wouldn't like her answer.

She stared into space for a moment then glanced at Dorothy before rising from the sofa. A few seconds later she had opened the door to a room at the back of the house and called up the stairs.

Ilka's father straightened up in his chair. Dorothy had

laid a blanket around his shoulders, and it slid to the floor when a woman showed up in the doorway.

"This is my youngest sister, Jane-Maya," Lydia said.

Ilka gaped at the woman. She was in her late twenties, maybe thirty. Two girls still in their nightgowns walked in behind her. Ten and twelve? Ilka wasn't sure; guessing ages wasn't her strong suit. The daughters stared down at their bare feet.

"They're going to have a new life now, outside of the cult," Lydia explained.

Dorothy carried in an extra chair so they all could sit down. She brought in more coffee and two glasses of fruit juice for the girls. They sat glued to each other and their mother on the sofa, hands folded in their laps and eyes averted. Their hair was gathered in ponytails that hung all the way down their backs.

Ilka took note of a large, reddish-brown splotch on the skin of the oldest girl, just above her nightgown's collar. A burn mark, or a wide scar. Suddenly she felt Lydia's eyes on her and realized she was staring at the girl's neck. She quickly looked away.

"My sister and her girls are going up to Canada, where our other sister lives."

It was obvious the two were sisters, Ilka reflected. They had the same delicate features and flat nose. Jane-Maya wasn't much taller than Lydia, either, though her eyes were light blue and Lydia's were brown. She had the same long ponytail as her daughters, and she wore a long dress buttoned up to her neck.

"We got her out four months ago, and now she's found a place up there for all of them. She has three kids, so they need quite a bit of room."

Lydia smiled tenderly at her sister and nieces; the warmth in her eyes became her. Ilka listened as Lydia explained that her two sisters had stayed with their mother at the cult's headquarters in Utah until a few years ago, when she'd finally managed to contact them through one of Alice Payne's friends, a lawyer.

"It took a long time for us to find each other. In more ways than one." Leaving the cult had been a difficult decision, Lydia explained. "Both my sisters were married to Isiah Burnes, and that gives you status and a better position in the hierarchy. But it also makes it much more difficult to get out."

"But wasn't Isiah Burnes your father?" Ilka said.

The steely look returned to Lydia's eyes as she nodded wordlessly.

Ilka left it at that. Something inside her softened up; she'd never seen Lydia this way, sensitive, emotional, so different from the desperate and angry woman she'd been down in Kentucky.

"I can't go with Jennings until I get Jane-Maya and my nieces to Detroit. Our sister will pick them up when they cross the border."

Ilka had no idea where Detroit was in relation to Racine, nor did she know the city was located on the US-Canadian border; geography was another of her weak points.

"I can drive them there." Ilka glanced over at Jane-Maya, who was looking away. "How far is it?"

"It's a six-, seven-hour drive from here," her father said.

"Can we borrow the hearse?" Lydia asked.

Suddenly Ilka understood why it had looked so routine when Lydia had crawled up into the coffin, back when they fled from the Rodriguez brothers. "You want to smuggle them out of the country in a coffin!"

Her hand flew to her mouth; she shouldn't have said that out loud, in front of the woman and her daughters. But they showed no reaction.

"It's the only way. They don't have passports or IDs. Isiah Burnes doesn't allow it."

Ilka nodded thoughtfully. Of course Lydia could forge the necessary papers, she thought; after all, she'd forged her father's death certificate.

Ilka had made up her mind. "I want to do this. When do we leave?"

Jane-Maya and her daughters on the sofa didn't look like they cared who drove them, but Lydia thought it over.

"Tomorrow," she finally answered. "If you're serious about this. You should leave around ten; that way you'll hit the Detroit-Windsor Tunnel around rush hour."

Ilka nodded. That meant Lydia could leave with Jennings tomorrow too, as soon as Ilka took off.

"But there are a few things to do first," Lydia said. "I've rented a storage unit in a warehouse three blocks away from the funeral home."

Ilka knew that must be in the industrial zone farther out from downtown, though she'd never been there.

"There's a large coffin inside, an XL, or oversized as we call it. It's easy to get to. There's also a cart to roll it out on, but you can back the hearse up all the way to the door."

"I can go with you," her father said, but Ilka shook her head and said she could handle it.

"While you're driving here in the States, they can sit up in the coffin if you close the curtains in back. Just so no one can see inside. But when you get to the Canadian border, to customs and immigration, they need to be lying down inside the coffin. As long as the papers are in order, they won't check inside."

Bizarre, Ilka thought, but she nodded. "We could even leave today." She glanced over again at Jane-Maya.

Lydia shook her head. Everything had been coordinated with their sister in Canada, she explained. Then she stood up and asked Ilka and her father to follow her outside.

"They came directly from Alice's," she said when they reached the front steps. "The plan was for them to stay with Fernanda a few weeks before going on, but Alice couldn't get hold of her, and neither could I. So she drove them up here. Usually Alice drives a cult member down to Key West when she gets them out. It helps to have a place they can relax for a while with no pressure. It's an enormous change in their lives, especially for us who were born into the cult. It's all we've known."

Ilka noticed that her father had closed the front door.

"Then when we decide they're ready to go on, Alice drives them up here to Racine, to me. But they only stay for a night, two at the most, before I take them to their final destination."

"Where's that?" Ilka caught herself whispering, though there was no one else around.

"Usually they go to other women who have escaped from some religious group, not necessarily God's Will. It could be Mormons, Scientology, the Family. The feeling that you're in prison, it's the same. And no matter what group you've escaped from, you want to help others in the same situation."

Ilka nodded. Yes, she could see that.

Lydia turned to Ilka's father. "I'm worried about Fernanda. Is there anyone in Key West you know well enough that you could ask them to check the house? To make sure everything's okay?"

He ran his hand over the top of his head and thought a moment. "Nick. I can ask him to run over there."

He turned to Ilka. "He's the one you met, the guy behind the bar. Could you look his number up for me? The name of the bar is Mudville."

Ilka fished her phone out of her pocket and googled the bar.

"When did your sister and nieces get here?" She thought about her own desperate search for Lydia.

"Yesterday evening. I talked to Alice the day before yesterday, which is when she told me she couldn't get hold of Fernanda. I couldn't put them up in the funeral home this time, obviously, so I asked Dorothy if they could stay here."

Ilka nodded. Of course Lydia knew Dorothy well enough to feel comfortable asking her.

"Our sister in Canada is so happy they'll be together again. After she picks them up, it's another five hours to the house she's rented, so it's going to be a long trip for the girls."

Ilka found the number of the bar and handed her phone to her father. She pulled Lydia aside. "There's something I need you to do for me."

Without mincing words, she described Artie's situation and what had happened with his insurance. "I know you've already put a lot into his hospital account, but it's not enough. I don't understand at all how it can be so expensive, and I've racked my brains, but now I'm at the point where I don't know what to do."

"Don't worry about it, Artie is my responsibility. I'm the reason he's in this terrible mess, it never should've happened. I'll make sure he doesn't lack for anything. And if the Rodriguez brothers get their hands on me before we can put them behind bars—well, they'll just have to get by with a lot less money, won't they!"

Ilka had never heard this sense of humor from Lydia before, even in her disguise as Sister Eileen. It must be an enormous relief for her, she thought, knowing that all the years of living underground in constant fear of being found were coming to an end. Finally, she wasn't alone.

"Thank you," Ilka said. She was about to turn back to her father when Lydia reached out and held her arm. Ilka stared at the edge of a round burn mark that was now exposed, just visible above the petite woman's collar.

Lydia let go and let her arm fall to her side. "We all have one."

She tugged her blouse up to cover the scar. "It's part of the baptism ceremony, the day you turn twelve. That's the day your childhood ends and your adult life begins. And everything that comes with it. Jane-Maya's oldest daughter just turned twelve, so her brand hasn't healed yet. It was part of the reason my sister worked up the courage to run away, before her younger daughter had to go through the same ritual, and before they both were married off."

Lydia pursed her lips. "I think I've always hoped that someone someday would step forward and let the world know how much evil Isiah Burnes has done. Look at my little nieces. I can't say for sure they've already been abused, but it wouldn't surprise me. That's what we're up against. We're fighting the pain, all the damage done to the women and children in the cult, every single day. And I'm well aware how it's so unreal to all of you on the outside, that such things can even take place, that more people don't get out. But when you're inside the cult, it's hard to imagine life being any different."

"But they rape small children—surely every parent can see how wrong that is."

Lydia nodded. "You'd think so, but that's not how it

looks on the inside. Burnes convinces us the lives we lead are full of love, that we are being broad-minded. However perverted it sounds, the cult looks on open sexual relationships as universal love given to all the members. He brainwashes everyone into thinking that evil exists only outside the cult. And people believe him. It's going to take a man like Calvin Jennings to stop Burnes. Otherwise there's no hope."

"You are so brave! And you're doing the right thing by going with him. I'll make sure your family gets to Canada."

Lydia nodded and glanced over at Ilka's father, who was still speaking on the phone. "Just give me a minute, I'll get the money for you."

She headed for the door as he handed the phone back to Ilka. He looked worried.

"He's going over there to check on them," he said.

Ilka squeezed his shoulder. When she was down in Key West, she'd seen how close he'd become to Fernanda and Ethan. And it had been equally obvious how the boy felt about her father.

She told him Lydia was upstairs getting the money. "Do you want to go along to the hospital, to pay them? Or would you rather stay here?" She could pick him up on the way back; that would give her time alone with Artie, so she could explain things to him.

He shook his head. "No, I'll go with you. Her nieces have been through enough, and a strange man around the house might upset them even more. They need all the rest they can get. They've got a long trip ahead of them tomorrow."

"I don't think you're upsetting them, I think it's the whole situation. I just can't understand how something like this can take place. Especially when the authorities know about it."

Deep down, she almost had trouble believing the cult was as bad as Jennings and Lydia described it; on the other hand, she'd seen the look in the eyes of Jane-Maya and the two young girls. And now she saw the same darkness in her father's expression.

"Several years ago, another cult leader was arrested," he said. "He got life plus twenty years. They called him one of the worst sex monsters in history. But even from prison he managed to control his followers. That says something about the strength of people's belief. He had over fifteen thousand followers."

"But what about people on the outside, why don't they do something about it?"

Her father shook his head. "They called him the Prophet of Evil; he owned an enormous amount of land close to the border between Utah and Arizona, worth something like a hundred million dollars. Some of the local police were members of his cult, while he was on the FBI's Most Wanted list."

He shook his head again. "It's hard to understand, I know, but I'm sure everything Lydia says is true. It's all happened before."

Lydia came back with the money in a plastic sack.

"This will cover everything he wants or needs. Whatever's left when he gets out of the hospital, put it in his bank account."

She looked at Ilka. "I'm very sorry, I didn't know Artie had these problems."

Ilka knew it was the closest she'd come to apologizing for how all the problems had been dumped on Ilka.

At the hospital, Ilka asked her father to wait in the hallway while she went into the office on Artie's ward. The woman she'd spoken to last time was behind the counter, and she didn't look particularly happy to see Ilka. But she nodded and waved her on in.

"The hospital administration has entered into an agreement with Sorvino and his bank." The woman obviously wanted Ilka to keep her nose out of it. "His house has been put up as collateral, and we won't demand payment on what we are owed until the house is sold."

"That won't be necessary." Ilka began unpacking the money. "What's the status of his patient account?"

It seemed to take a superhuman effort for the woman to lean over and check his account. "He owes four thousand nine hundred dollars, as of today. But now that his house has been put up as security, he can continue with his rehabilitation. We've also planned a follow-up scan for next week."

Ilka brought out the bundle of hundred-dollar bills and counted out forty-nine of them.

The woman behind the counter stared at the money.

"I want to close his account," Ilka said. Her father appeared in the doorway. "We would like to move Artie over to the private section of the hospital. Would you mind checking if there's a vacancy? Preferably with a balcony, so he can get some fresh air."

The stack of bills filled her hand. Artie wasn't going to lie one second longer in that eight-bed room with the threat of being thrown out of the hospital hanging over his head. He was going to have a private room, a balcony for smoking, and the same special treatment as Amber.

The Rodriguez brothers had chosen the wrong people to go up against, Ilka thought, feeling enormously satisfied.

"Would you like him to be transferred immediately, today?" the woman asked, holding the phone to her ear while eyeing the stack of bills.

"Yes, thank you."

"The patient transfer is effective as of today," the woman said over the phone. She informed the private section that payment would be made in cash.

She glanced up at Ilka and nodded to confirm there was a room available. Ilka felt any lingering bad conscience fading as relief spread through her. The only thing that still bothered her—a bit—was that those Rodriguez assholes would never know the money they were after would be paying for their latest victim's comfort, the best the hospital could provide.

The woman still held the phone to her ear. "Does

he have any special preferences as to his menu? Vegan, vegetarian, gluten-free?" Suddenly she could hardly be more friendly and helpful.

"Put him down for fish and meat," Ilka ordered, adding that vegetables weren't so important.

"If you offer any special additions to menus, we'll take them too," her father said. He made it sound as if they were booking a Caribbean cruise for Artie.

Ilka smiled and nodded.

"We do have a vacant room with a balcony," the woman confirmed. "We'll get going on his transfer, and as soon as the papers are in order, a porter will come by to take him over. Mr. Sorvino will be discharged here, and we will notify the bank we no longer need his house as security."

Ilka thanked her. She googled Happy Homes to get their number. It was time to call the real estate agent and tell him Artie's house wasn't for sale.

Artie was sitting up in bed when they walked in. His black stocking cap was nowhere in sight, and his head had been freshly shaved. So, Ilka thought, he had finally relented. She felt sorry for him. He looked sullen as he stuck a plastic spoon into a small cup of yogurt.

Ilka hadn't seen him since he'd found out she'd been lying about his insurance. She'd thought it would feel so satisfying to tell him the hospital bill was no longer a problem, and that he'd be transferred to a private room, but suddenly it didn't seem that easy.

Her father nudged her aside and walked over to the bed. "So, what do you think? Are you ready to get going?"

Artie was about to answer when he spotted Ilka in the doorway. He looked away and laid the cup of yogurt on his night table. "I think I've got a handle on things." He told them about the real estate agent. "They've promised to keep me here."

Ilka approached the bed and spoke quietly, so only her father and Artie could hear. "I'm so sorry, I should have told you what was going on. But now we have everything under control. Sister Eileen says hello and to focus on recovering."

Artie took her hand, and she felt her father's eyes on them when he squeezed it. Maybe she was imagining it, but his cheeks seemed redder. And he looked more alert. Ilka thought they might have cut down on his meds. His face still fell off to one side when he spoke, though.

Two porters walked in the door, and before she and her father could explain what was going on, they asked Artie if he had any belongings in the locker. One of them unhooked an oxygen hose from the wall while the other laid a clothes bag on his blanket. Ilka supposed it was the clothes he was wearing the day he was attacked. She asked him if he had anything in the drawer of the night table, but Artie shook his head.

"I don't understand, what—what's going on?"

Her father gave him an arm and helped the porters move him onto a wheelchair. "We're moving you."

When Artie rolled into his new room he immediately headed for the balcony door, then asked Ilka if she had a cigarette. Flowers and a small woven basket with some fruit stood on the night table. They'd been told that a doctor and nurse would come in to say hello and give him an introduction to the ward.

He and Ilka sneaked a smoke on the balcony while her father left to check on Amber. When he returned, two of the ward's personnel followed him in. They asked if Ilka and her father wanted to stay for their meeting with Artie, but he declined and told Ilka to come with him.

"Someone wants to say hello to you."

Ilka glanced back at Artie. A nurse had already helped him into bed and was explaining how to call someone for help.

Artie nodded and said it was okay for them to go, that he actually would rather they didn't hear about all the stuff wrong with him. Ilka was relieved; she wouldn't have to feel she was sticking her nose deeper into his private life.

Mary Ann sat in her wheelchair next to Amber's bed, her back to the door, holding her daughter's hand. A shawl covered her shoulders, and she had on the same clothes as when she'd been arrested. She looked thin, gaunt even, and her skin had turned sallow from her time in jail.

Her father stepped aside and let Ilka into the room. She stood quietly for a moment, then walked over and knelt down to hug her father's wife.

Mary Ann's eyes were moist when she looked up at her husband. "She's having a boy." She turned back to Amber. "And you're sure he's okay? Nothing happened to him when the horses ran over you?"

Amber nodded warmly. "He's fine. They even think I can go home, if I can get some help. I still have to stay in bed. And I'm not supposed to lift anything."

"I'll be there," her mother blurted out, even though she wouldn't be much help in the lifting department.

"Tom is there for me too, you know," Amber said. "We can live together out on the ranch."

Mary Ann looked determined. "You're going to stay with me. Where there is good access to doctors and midwives."

Ilka opened her mouth to back up her half sister, to say she needed to be with the baby's father, but Mary Ann beat her to it.

"You can take over the ranch when you're a family, after the baby comes." She made it sound as if she'd already planned everything out.

This was obviously news to Amber. She glanced at her father, but he simply nodded in agreement: She and Tom could live out at the ranch and run the stables.

"If that's what you want," her mother added.

Amber nodded enthusiastically. To Ilka it looked like she was eager to seal the deal before anyone had second thoughts.

"We want to, very much." She hesitated a moment. "Of course, I'll have to talk to Tom about it first. He's sort of overwhelmed, since he's taking care of the horses by himself."

"By himself?" Mary Ann said.

"Nobody else has been out at the ranch since what happened with Grandpa."

"What do you mean?"

"Everyone just stopped coming to work."

Mary Ann turned to Ilka's father. "Paul, you have to help our son-in-law. Hire some stable workers who can start immediately."

Ilka thought the best thing to do would be to call Frank Conaway and ask him to step in. He'd worked several years for Fletcher, and he was familiar with the horses and the stable.

Not that Mary Ann oozed with motherly love, but by now Ilka knew her father's wife well enough to understand that she expressed her feelings through actions. It moved her to see how Mary Ann swept everything aside to take responsibility for her daughter and coming grandchild.

After her father walked around the bed and sat in the easy chair, Ilka asked, "When were you released?"

"An hour ago. The lawyer drove me straight here. I haven't even been home yet."

Mary Ann looked Ilka right in the eyes before lowering her head. "Thank you," she murmured.

It wasn't so much those two little words as the brief, intense look Mary Ann had given her. Ilka smiled.

Mary Ann reached for her daughter's hand, and Amber responded by grabbing her father's hand. Without speaking she looked back and forth between them, as if she needed to get it through her head that they were both still alive and there with her.

"What about Leslie?" Ilka asked Mary Ann. "Does she know you've been released?"

Mary Ann let go of Amber's hand and shook her head. "Not yet. Paul's going to tell her, and then I hope I can have a talk with her."

Ilka could hear it in her voice: It was going to be a difficult conversation, and not only because of the traumatic events at the ranch. Nothing could erase all the lies Leslie had grown up with. Mary Ann was going to have to convince Leslie that she'd sacrificed being with the man she'd loved to protect her. That she'd lied to give her daughter a secure childhood.

Her father's phone rang, breaking the silence in the hospital room. He fumbled around in his pocket and excused himself as he walked out on the balcony.

Moments later he returned with a grim look on his face. "We have to go," he told Ilka. He glanced only briefly at Mary Ann and Amber on his way out of the room.

Ilka followed him. "What happened?" she asked when they reached the hallway. She struggled to keep up as he hurried past Artie's room to the exit, where he stopped and turned to her.

"Fernanda is dead." He opened the door for her. "And Ethan is missing."

26

W hat do you mean, he's missing?"
Ilka clamped onto her father's arm and made
him stop. "And what about Fernanda?"

Despite his Key West tan, her father looked pale. He
seemed a bit confused as he squinted and took a deep
breath, as if he were struggling to get hold of himself.
Ilka supported him as they began walking again, slowly
this time down the hallway toward the hospital's main
entrance, where the car was parked outside.

"The police are down there now," he said, his words
catching in his throat. "She was shot. They found her on
the steps out back."

Ilka was stunned. "And Ethan?"

Her father kept his eyes on the tile floor, concentrating
on his every step.

"What did they say about him? Did they contact his school, his friends?"

They reached the car, and Ilka opened the passenger door and helped him in.

"They don't know where he is," he said. The corner of his mouth trembled as he stared straight ahead.

She backed out of the parking space. "If he saw what happened, maybe he's hiding somewhere?"

"His schoolbag was in his room, and they found his phone on his bed." Her father reached in his pocket for a handkerchief and wiped his nose. "They sent out an APB, and the police have my number so they can call if there's any news."

Ilka noticed her hand trembling when she squeezed his arm. Her father swiped his eyes dry with the handkerchief and shook his head.

Ilka thought of Fernanda, her coal-black hair, the smile that spread from her eyes to her lips. A beautiful woman. "Did she have a black hood over her head when they found her?"

He whipped his head around to look at her. "Why do you ask that?"

"Forget it." What if the Rodriguez brothers had found something when they searched Lydia's apartment? Something that led them to Fernanda. Whom they killed to put pressure on Lydia. First Artie, and now Fernanda. "Don't say anything to Lydia."

"But I have to," he said, his voice thick, hoarse. "Fernanda and Ethan are family to her. I have to tell her what happened."

Ilka ran over the curb at the funeral home's front parking lot and braked so hard that her father's knees rammed into the glove compartment.

The parking lot was nearly full. "What in the world's going on here?" She turned to her father, but his face was blank as he surveyed the rows of cars.

Ilka found a spot at the far end of the lot. "If the Rodriguez brothers are responsible for this with Fernanda and Ethan, they did it to frighten Lydia, so she'll give up. And if she hears about what's happened, she won't go back to Texas with Jennings."

She laid her hand on top of his. "And if she doesn't go back, to testify against Isiah Burnes, she'll never be free. Fernanda would never have wanted that. The only people who *do* want that to happen are the Rodriguez brothers and Burnes."

Her father was even paler now, and Ilka watched him fight back tears. Another car parked in the spot beside them. Two older women got out, one of them carrying a Tupperware container. Ilka watched as they walked briskly to the front door.

"You're probably right," her father finally said. He was about to add something but thought better of it. He shook his head and folded his hands together.

Ilka didn't feel like leaving the car, and apparently, he felt the same way. She could hardly bear the thought of walking in and seeing what it was her mother and Jette had done to attract this horde of people. But finally she got out and walked around to help her father.

"It could be someone other than the Rodriguez brothers," he said after Ilka had locked the car. "It could be a burglar, she might have surprised him. Or..."

Ilka agreed, someone else could have done it. *Could* have. Regardless, though, she was afraid that someone was targeting Lydia, attacking her where she was most vulnerable.

"Ethan's a smart boy," her father mumbled. "A good boy. He knows a lot of people down there. Has a lot of friends. There's a lot of places he could go to for help."

His voice broke.

He was trying to keep from falling apart, Ilka understood that. But the monotonous way he mumbled, almost a chant, grated her nerves like a fingernail scraping a backboard.

Another car pulled into the parking lot, and a man her father's age stepped out and headed toward the front door.

"There you are!"

Ilka stopped and turned at the sound of her mother's cheery voice. She'd come out from around the back, and now she was waving at them.

"So many more have shown up than what we counted on." She looked at Ilka. "Dear, would you please pick up more milk for us? And a few more packs of napkins."

"What's going on?" Ilka's father asked.

"It's the Danish evening, the one we planned. It seems that the flyers we put out the other day found their way onto Facebook, a special Racine group, and now people are flooding in. We weren't at all expecting so many, isn't it wonderful!"

Ilka nodded then asked what she should buy, skim or whole milk.

Her mother held her hand out to her father and frowned at Ilka, as if her daughter had said the completely wrong thing. Ilka watched them disappear inside the funeral home, then she got back in the car.

At least thirty people had shown up, maybe more, Ilka guessed, when she returned and entered the memorial room. The retractable partition wall had been pulled out, as only the front half of the room was being used, and three long tables covered with white tablecloths lined the wall. Plates and cups were stacked on the tables, which were covered with cakes. Leslie was busy cutting and handing out generous portions with a big smile on her face.

Ilka watched her for a moment, then walked over with the milk and asked if there was anything she could help with. Her mother and Jette were setting out more chairs while smiling at all the unfamiliar faces and urging people to come inside. Gregg, the old undertaker, was standing up front with rolled-up sleeves, fastening a large screen to a stand. The whole production reminded Ilka of her school days back in Brønshøj. She noticed the machine on the table beside him, and for a moment she thought they were going to show slides. Then she realized it was a film projector.

"What are they showing?" she asked Leslie, who was unpacking napkins.

"I think it's something about Hamlet and Crownburg." It took Ilka a moment to realize she was trying to pronounce Kronborg, Hamlet's castle. "But your mothers were also talking about some woman named Leonora Christine, who sat up in a blue tower."

My mothers and a blue tower. Ilka was already tired. But she also felt overwhelmed by the same warmth she'd felt before, the evening her mother and Jette had showed up at the funeral home. There was something reassuring about how they were itching to tell their stories, as if their class had just come in from recess. Their energy—moving chairs around and helping people they'd never met—distracted her for a moment, made her think everything would be okay. But there was a morgue down in Key West with Fernanda inside.

Ilka nearly jumped when Leslie said, "During the break I'll hand out the folders. I'm afraid we don't have nearly enough, there's so many people here. Do you think it's okay if I ask people for their email, so I can put them on our mailing list and send them our newsletter?"

"Newsletter?" Ilka tried to focus. "What's the news you want to get out?"

Leslie stared at her. For a moment Ilka noticed the same expression of contempt she'd been met with the first few times she'd seen her half sister. But then Leslie cleared her throat and explained that this whole program was part of the effort to lure people back to the business. It was a marketing strategy, offering something special to counter the American Funeral Group, which was trying to squeeze out all the other funeral homes in the city.

"This is it," she said, emphasizing every word now. "This is what *we* have to offer. We can be personable, tell stories that people are interested in hearing. We have something to offer that no one else does: Danishness. We can *hygge* with people. History still means something to a lot of folks in Racine; a lot of them have Danish blood, you know. And look around, all these people meeting up here—that speaks for itself."

Ilka could see Leslie's mouth moving still, but she'd stopped listening. She eased her way out of the conversation and back toward the door.

Her mother stood up at the lectern and clapped her hands, and in her pleasant British accent she addressed her audience.

"*Hjertelig velkommen*," she said. "Welcome to our Danish evening."

Ilka glanced around for her father, but he was nowhere in sight. She grabbed her jacket and made sure the pack of cigarettes was still in her pocket. As she fished around in her bag for her lighter, someone from behind called her name. She whirled around and saw Calvin Jennings coming in from the foyer.

"Am I late?" He smiled at her.

Ilka shook her head and said they were about to start.

"Your mother invited me. I ran into her down at the

hotel. Interesting; it's like this place is a colony of Scandinavians, all these descendants. I didn't know."

He was wearing a light-blue shirt, newly ironed, and the same narrow tie from the first time she'd seen him. Ilka tried to remember—was that tie in style back in the 1980s? But back then she had been too young to have noticed things like fashion.

"We're serving cake and coffee in there, if you'd like." She pointed at the door. "I just need some fresh air before she gets going on Hamlet and Ophelia."

Jennings headed for the memorial room while Ilka walked out back, still searching for her lighter in the front compartment of her bag.

Ilka loaded up on cake and coffee during the break, then made her way through the crowd to where Jennings was sitting, clear in the back.

She handed him the coffee and plate. "Lydia told me about your daughter."

Her mother and Jette were up at the podium, trying to stop the projector from spitting out its stream of pictures, while Leslie was busy at the cake table, making sure every person she served cake also was given a folder.

The mention of his daughter didn't seem to bother him. He simply nodded and said that even though it had happened years ago, it was still there with him.

"You know how it is when you've got a rock in your shoe? This might be hard to imagine, but it's like getting that rock stuck in your heart. It reminds you all the time that something's not right. The pain doesn't go away, it's always there. That's how it is for me."

Ilka knew all about loss. Flemming's death had made her incredibly vulnerable. She'd never felt it as a rock in her heart or as a constant reminder, yet she still understood what he was talking about.

"Emma was a quiet girl. Once in a while her mother and I talked about it, that being so shy might be a problem for her someday. When she got older, we both felt it might help her to have a boyfriend, but then she met Josh."

He showed no sign of it being difficult for him to talk about his daughter. On the contrary, he spoke as if he'd done so many times.

"She was seventeen when they met, and nineteen when she took her own life. That last year we only saw her once. That was tough, really tough, maybe especially for my wife, because she felt Emma was turning away from us."

He shook his head. "I tried to tell her that wasn't true, that it was Emma turning *to them*. That it was no conscious choice on Emma's part, cutting us out of her life. It was just that Josh and the cult became everything to her. God's Will was her life. At the start she wrote us letters, she seemed happy, a lot more open than the girl we'd known. But the letters gradually stopped coming, and then one day a guy at my station came into my office and told me what had happened."

Ilka set her untouched coffee down on the floor.

"They'd already burned her by the time we found out. Josh disappeared right after she died. I don't even know what happened to him."

Ilka tried to imagine what it must have been like, watching as their daughter disappeared into God's Will.

Their conversation shifted to his plans for their return to Texas. "First we're going to talk to a lawyer. I've got one lined up, one I've been using, to run interference for us before Lydia goes in and makes her statement. It's mostly to make her comfortable with the situation, so she doesn't feel like she's walking into a lion's den. The police are planning a raid on God's Will, but it's all got to be coordinated so Burnes doesn't slip away. It's happened before. They have a private plane and landing strip. He'll try to get out of the country, no doubt about that, if he finds out the police know where he's at. For a long time, everyone thought he was staying at their headquarters in Utah, but some months ago we got a tip that he might have moved to their place in Texas, along with a lot of his family."

Ilka told him that Lydia had helped her younger sister escape. "Both sisters are married to him. They had moved to Texas recently, and they'd counted on meeting Lydia there, but then they were told she'd run away. After that, Alice Payne got into contact with them."

Jennings nodded. He'd heard they were planning on settling in Canada, he said.

"It must be a big risk for Payne," Ilka said. "It can't

be that hard for the God Squad to keep an eye on what she does and where she goes."

He shook his head with a glint in his eye. "It's not that easy. Alice Payne knows what she's doing, and her network of people are loyal. The second a woman gets free from the cult, they're right there to make her vanish. Then when they're absolutely sure no one's on their trail, Payne sets the wheels turning in the network. And the women are on their way."

"Make them vanish?" Now Ilka noticed the guests returning to their seats. Her mother had managed to get the projector under control, and Jette was glancing through some of her notes.

He lowered his voice. "They send an undertaker, and then it all starts. The coffin is driven from a morgue to a funeral home or a private home, then to a church or a crematorium. Along the way the women and their children are hidden in the coffin. It can take a few days, or even a week."

Ilka stared at him, but he just nodded. "That's it. They vanish while the coffin gets driven around. Just like a shell game. You know, with a coin hidden underneath one of the shells. Suddenly it's gone, and no one knows when it happened. Pallbearers, is what Payne calls her helpers."

Ilka's mother clapped her hands again and thanked everyone for their interest and the excellent turnout. "We plan on holding a program once a month, and everyone will have the opportunity to register, if you go into our funeral home's website and then to 'Danish Evening.' Naturally you're always welcome to stop in, and we'll be glad to tell you about what we have to offer. We always have coffee ready and time for a chat, and we also are happy to help with information, such as finding out where your families in Denmark originated from."

Jette stepped in, and an image popped up on the big screen: a Danish kringle.

The audience laughed. Jette gave a thorough account of the pastry's history, starting with an Austrian baker's apprentice who traveled to Copenhagen, back when the pastry's form was that of two crossed arms…Ilka stopped listening. There was something she'd read, shortly after arriving in Racine. Something about the town playing an important role in the Underground Railroad that helped slaves escape from the South in the mid-1800s, bringing them to safety. Sometimes to Canada. That was back then, she thought. Now they were using closed coffins, but Racine was still a vital link in the network. The need was still there.

After the guests left, Ilka helped clean up and put away the chairs. Jennings had offered her mother and Jette a lift to the hotel, and Leslie headed for her room after all the cake pans had been returned to their owners. Her father had gone to his room during the break, and now Ilka felt bone-tired. Ten minutes later she crawled under the covers and texted Lydia, telling her that Jennings had everything under control. He would be picking her up at eight, and the long drive would take somewhere around two days.

She turned out the light in her tiny room and set the alarm. Then she searched for the Detroit-Windsor Tunnel on Google Maps and saved it for her trip the next day.

27

Ilka slept like a log, and after two cups of coffee and a piece of chocolate cake left over from the previous evening, she drove to the warehouse and backed the hearse up to the wide door in back. She found the code and keys to the storage room Lydia had rented. The place looked deserted, which was a relief to her, because she was going to have to grapple with the enormous coffin to get it into the vehicle. An iron hasp had to be pushed to the side before the heavy door could be raised. Lydia couldn't weigh over 120 pounds or so; the door must have been hell for her to open.

A stale, musty odor met Ilka head-on when she stepped inside. Sunlight fell on the dusty concrete floor, and she glanced around a moment before heading for the far end of the building. Her footsteps echoed in the cavernous warehouse. She kept an eye on the letters attached to the row of identical iron doors on her right.

When she reached C, she switched on her phone light and punched the code in. A hollow echo pinged around up in the rafters when she stuck the key in and turned it.

The storage room was empty except for the dark-blue coffin. Not only was it twice as wide as the standard models Ilka was familiar with, but it was quite a bit longer, too. It stood on a catafalque. Her actions felt routine as she unlocked the wheels and pulled out a narrow handle, all the while hoping she'd be able to wrestle it into the hearse without too many scratches.

Slowly Ilka pushed it through the doorway. The coffin seemed ready to slide off when she hit a small bump, and she leaned over and nearly lay on it the rest of the way. She locked the wheels again when she reached the hearse and opened the rear door. An extra pair of hands would have been nice, she thought, as she pulled out the rack in the back of the vehicle. She cursed as she raised the catafalque and shoved the coffin inside. But if Lydia could do it all by herself…

Lydia and Jennings were on their way to Texas by now, she figured. Ilka had been thinking of her that morning. Her skin tingled, as if she were the one headed down there, not Lydia.

As she secured the coffin, Ilka noticed the round ventilation holes hidden by the coffin lid that had been drilled all around the upper edge. Big enough for air to come in, she realized. She slammed the rear door shut.

Even though the coffin looked gigantic in back, she hoped Jane-Maya and her two girls weren't prone to claustrophobia. They would be packed like sardines until they reached Canada.

Before leaving the funeral home, Ilka had texted her mother to congratulate her on the previous evening's success. She wasn't sure the two Danish women would be there when she returned to pick up her father and take him to Dorothy's. He'd been devastated by Fernanda's death, and while seated during the program he'd held his phone in his hand, hoping for news about Ethan.

Ilka had written her mother that she would be gone all day. Will be back this evening. Mary Ann out of jail, Leslie doesn't know yet.

Maybe it was stupid to let her mother in on that, but Ilka couldn't bear the thought of Leslie not knowing while Mary Ann sat at home, planning what to tell her daughter. And if anyone could prepare Leslie for what was coming, it would be her mother and Jette. The three of them seemed to be getting along very well together.

After rolling the catafalque back to the storage room and making sure the door was locked and code punched in, she climbed in the hearse and checked her phone. Her mother had written back.

Leslie moving home to mother later today. She's with her now. They hope Amber can come home from hospital, they can take care of her. We're with Eric and Elly.

Ilka stared at her phone. It was barely past nine, and already everyone seemed to be on the go. It stung a bit to realize they were doing just fine without her, but on the other hand, it did lift some of the weight off her shoulders. They could figure it out. They could handle things. Even with her sitting in a hearse with an XL coffin in back.

On the way back to the funeral home, Ilka thought about grabbing one more cup of coffee before she and her father headed out to Dorothy's. She had a long drive ahead of her with Jane-Maya and the girls. They planned on leaving at ten, which would put them at the Canadian border around five that afternoon, even with several stops along the way. The traffic might be heavy at times, but she'd taken that into account too. Her passport was in her bag, and Lydia had filled out the documents to be shown at the border.

Ilka hadn't known she needed a visa to enter Canada, but Lydia had taken care of all the details. All Ilka had to do was bring along a stamp from the funeral home, to be used when she handed their false documents over. She had to remember that when she picked up her father. False documents, forgery—Ilka hadn't even considered the consequences if she were caught. It wasn't anything like smuggling drugs in embalmed baby corpses, she told herself, but she still could be charged with human trafficking, even though it would have been perfectly legal for Jane-Maya and her daughters to leave the country, had they had passports. But Lydia claimed they'd never lifted the coffin lid before. It was just a matter of the corpse passport and other papers being in order.

Nevertheless, Ilka was nervous. She straightened up and tightened her grip on the enormous leather steering wheel; no sense in worrying about it yet, she decided. She rolled her window down and lit a cigarette.

She stepped out in front of the garage and glanced up at her father's open upstairs window. He was waiting, ready to go, and Ilka had almost reached the back door when she noticed the small body, lying on the ground like a dark shadow. Motionless.

She heard herself scream, and in two long strides she was beside him, kneeling down. Only when she leaned over could she hear his faint sobbing. The way his frail body shook, he seemed to be trying to hold in some unbearable pain. The October morning was chilly, but all he had on was a T-shirt and a pair of knee-length shorts.

"Ethan," she whispered.

He was tied hand and foot, and a rag had been stuffed in his mouth. He stared at her with terrified eyes.

"Ethan," she said again, then began speaking quietly to him. Repeated his name, explained that he was at Paul's house and everything would be fine now. She spoke soft words, a blanket of sound to calm him. And her, too—she'd been shocked, horrified at finding him.

"Okay, now I'm going to take the rag out of your mouth." She reached for him slowly. "I promise, no one's going to hurt you."

He felt warm, very warm, and his small body was cramping up. Ilka loosened the gag, and instantly the boy gasped for air. His eyes darted around as she tried to free his hands. They were bound only with a light plastic line, but the knots were too tight for her to undo. She threw her coat on the ground then explained that she was going to carry him inside. Instantly he raised his hands in front of his head in self-defense and began crying. The odor hit her when she reached down to lift him up: sweat and something else, something piercing. She pulled her arms back and noticed the dark blotch on his shirt.

She spoke as calmly as she could. "I'm carrying you in, Ethan, and I promise to be very careful."

She'd begun crying herself, she noticed, as she gently wriggled her arms underneath the boy and lifted him without touching the bloody spot on his chest. As smoothly as possible she carried him to the door and managed to press the handle down with her elbow. Then she maneuvered her hand under his knees and stuck the key in, still taking care not to touch his wounds.

Inside she called out for her father, but all she heard was the shower running in the bathroom. Ethan was still trembling, though now Ilka wasn't sure if it was from fear or fever. He was terribly hot, that she knew. Ilka took baby steps as they passed the preparation room and coffin room. When she opened the door to the memorial room, his breathing was so rapid that she feared he was going into shock, or about to lose consciousness. His eyes were closed, but his muscles quivered with tension.

"It's over now," she whispered as she laid him down

and tucked a pillow under his head. "All over. You're safe here with us."

He was crying again, this time quietly, with his eyes still closed. Ilka wanted to grab him and hold him close, but she didn't dare. He was obviously in great pain, with blood still seeping through his shirt, mixing with dried blood and the stink of burnt flesh.

Ilka rushed into the office for a pair of scissors, then snipped off the plastic line around his hands. The line had cut deeply into his wrists, and for a moment she sat blowing on them. Then she leaned down and cut the lines binding his feet.

She thought about taking his shirt off, but no, she didn't dare touch him there. She hurried out and grabbed a blanket and covered his bare legs. Carefully she stroked his burning forehead. When she told him she was going out to get Paul, he clearly reacted to the sound of her father's name, but he kept his eyes closed.

Ilka left to find him.

"Follow me, right now," she said, when her father stepped out of the bathroom, fully clothed and ready to go. "Something terrible's happened, Ethan is here, and we have to get him to the hospital."

"What—"

He walked into the room and spotted the boy on the sofa. "My God, what...what's happened?"

"They branded him." Ilka kept her distance, hoping the boy would feel safe now that someone he knew was with him.

Her father sank to his knees beside the sofa. "*They?*"

"The cult. I don't think the Rodriguez brothers killed Fernanda, I think God's Will found them. And they used Ethan to let Lydia know they're after her."

Her father jerked his head around; tears welled in his eyes, and he looked pale as a ghost.

Ethan seemed so small lying there. Much smaller than she remembered him in Key West. She joined her father when he tried to lift the boy's shirt up, but it was stuck to his skin where he'd been burned.

"I'll bet it's the same brand Lydia and her niece have," Ilka said. And Jane-Maya too, she thought, underneath the dress she wore buttoned to her neck.

Her father struggled to get up off the floor and sit on the edge of the sofa. Ilka went into the kitchen to get the boy a glass of water. She leaned against the counter and closed her eyes. If it was Isiah Burnes who had found Fernanda, he was almost certainly looking for Lydia too. Ilka was so, so grateful that she and Jennings had left before Ethan had been dumped.

"Ethan says he'd just come home from school, and he took his bag up to his room, and he heard the shots," her father said, when she came back in with the water. "He didn't see the two men before they were in the doorway. They grabbed him and left, and on the way, he saw Fernanda lying on the ground."

While he spoke, the boy stared up at him, his eyes bulging with terror. He was still quivering, as if his muscles were somehow plugged into electricity.

"They stuffed something into his mouth when he started crying. A man sat in the backseat and held on to him while they drove away. At some point they stopped, threw Ethan out on the ground, and tied him up."

Her father gazed lovingly at the boy as he stroked his hand. Ethan stared at the ceiling while he listened to her father's voice. He seemed to be shaking less now, even though his forehead was covered with small pearls of sweat.

"Let's get him to the hospital," Ilka said. Her father nodded.

"No!" The boy reached for Paul as if he were about to fall.

"It's okay," her father said. "I'll go with you. You've been injured, and we need the doctors' help so it doesn't hurt anymore."

He turned back to Ilka when Ethan calmed down a bit. "He has trouble remembering what happened after that. But later the car stopped again, and they blindfolded him and carried him into a house. It was hot, and it smelled like when Fernanda started the woodstove. The next thing he remembers is the pain in his chest, as if he'd been stuck with a sword made of fire."

A tear ran down her father's cheek.

"Maybe they gave him something to knock him out," Ilka said.

Her father nodded. He turned to Ethan and whispered that they had to get his shirt unstuck from where he'd been burned. Very carefully he lifted the shirt; the brand came into sight.

It was as big as a fist, and it looked grotesque against the boy's sensitive skin. The wound was open and bloody. In the middle, where the white-hot iron had been pressed into him, a scorched black mark stood out, identical to the one Ilka had seen under Jane-Maya's daughter's neck.

"We have to get Jane-Maya and her girls away from here," her father said. "You need to go. They probably thought this is where Lydia was hiding them. Go, I'll take Ethan to the hospital."

Ilka glanced at the clock. Her phone rang: Dorothy, she thought, wanting to know where she was, maybe. But no, it was Lydia. And she was upset.

"Jennings hasn't shown up yet. He should have been here two hours ago. And I can't get hold of him."

Ilka hurried out of the memorial room. "Where are you?"

"I'm on the way to the hotel. Meet me there."

"I'm on—"

Lydia hung up.

Back in the room, she said, "You're right, I have to go."

Her father nodded and told her to tell Dorothy why he hadn't come along.

Ilka stopped herself from passing on what Lydia had just told her. "Okay."

He had enough to do; there was no reason to burden him more before they knew why Jennings hadn't shown up.

The moment Ilka got behind the wheel, she called

the number Jennings had given her. No one answered, and a few minutes later she stopped in front of the hotel entrance in a no-parking zone and hopped out. She'd parked there before, thinking that allowances would be made for a hearse. Today she didn't care. The oversized coffin would draw attention, no doubt, but she slammed the door shut and ran inside anyway.

Lydia stood at the window, but she turned when Ilka walked in. She looked worried to Ilka, nervous, as they approached each other. The only other people in the foyer were a couple with two small children at the reception desk and an elderly woman sitting on a sofa, studying a city map.

"Come on." Ilka reached for Lydia. She recognized the receptionist, who'd been on duty when Jette had asked for an extra bed. She told the woman she had Jennings's phone, that he'd forgotten it at the funeral home the evening before. "What room is he in?"

"Room One Fourteen." The receptionist pointed down the hallway.

"His car is in the parking lot," Ilka said as they passed an ice machine set back in a shallow niche. All she could hear in the dark hallway was the machine's growl, drowning out the sound of her nervous breathing.

They stopped and pounded on his door. No answer. Ilka pounded several times again, then she pulled her phone out of her pocket to see if Jennings had texted her.

Lydia paced the hall, checking her watch as if time were running out for her. "Jane-Maya."

Ilka spoke quietly, hoping to calm her down. "Don't worry, I'll get them to Detroit. We'll just have to drop one of the stops I planned on. But first we have to get you on your way."

Lydia took a deep breath. Ilka knocked again then put her ear to the door. Silence.

"He's not in there," she whispered. "Wait here."

Ilka ran back to the reception desk. The family and the elderly woman were gone, and the foyer was empty. The receptionist looked up from her phone under the counter and asked if she could be of help.

"I'm wondering if Calvin Jennings has checked out?"

The girl shook her head as she peered at the hotel's computer. "No. Mr. Jennings is checking out today, I see, but he hasn't left yet."

She was a young, plump girl who looked as if she should still be in school instead of playing *Bejeweled* on her phone, but she was on the ball enough to call his room. Ilka heard the phone ringing; two rings were enough for her to know he wasn't going to answer.

"May I have a key?" She was about to explain why she had the authority to enter the man's hotel room, but before she could get started, Lydia marched in from the hallway and pulled her away. Without a word she led Ilka back to Room 114. The door was open a crack. She glanced at Ilka, then she pushed the door open.

Jennings was hanging from a ceiling pipe to the left of the window. A floor lamp had been knocked over, and his things were scattered on the floor. For a second Ilka stood frozen, staring at him, then she pushed Lydia away from the door and jumped over to him.

"He's dead," Lydia mumbled. Ilka turned; her eyes looked empty as she pointed at his open shirt. That's when the stench hit her.

Charred skin, sweat. She didn't need to open his shirt, but she did anyway. The brand was identical to Ethan's, only deeper. As if the branding iron had been pressed harder into his flesh.

"They took the papers," Lydia said. "All the evidence."

She'd already picked the empty briefcase up from the floor. The dark-brown leather case had been cut open lengthwise, a contemptuous message: They'd gotten what they'd come for.

Ilka's knees buckled. She doubled over, and a croaking sound shot out of her throat, as if the air had been knocked out of her. She knelt and hid her face in her hands, her stomach cramping at the sight of Jennings's dead body.

Lydia closed the door behind them. "Jennings was ready to leave, he'd already packed."

Ilka peered at the overturned suitcase on the floor by the desk. Neatly folded pants and shirts. Socks and sweat suits.

Ilka slowly got to her feet and sat on the bed. She told Lydia about Ethan. "My father will take him to the hospital. But we're going to have to call the police."

Lydia stared in horror at Ilka. "Is it bad?" she whispered.

Ilka nodded and turned to Jennings, even though she could hardly stand looking at him. She wanted to cut him down, but she knew they couldn't touch him before the police came.

"Ethan has the same brand burned on him, just not as deep."

She also had to tell Lydia about Fernanda. "Sit down."

Lydia leaned forward and held her head in her hands while she listened. Ilka wanted to put her arm around her shoulder, but she had to call the police. She brought out her phone.

"Wait," Lydia said. "If we're still here when they come, they'll arrest me. Let me get my sister and the girls out of here before the God Squad finds them. If Burnes manages to stop us, they'll never be free. And they'll be punished for leaving him. Severely punished."

Ilka understood. It was unbearable watching the woman sitting there, staring up at the man who could have saved her. She stood and slowly walked over to Lydia, folding her arms around her. The frail woman's body collapsed as she silently sobbed.

28

After leaving the hotel, they called the police. Ilka asked for Stan Thomas, and she explained that she had information about a man who had been hanged in Room 114. She gave him Jennings's name and told the officer what she knew about him: He was in Racine because he and the police in Texas were building a case against Isiah Burnes. She gave him Lydia's name but didn't mention that Lydia Rogers was the nun he was familiar with from the funeral home. When Thomas asked what connection Ilka had to this Jennings, she raised her voice, shouted that he was fading out, she couldn't hear him.

"I'll call you back later," she shouted. She hung up.

Lydia sat staring out the passenger-side window.

"Do you think they're looking for you?" Ilka asked.

Lydia shook her head. "I think Jane-Maya and the

girls are the ones they're after." Her voice was still list-less, monotone. "Burnes will not tolerate disobedience in his wives, and there's no limits to what the God Squad will do, when it comes to carrying out his orders. These are boys born into the cult, and they're given no physical contact whatsoever from the time they're born. No one holding them, comforting them. When they cry, they're hosed down with water until they stop. If they get sick, God determines if they're strong enough to sur-vive. Only the girls get medical help. The men chosen to serve Burnes have no empathy. And their only job is to protect the cult."

The crematorium chimney came into view over the fields. Ilka slowed down and once again checked her rearview mirror. She'd kept a close eye on other cars since leaving Racine, but no one seemed to be following them. Before leaving the hotel, she'd thought about call-ing Jeff and asking for an escort, but they hadn't spoken since their argument outside Artie's house.

She signaled to turn and drove slowly down the gravel lane to Dorothy's place, then on through the gravel park-ing lot and around to the back of the house and out of sight. She parked the hearse and Lydia hopped out. Ilka followed her to the back steps. Before opening the door, she turned to Ilka.

"I'm sorry. Sorry that I let you believe your father was dead. I didn't know you were in his will, and when I found out it was too late. I didn't know how to handle the situation, so I just went on with the charade."

"But why? Why wasn't the story about him being in rehab good enough?"

"I was scared. I knew they'd keep looking until they found him. I care so much about your father. He took me in, gave me a life, a place where it felt like I belonged. I had to protect him. I was hoping he'd be safe down there, that the Rodriguez brothers would eventually stop looking for him."

Ilka listened, but she couldn't meet Lydia's eyes; somehow it all felt too personal.

"But it was wrong of me to keep you in the dark, and I apologize for that. I'm sorry."

"Thank you." Ilka felt there was nothing more to say. Lydia had put her through so much, and Ilka wouldn't have believed her own bitter anger could just vanish with a simple apology, but apparently it could. It felt good to know Lydia was aware that she'd been wrong, and the anger just wasn't there anymore. Strange. Ilka thought it also might have something to do with Jennings's murder, the shock. Maybe she couldn't really feel anything.

They heard a key being turned on the other side of the door, and a moment later Dorothy hugged them both. She whispered to Ilka that her father had called and told her about Ethan.

The police must be at the hotel room now, Ilka thought. She owed Thomas an explanation about how she knew Jennings, but that would have to wait until they left.

"I haven't said anything to Jane-Maya, she doesn't

know yet that Burnes has uncovered the escape route. I think it's best this way. She's so happy about getting back together with her sister in Canada, and the girls are excited about the trip. I just didn't want to make them nervous."

They stood in a small back hallway, which had several pairs of rubber boots lined against the wall. Ilka could see Jane-Maya and the girls through the kitchen door, waiting on the sofa with three small travel bags in front of them. Each girl had a book on her lap, but they looked up when Ilka and Lydia walked in. The fright in their eyes was gone; now they were curious and eager.

Ilka smiled at them, even though she felt shattered inside. To counter the image of Jennings's body that kept flashing through her mind, she tried to focus on the long drive in front of her. She'd already ignored three calls from Thomas, and now he was calling again, but instead of answering she texted her father that they were at Dorothy's and would be leaving soon.

Lydia had gone upstairs, and now she came down carrying a stack of bills.

"Come with us," Ilka said as she stuck the money in a black billfold. "You have to leave, it's too dangerous for you here."

Lydia shook her head. "I'm not leaving Ethan. I'm staying until he's well enough for us to leave together."

Since finding the boy at the funeral home, Ilka had felt an odd fluttering anxiety in her chest, but now it was a knot of pure fear. "You can't stay! You have to come with us to Canada. We'll take care of Ethan, he's safe with my father, and we'll bring him to you when he's well enough to travel."

Lydia considered that for a moment, but then she shook her head again. "If it wasn't for Ethan, I'd turn myself over to the police and get it over with. But I'm the only family he has left. I thought it was too dangerous for him to live with me, I knew someone might track me down someday, so I made the deal with Fernanda back then. So he'd be safe, somewhere far away. But he wasn't anyway. I didn't take good enough care of him."

Her eyes were tearing up.

It was hard for Ilka to see Lydia so emotional.

"I'm staying with him until we can leave together," Lydia repeated.

She walked over to the bureau between the windows facing Dorothy's parking plot and took out a plastic folder. She handed it to Ilka and explained that they were the papers she'd need for the trip. A transit permit for the fictional corpse in the coffin, the black billfold with the money, and a death certificate. Plus, a visa that she had procured via the internet.

"And you have your passport?" she said.

Ilka nodded and looked over the fake documents. Through the haze of thoughts in her head she heard Jane-Maya ask her girls if they needed to pee before they left.

She looked up and saw Lydia in the kitchen now with Dorothy, who was dabbing her eyes with a white handkerchief. Dorothy walked into the living room to say goodbye.

Jane-Maya was standing at the staircase. "Someone's coming."

Lydia stiffened, then quick as a flash she was at the window. Ilka looked past her at a car roaring down the driveway and recognized it at once: Jeff's black BMW X5, the one she'd ridden in out to Artie's house.

"It's Jeff," she said, then walked out into the kitchen. "I'm the one he wants to talk to."

Ilka explained that she owed him money for helping find her. "It was about the money for Artie, I had to find you."

"But he didn't find me." Lydia seemed more annoyed than worried that someone was showing up just as they were about to leave.

"In a way he did. He knew you were staying in Artie's house. We just got there too late."

Lydia brought out a bundle of money; it was clear she wanted him out of the way, and as soon as possible. "How much do you owe him?"

"Ten thousand dollars."

He could forget about the bonus, she decided. Had the present situation been different, she'd have told him he hadn't done what he promised, and he wouldn't get a cent. But like Lydia, she just wanted him gone.

Out of the corner of her eye, she noticed Jeff getting out of his car and staring up at the house for a moment before turning back to the lane. Lydia handed her the money, and she strode over and opened the front door. "You didn't find her," she said, before he could say a word.

He seemed surprised to see her. His eyes moved down to the roll of bills in her hand. "What are you doing here?"

Ilka was puzzled, but she told him she was visiting one of her father's friends.

"You need to leave," he snapped.

His animosity confused her. "Here's your money."

Jeff ignored the bills and opened the car door. "Get over here, now!"

"Why in the world should I do that?"

"Because I say so!"

His voice was like a whip, and Ilka noticed his eyes darting around as he reached out to grab her.

She heard the cars. "What have you done?" she yelled.

Jeff told her again to come with him.

Their eyes locked, and she froze when he said, "I find people. That's what I do. That's what I've done."

29

Three black cars appeared on the lane: Two four-wheel drives in the lead and rear, with an elegant limousine in the middle. Not a stretch, but a large black vehicle with tinted windows. For a few moments it seemed as though all the sounds around Ilka vanished, but then the car engines broke through the silence. It felt as if an army was invading.

Jeff had started his car and made a quick U-turn, so he was ready to take off when the black armada arrived. He ignored Ilka, who was shouting at him now even as she returned to the house, the money still in her hand. She ran into the kitchen and slammed the door, then looked for Lydia. Jane-Maya rose up from the sofa. A stunned silence had fallen over the house.

Out in front, the limousine driver got out, walked around to the passenger door, and opened it. Ilka hid behind the window's long curtain, barely breathing as a tall man wearing a black suit stepped out and surveyed the windows of the house. Immediately she recognized Isiah Burnes from the searches she'd done on the net, but seeing him in person was much more frightening. She heard Jane-Maya let out a long groan behind her, as if the life was seeping out of her. Ilka reached out to her and clasped Jane-Maya's hand as they watched the old man outside.

Ilka studied Isiah Burnes. Even though she knew he couldn't see her, it felt like he could, in a way that sent shivers down her spine. The cult leader folded his hands in front of him and stood majestically, tall and erect, as he waited for his four men from the other cars to assemble behind him. They looked fearsome in a primitive way. There was nothing of the well-groomed, muscle-bound look of Raymond Fletcher's security people. The men in Isiah Burnes's God Squad wore hooded sweatshirts and jeans. Ilka couldn't see if they were armed, but they looked so threatening that it didn't matter. Burnes nodded almost imperceptibly at the driver, and one of the backseat windows in the limousine slowly rolled down. A woman leaned out and looked up toward the house.

Ilka heard a muffled scream and turned; Jane-Maya's hands had flown up to her mouth in terror at the sight of the woman in the car. Dorothy quickly herded the two girls into the kitchen.

Lydia joined them in the living room and stopped

abruptly, petrified by what she saw. "No," she whispered. The blood drained out of her face. Jane-Maya stared in wide-eyed shock, her arms now clutching her chest.

Nobody moved, inside or outside the house. Ilka's mind raced—was it possible to get everyone into the hearse before the God Squad forced their way inside? But even if she could hide them all in the coffin, it would be impossible to get away.

Lydia took a deep breath, and before Ilka could react, the short, slight woman was standing in the doorway, her arms folded in front of her. "You're not welcome here." Her voice was surprisingly forceful, with no sign of the fear that had to be gripping her.

"We're here for my wife and daughters." Ilka was shaken. Burnes was lean, practically skinny, but the mesmerizing authority in his voice made her step forward for a better look at him.

Lydia was doing everything she could to appear unruffled, but when Burnes spoke her arms loosened, and she held on to the doorframe as she began shaking her head. Her lips moved, but no words came out. She was struggling to maintain her strength.

Ilka's lungs began to sting—from holding her breath, she realized. The tension outside, the electric atmosphere seemed to have penetrated the walls and filled the living room. She should go out and stand behind Lydia, but she couldn't leave Jane-Maya, whose eyes were locked on the woman in the car.

"Get in your cars and leave," Lydia said, her voice acid with hate. "You're not welcome here. And you," she shouted, now staring at the woman in the backseat, "you are *absolutely* not welcome."

Ilka took a few steps toward the door.

"No one can turn from God," Burnes proclaimed, his bass voice booming. "My wife belongs to God and our brotherhood. Turning away is a mortal sin. You of all people must know that. No one who stands alone finds love."

The cult leader pointed over to the woman in the car. "But even for those who in moments of weakness turn from God, there is a way back," he said, so slowly that every word felt like the blow of a hammer. "And that pathway is open for Jane-Maya and our daughters. For you, though, there can be no return. Your sins will forever haunt you. Heaven will forever be closed to you."

His voice changed; it was as if he were reciting a prayer for a congregation. "I have come for my wife and my daughters."

Again, Ilka felt the chills down her spine. The men behind him stirred, as if Burnes's proclamation was a signal.

Jane-Maya turned to Ilka, then glanced back out at the car window. A look came into her eyes, but before Ilka could read it, the young mother's fingernails had dug into Ilka's arm. "Get my girls out of here, take them away and make sure they're safe," she whispered.

Ilka glanced at the two terrified girls in the kitchen

doorway watching Burnes, who now took a few steps toward the house.

"Get them out," Jane-Maya repeated, pleading now, tugging at Ilka. Then she walked over and kissed both of the girls.

"Is there another way out of here?" Ilka asked Dorothy as they hurried into the back hall.

Dorothy shook her head. "If you take the hearse, you'll have to drive over the fields, and they can't help but see you."

The hearse was no match for those four-wheel drives, Ilka could see that. It could hardly even make it up over the hill.

"Run down along the fence line to the crematorium, hide the girls in the oven," Dorothy said. "When the oven door shuts, it can only be opened if you know about the mechanism under the door, you have to slide it to the side. It's a safety measure for when the oven gets hot."

They turned at the sound of Jane-Maya's shrill voice; she was standing beside Lydia now.

"You betrayed us!" she screamed at the woman in the backseat. "You turned against your own family."

"Run!" Dorothy whispered

"You'll never ever get them..."

Jane-Maya's voice faded away as Ilka and the girls ran down the path to the crematorium, hunched over and hidden by the bare yet thick bushes lining the property's boundary.

The girls ran as fast as they could, their legs pounding

the ground like drumsticks. Their eyes were shiny from terror, but they didn't hesitate when Ilka pulled open the heavy crematorium door and grabbed their hands before entering the dark building. They hurried to the back room where the oven stood like some prehistoric monster in the middle, emitting a charred odor. A green handle used to start the oven stuck out on the right side, with a temperature gauge below it.

"I promise, you'll be safe here," Ilka whispered, panting for breath. "Nobody can find you; just be quiet, completely quiet. Promise me you will be, that if they come in here, you won't make a sound."

She looked at the girls and saw that promises weren't necessary. What they were running from terrified them much worse than being locked up in the dark.

Ilka jerked the wide iron door open. The oven was cold, and the girls scrambled up onto the sooty iron sheet. They sat hugging their knees in silence.

"You two are the bravest girls I've ever known," Ilka said. She wasn't sure *she* could let herself be locked up in there. "I'll come get you as soon as they're gone. I promise, nothing's going to happen to you as long as you stay quiet."

Both girls nodded at her, then Ilka closed the oven door. She heard a click when it locked, and she stared at the door a moment before running back and pulling the crematorium door shut behind her.

She spotted two of the men in sweatshirts walking into the house, and she took off running, hunched over, nearly parallel to the ground. On the other side of the property line, she followed a tractor path shielded by a low embankment. When she reached the back of the house, her lungs were burning and a metallic taste had spread inside her mouth as she gasped for breath. She edged over to the back door and stood on tiptoes. In the living room she glimpsed a pant leg as it disappeared up the stairs. The other man was nowhere in sight, but the three travel bags were still on the floor, and the documents and billfold Lydia had left for her remained on the table.

Ilka crept inside and froze. She heard footsteps upstairs—both men or just one? She couldn't tell, but she slipped over and grabbed the bags and documents and billfold, and seconds later she was outside, hiding behind the hearse.

Loud female voices rang out from the front of the house. Ilka pushed the bags under the hearse and stuck the documents and billfold inside her blouse; then she stood up straight and took a few deep breaths before walking inside. Out the front window she saw the other two members of the God Squad headed for the crematorium. She made a move to run after them, but Dorothy grabbed her.

"Let them go. They can't get the oven open. If you run after them, they'll suspect the girls are hiding down there."

Ilka knew she was right. But all she could see was those two girls, sitting cramped in the dark. What frightened her the most, though, was the fear she'd seen in their eyes when they saw Isiah Burnes outside the house.

Every nook and cranny inside the house were being searched. The two men had found a trapdoor to the cellar, and they were up and down and all over the house, peering behind furniture, inside closets. Their brutality as they searched scared Ilka; what would they do if they found the girls?

Next, they went outside and turned the hearse inside out. They left the coffin open and strode across the gravel parking lot to the barn on the other side. On the way one of them stopped and glanced inside Dorothy's car, and a moment later he pried open the trunk to see if the girls had been hidden in there. He left the trunk lid open and ducked into the barn with his partner. Burnes stepped toward Jane-Maya. The limousine's back window was still rolled down, but the woman inside was now out of sight.

"You're coming with me." He spoke calmly as he reached out for her. "If you choose to leave your daughters here, you'll never see them again."

There was no threat in his voice, only in his chilling words. Spoken gently, lightly, like a soft breeze on the skin.

Jane-Maya stared down at the ground.

"Thank your sister for seeking forgiveness and for her wisdom in blocking the pathway that led you all astray. God is willing to take you back."

"No." Jane-Maya's words were almost inaudible.

"What's going on?" Ilka whispered to Dorothy.

"It's their sister from Canada. She betrayed them. I don't get it, I heard Lydia talking to her this morning. Everything sounded fine. We thought she'd be waiting on the other side of the border, but I guess it was a trap."

"Come." Burnes motioned at Jane-Maya with out-stretched hand.

"My girls," she whispered.

He took another step toward her.

Ilka spotted the two men coming out of the cremato-rium. They'd left the lights on and the door open—and the two girls inside, apparently.

"Come," Burnes repeated. He moved smoothly, gracefully, almost as if he were floating, and now he was close enough to touch her.

Jane-Maya turned quickly to Lydia, and Ilka read her lips: *Take care of them.* Then she took his hand. Ilka bowed her head as Burnes led Jane-Maya to the car, and she kept it bowed even as she sat in the backseat beside her sister.

Ilka watched, not moving a muscle until finally she wiped a tear off her cheek. Once more the world grew quiet around her as the men returned to their cars and slammed the doors.

Then suddenly it was if somebody had turned the sound back on.

"Nooooooo!" Lydia screamed.

She ran to the limousine, flung open the back door, and reached inside for the sister she'd helped get to

Canada. Maybe it was her anger. Or maybe it was desperation, or maybe a bit of both that gave her the
strength to pull the woman out of the car and onto the
ground.

"Traitor!" Instantly Lydia was all over her; the
woman tried to protect her face with her hands. "How
could you do this?"

Ilka's chest tightened as Lydia screamed in rage. Before
she knew it, the four men jumped out of the cars. One of
them held something against her neck, and a second later
Lydia's body jerked and lay still. It took a moment for Ilka
to understand: They'd used a Taser on her.

Ilka bit the inside of her cheek so hard that it bled
when Lydia collapsed. She caught a glimpse of Jane-
Maya hiding her face in her hands and sobbing before
the backseat window was rolled all the way up.

What happened next took place in slow motion for
Ilka, and would stay with her for a long, long time.

The four men in sweatshirts lifted Lydia up, and a rear
door of the lead car was opened. Ilka screamed and ran
over to try to stop them, but she was knocked unconscious by one of the men. When she came to, the three
cars were on their way up the lane.

Dorothy was kneeling beside her with an arm around
her shoulder as they stared silently, watching the cars
vanish over the hill.

They'd taken Lydia with them.

"We need to get the girls to safety," Dorothy said. She
held her hand out and helped Ilka to her feet.

Ilka's legs felt weak when she stood up. Her whole body had been wound tight since sneaking the girls over to the crematorium, and now her tendons felt as if they were sticking out of her skin.

"The girls," Ilka said. She remembered Jane-Maya, her head in her hands. "How could she leave them behind?"

"She's trying to save them," Dorothy said as she helped Ilka into the kitchen. "I saw it in her eyes when she said goodbye. She doesn't expect to see them again."

"What do you mean?"

Dorothy wrung out a wet dishtowel and held it against Ilka's temple, which was still bleeding. "I mean that Jane-Maya is sacrificing herself so her girls can live in freedom. And it's our responsibility to make sure they're safe."

"They can't get by without their mother."

They left the house and headed for the crematorium, Dorothy leading the way.

"Yes they can," Dorothy snapped. "They can if it means not being raped and married off while they're still children."

Ilka felt dizzy. "But...but Jane-Maya had just been talking about how happy their sister was for her new life in Canada."

"Escaping is one thing, making a new life is another." Dorothy's face showed both anger and sorrow. "Their sister wasn't tough enough to do that, it looks like. She ratted on her family so they would take her back."

Ilka nodded to herself, only then understanding what had happened.

"We have to get hold of Alice Payne," Dorothy said. "Her network will have to help the two girls. But right now, I'm more worried about Jane-Maya and Lydia."

They were just outside the crematorium. Her voice seemed to float away with the wind. Ilka was glad Dorothy was walking in front, unable to see her sobbing. The bleeding hadn't stopped, but no matter, she wanted to be there with the girls. She couldn't shake that look on Lydia's face at the sight of the third sister in the back of the limousine.

"The girls can stay with us for the time being," Ilka said as they stepped inside. She lowered her voice, as if the men might still be around.

Dorothy shook her head. "No way. The cult knows about the funeral home. They might come back looking for them."

"The ranch, then. It's already like a fortress out there, and with Lydia's money, we can rehire people to make sure they're safe."

She paused a moment. "And I could ask Mary Ann and Leslie to move out there. Someone would always be in the house with the girls."

Ilka had dried her eyes, but she still felt like crying. She couldn't bear thinking about the two sisters' future.

Dorothy looked at her in surprise. "Do you think Mary Ann and Leslie will do it?"

Maybe that was too much to hope for, Ilka thought,

but she wasn't going to shy away from asking. And something had happened to Leslie. Something good. As if her half sister had realized she could do more than stay at home and take care of her mother.

Dorothy pushed the bolt lock aside and opened the oven door. Jane-Maya's daughters sat in the dark with their hands on each other's shoulders, leaning against each other, forehead-to-forehead.

Ilka took a step back at the sight of the two young girls practically entwined. It was poignant, to be sure—so much so that it made her throat hurt—but what struck Ilka most was that they'd obviously done this before, clung to each other this way to fight off their fear. She heard Dorothy's voice, and she watched her help the girls out and down to the floor, but her legs felt paralyzed when she tried to step over and help.

"Are they gone?" the older girl whispered.

Dorothy nodded. "We have to leave too."

She spoke without drama, in a natural tone of voice, and Ilka felt a moment of calm.

"We don't want to go back to the family!" The girl was nearly shouting now.

The younger girl clung to her sister and said nothing. Ilka stroked her hair as she debated how to tell them their mother wasn't coming back.

"You won't have to, we promise," Ilka said, adding that they'd done a great job by being so quiet.

She decided that if Mary Ann and Leslie wouldn't step up, she would move into Artie's house with them.

The problem was that it would be just as unsafe as the funeral home. It was much easier to keep people away from Fletcher's ranch.

"Did they take Mom away?" the younger sister asked meekly.

Ilka shot a quick glance over at Dorothy, then nodded. "Your mother and aunt went with them." There wasn't any good way to say it, really.

But the girls simply nodded back, and the older one took her sister's hand.

30

They divided everything between two cars. Dorothy took the cardboard box with Lydia's money and laid it on the passenger-seat floor. Burnes's man had ruined the lock on the trunk, so she tied the lid down with twine. Ilka drove the hearse with the girls hidden in the coffin.

She couldn't get Lydia out of her head, the sight of her lying on the gravel. Also, Jane-Maya, hiding her face in her hands. More than anything she wanted to scream, but she had to hold back for the girls' sake; she couldn't show any sign of how bad things really were.

Earlier she had called Stan Thomas. Her first thought had been to call her father, but she simply couldn't tell him what had happened to Lydia. She couldn't even handle it herself.

"They took Lydia," she'd said through her sobbing.

She'd struggled to get hold of herself, so she could give the officer a description of the three black vehicles.

At first, he seemed most interested in knowing if what had happened at Dorothy's place had any connection to Calvin Jennings. When he told her that Jennings in all likelihood had been dead when he was hung, the dam broke for Ilka. The words streamed out of her, and she told him about the cult and Lydia's escape, as well as the whole story of God's Will and the Rodriguez family murdering Lydia's brother and his family.

He listened in silence.

"She's facing the death penalty," she repeated, explaining what Jennings had wanted to save Lydia from. "He had proof that she wasn't the one behind it all, and he believed she'd acted in self-defense at her brother's house. He wanted to help her, and now they've killed him."

Again, she started sobbing; she couldn't help it, but Thomas waited patiently until she could tell him about Ethan and Fernanda's murder.

"Is the boy still in danger?" he said.

"I don't know."

Her fear of what would happen to Lydia took over, it crept into her bones, and she walked around in small circles to keep herself from going crazy.

Thomas sensed the state she was in, and he told her he would send a patrol out to escort them away.

"We can't wait," Ilka said. "We have to leave, now."

Dorothy had placed the girls' small bags behind the front seat. She was helping them into the coffin.

"Lydia is in one of the four-wheel drives," Ilka explained. "Jane-Maya is in the limousine with Isiah Burnes. Find them, and we'll be okay."

"No," he said, "it's too dangerous!"

Ilka heard activity in the background, and she realized he was still at the hotel. "We're leaving now, for the ranch." She promised to call when they got there.

"I'll send a patrol out to meet you on the way."

Ilka dried her tears with the back of her hand.

"Lydia," she whispered. "Just find Lydia."

31

Ilka clutched the wheel. Dorothy was leading the way, and it felt as if her car was pulling the hearse over the hill. Her eyes darted across the surrounding fields; they were visible from practically any direction, which made Jane-Maya's daughters an easy target if Burnes's men were still around.

They turned onto the main road, and Ilka's eyes lingered on every car that passed them.

A text buzzed in from Jeff. Turn around. Get away from town.

Ilka called him and screamed, "Who the hell do you think you are, you asshole! Do you even know what you did?"

"Turn around," he insisted.

Ilka noticed his black BMW, parked on the side of the road up ahead.

"Don't go into town," he said. "There's two cars at the funeral home, and they're out at Artie's house too."

"Okay, smart-ass, if they wanted us, why wouldn't they just wait here for us?" She was so mad that for a moment she forgot how desperate she felt.

"I'm helping you get away," he said, unaffected by her anger.

"Helping!" Ilka screamed. He got out of his car and stood beside the highway. She blinked her lights and signaled to Dorothy to pull over on the shoulder. Dorothy peered at her in the rearview mirror, uncertain what to do, so Ilka pulled over and jumped out of the car. Dorothy rolled down her window.

Jeff began walking back to them, but Ilka strode up to him and smacked him in the face before he could say a word. She wanted to pummel him, to pound him into the ground, but she couldn't stop the tears and wailing, and she felt she was crumbling right there in front of him. She had so much she wanted to say, but it all drowned in the desperate sorrow mounting inside her. She was in shock, and everything seemed so unreal. Suddenly she remembered her mother and Jette, both at the funeral home.

"My mother," she said. She felt Dorothy's arm around her now.

"I put some guards at the funeral home," Jeff said. "In front and back. And we told your mother to stay inside."

"But really, if Burnes wants us, why didn't they just wait here and stop us?"

"They figure you've called the police," he calmly explained. "Right now they're keeping a low profile, but they're waiting for you, you can be sure of that."

She stepped back and looked him over. "How could you ever think I can trust you, after what you've done." Her anger began churning again. "You sold Jane-Maya and Lydia! How much did they pay you for trapping us?"

"This isn't about money, it's about getting you out of here, to safety."

"And then what happens?" Dorothy stood with both hands in the slanted pockets of her coveralls.

"You disappear into thin air, and they don't have a prayer of finding out where you've gone."

"But—"

Dorothy grabbed Ilka's arm and pulled her back a step. "We'll do it. Let him help us. At this moment, all that matters is stopping them from getting their hands on the girls. We've got to get them to safety. And we just have to hope the police will do what they can to stop Isiah Burnes."

Ilka shook her head but realized she was already wavering, about to change her mind. "What if he's bluffing?" she whispered.

"Let's all get turned around, and then both of you follow me," Jeff said. He started back to his car.

Ilka let Dorothy lead her away, but before she reached the hearse, she turned and shouted back at Jeff, "What's in it for you?"

He stopped as he was about to get in his BMW. "A job, I hope."

Ilka felt like slapping him again, but she felt Dorothy's eyes on her. She was right; they needed his help.

He whipped a U-turn in his BMW and waited. When both vehicles were lined up behind him, he took off. They passed Dorothy's driveway and continued on past autumn-gold fields on both sides of the road. A few miles farther he slowed and signaled to turn right. Ilka checked all around for black cars before following him toward a patch of woods that swallowed up the road.

Jeff slowed down again when he entered the woods, and Ilka glanced in her rearview mirror; Dorothy was following, and nothing seemed amiss. They drove down the bumpy road through the woods, where the treetops curtained off the gray daylight above. Several minutes later, Jeff stopped and shut off his engine.

"What's happening?" Ilka shouted as she jumped out of the hearse. She glanced back at the coffin inside.

He followed her eyes. "Let the girls out," he said.

Ilka instinctively took a step back to guard the coffin, but Jeff simply explained that he knew what Burnes was after, and he'd seen that Burnes hadn't taken the girls with him.

"How?" Ilka said. "How do you know what happened? All the windows on those cars are tinted. You're lying."

Suddenly her anger gave way to fear. She'd never really felt sure about where Jeff stood, and right now it looked like trusting him had been a terrible mistake.

"I saw what happened," he said.

"How?" she shouted.

He shook his head and motioned to Dorothy to get out of her car. *This feels all wrong*, Ilka thought, and she looked for somewhere to run. It was a trap he'd set up. She grabbed Dorothy and pulled her close, then turned to Jeff.

"Why? Why are you doing this? What is it you want?"

Dorothy wrenched free of her grip and stepped toward Jeff. "We can pay you. What will it cost to get you to follow us out to Fletcher's ranch? Two young girls have just lost their mother, and it's time for you to show some compassion. And we have the money—just say how much."

Ilka stepped back toward the hearse. This wasn't going to end well; when Jeff realized how much money Dorothy had in the car, he would pressure them. Or else take the money and leave them here in the woods. She was panicking, she knew that; how could she ever get the girls out of the coffin and away from there without him realizing it? She shut the voices out and took a few deep breaths before cautiously lifting up the rear door of the hearse.

"I don't want money," Jeff said. "I just want my old job back."

"But there's nobody left to take care of," Dorothy answered.

"Sure there is. I want to be in charge of the family's security."

Ilka couldn't believe her ears. She looked at him and stepped away from the hearse, close to laughing at him. "You of all people must know, you have to be able to trust a security chief. You have to know he has your back, that he'll do anything to protect you. But you, you have us in the palm of your hand. It would be so easy for you to deliver us to Burnes and his God Squad."

"I'm here to help you. All I want is my old job back."

"You can't threaten your way to a job like that. You have to earn it, by being someone people can trust. And we don't, we can't trust you, don't you get it?"

"What will it cost?" Dorothy asked again.

He was getting impatient. "It won't cost you anything. C'mon, let the girls out, just trust me."

Ilka froze. She heard the growl of an engine nearby; then it stopped. All three of them turned and stared back at the narrow road. Ilka glanced in fright at Jeff before slamming the rear door shut. Dorothy locked her car and stood in front of the passenger-side door, where all the money lay.

They heard the engine start again, a deep rumble that soon became a wall of sound slowly moving through the woods.

Jeff's car blocked them in front, and now they were being cut off from behind. They were caged in. Trapped.

Ilka tried to make eye contact with him, but he seemed unaffected as he stared quietly in the direction of the noise.

"Let the girls out," he repeated. The vehicle plowed through the woods, snapping off branches as it approached.

Ilka's mind raced; how far away could she get with the girls? But they were too small, they could never outrun Jeff. And anyway, that would be abandoning Dorothy.

Suddenly the back end of a broad white truck appeared. Ilka held her breath as it bulldozed its way toward them, laying waste to small trees and bushes on both sides of the narrow road.

Jeff clapped his hands and started over toward them. "Let's go, get the girls out of the coffin."

Dorothy and Ilka froze; all they could do was watch the truck backing up.

"Now," Jeff yelled, waving at Ilka as the back of the truck slowly began lowering.

The smell of horses roused Ilka out of her stupor. She heard the driver's-side door slam shut as she stepped toward the ramp. Dorothy leaned up against her car with arms folded.

Ilka's mouth fell open as she stared inside the Fletcher and Davidson Raceteam's enormous horse trailer, and a moment later Tom, the stable manager, appeared and nodded at her. All the stall bars attached to runners on top had been pushed aside, and the trailer was one big open space.

"We need to get the cars inside," Jeff said, gesturing for them to get going. "The girls can stay in the coffin, of course, but they'll be more comfortable sitting in the backseat of the other car. Can you drive the hearse in yourself, or do you want me to do it?"

Jeff held out his hand for the key.

Ilka was still staring at the trailer. The fear that had nearly choked her only seconds earlier slowly drained away as she caught on to Jeff's plan.

Dorothy was the first to move. She opened the hearse's rear door, and Ilka heard her warn the girls that she was going to open the coffin lid. Suddenly Ilka could move too. She hurried over and flipped the steel latches, then they lifted off the lid. The girls were lying the same way they had in the oven, hands on each other's shoulders and foreheads together. At first Ilka thought they were sleeping; then she noticed their lips moving, as if they were reciting a rhyme together. When the lid was all the way off and the light hit them, they stopped and blinked their eyes open.

"Come on out," Ilka said, holding out her hand to the older girl.

The girl hesitated a second then took it. She sat up slowly and rested a foot on the edge of the coffin before being lifted out. Dorothy reached for the younger girl, and moments later they were standing outside, the girls staring in fright at the gigantic truck.

Jeff sat on his haunches beside them. "Have you ever ridden in a car inside a truck?"

Both girls backed off a step; the younger one grabbed

Dorothy's pant leg. Before Ilka could say anything, Jeff smiled and said that not very many people had, but they were going to get to.

"Together with Ilka and Dorothy," he added. He pointed at Dorothy's car and told them to hop into the backseat, and then they'd see how fun it would be.

The girls stared at him with eyes wide open, but Ilka nodded quickly and told them Jeff was right, it was going to be fun.

Dorothy unlocked the car.

"Come on," Ilka said. She opened the back door, and though the girls still seemed wary, they climbed in. Dorothy got behind the wheel, and Jeff nodded at her.

Ilka wondered if the hearse could even make it up the ramp. She turned to Jeff. "Maybe we should leave it here?"

He shook his head. "We can't leave anything behind. I'm driving mine in too. The hearse has rear-wheel drive, it'll make it up."

"Is it big enough for three cars?" Ilka said, and he explained that he would park his car beside Dorothy's to leave more room for the hearse.

Ilka gave him the keys, studying him out of the corner of her eye. He'd set all of this in motion to help them. He must have contacted Tom before stopping them out on the highway, and planned how to get them out of here.

Dorothy drove her car inside and parked inches from the wall of the trailer. Next Jeff drove his BMW in, and then he backed the hearse up the ramp as well.

"Thank you," she said softly when he hopped down and handed her the keys. "For this." She nodded at the horse trailer.

He nodded back. She thought she saw a glimpse of satisfaction in his eye, but there was no smugness, no *I told you so*.

"Where do you want to sit?" he said. "With the girls or me?"

Ilka shrugged.

"Tom has to be alone up front when we get to the ranch."

She nodded. It was as if a part of her still couldn't believe there was a way out. She felt like they were being airlifted out of danger.

"I'll sit in the hearse," she said. She needed to be alone, needed time to think things out.

At first she was afraid he'd try to talk her out of it, but he simply told her to get in before Tom raised the ramp.

Inside the hearse, she sank down into the driver's seat. Were you supposed to fasten your seat belt when being driven this way inside a truck? She did. Then she leaned her head back and closed her eyes.

The monster vehicle started moving. Tree limbs scraped along both sides, and the bumpy road tossed her from side to side, but Ilka soon didn't even notice. Her thoughts were with Lydia. Ilka didn't know if she'd ever see her again.

When she woke up, everything was dark and quiet. Ilka stared up at the ceiling for the longest time, not knowing where she was. Exhaustion kept tugging her back toward sleep, and she drifted in and out of consciousness until she began remembering everything that had taken place, at Dorothy's, on the highway, in the woods. Fear tugged at her chest again, crawled in under her skin, and Ilka's breathing became short and shallow.

Mary Ann and Leslie had been at the ranch to help when they drove in. Dorothy and the girls were given one of the guest rooms upstairs. Ilka tried to call her father several times, and when she finally got hold of him, he told her that Ethan had just come out of surgery. He was headed to the recovery room to meet the boy there.

"I'll call you back," he promised, but Ilka hadn't heard from him since then. Which was why she hadn't told him about what had happened to Lydia. Or to Calvin Jennings. He might have heard from someone else anyway, but Ilka wanted to tell him how Lydia had fought for Jane-Maya and her nieces. It wasn't something to talk about over the phone, though, she decided, as she waited for his call. She'd also tried to get hold of Stan Thomas, but his cell phone directed her to the station, where she was told he was out on an investigation. They couldn't divulge any further information.

Finally, Ilka had gone into the den and stretched out on the sofa, where she gazed out the windows into the dark until falling asleep.

Now it all slowly came back to her, and the more she remembered, the less she felt like waking all the way up.

She had no idea how she'd ended up in bed. Then Ilka realized she was still on the sofa, that someone had covered her with a thick comforter.

"Hello?"

The quiet voice startled Ilka. Her father was sitting in the easy chair beside the sofa, a newspaper in his lap.

"What are you doing here?" she snapped to cover up her shock.

"Waiting for you to wake up."

"I thought you were with Ethan," she said, still annoyed. But she softened when she noticed the worry in his eyes. "How's he doing?"

Ilka gathered the comforter around her and sat up.

"He's okay. They did a skin transplant on him, it went fine. He's getting out of the hospital soon. I left when he came back from the recovery room, but you were asleep when I got here."

"Have you heard about Lydia?" In all likelihood she already knew the answer to her question, judging from the sorrow written all over his ashen face. Her father looked even older.

He nodded. "Dorothy told me what happened and about Jeff and Tom helping you get out of there. We tried to wake you up, but you were sleeping like a log. She also told me about the third sister, how she betrayed Lydia and Jane-Maya."

The third sister, Ilka thought. She gazed up at the ceiling. Yesterday, for the first time, she'd felt like the third sister. When they all had stepped in to help, and she'd felt accepted, with no reservations. As if she belonged, as if she and Leslie and Amber were truly sisters. Amber's boyfriend had driven the horse trailer out into the woods to help them get away. And Leslie had been at the ranch, ready to help everyone.

"I tried to call you," Ilka said quietly. She could feel tears coming again. She was completely exhausted, but she tried to fight off her stupor, a hazy feeling of not really being present, as if she was trying to take a few steps back from the horrible things that had happened.

Her father glanced at his watch. "You've been asleep fifteen hours. We were getting worried."

Ilka simply nodded. She could have slept another fifteen hours if not for the dread gnawing in her gut. "When did you get back?"

"We got here about seven thirty yesterday evening, but you were already asleep."

"*We?*"

Her father nodded toward the door. Ilka turned and found herself looking at a white comforter that hung down over a rollaway bed behind the sofa. She straightened up and stared, dumbfounded at the sight of Artie lying back against a stack of pillows, watching her.

"Jeff didn't think Artie was safe at the hospital. He wanted Ethan out of there too, but the doctors said no, so he put a guard outside his room."

Artie didn't speak, he simply lay on the mountain of pillows, looking at her. It was as if all the violence had somehow locked him up.

"The ranch is like a fortress now," her father said. "We're safer than Fort Knox."

Ilka tore her eyes away from Artie and looked back at her father.

"Amber's here too," he said. "She and Tom moved into her house."

Ilka nodded. She knew her half sister had been living at the ranch from the time she started working for her grandfather.

"Have you heard anything?" She couldn't shake the feeling that something more had happened, that they were there to spare her when she woke up.

Her father nodded, while Artie shook his head.

"So far the police have arrested four people in town. They suspect these men are part of the God Squad, and that they were looking for you and Dorothy and the girls."

Finally, Artie spoke up, though his voice was hoarse. "We haven't heard anything about Lydia," he said, apparently knowing that was the question Ilka had wanted to ask.

"Dorothy contacted Alice Payne," her father said. "And Stan Thomas too. Nothing's come out in the media yet; the police don't want any supporters of God's Will to complicate the situation if they manage to locate Isiah Burnes's motorcade."

"How are you feeling?" Ilka wrapped the comforter around her, then stood up and walked over to Artie's bed.

He reached out for her hand and spoke in a small voice. "I'm afraid of what'll happen to Lydia. What if the police stop the cars and then they don't believe her?"

"She's going to be okay," Ilka whispered. She leaned over and kissed his forehead. "And we're here to back her story up. She's not alone anymore."

The door to the den opened, and Leslie came in carrying her iPad. "Have you heard?"

Everyone in the house was gathered around Leslie's iPad. The first thing Ilka saw on the small screen was a photo of Calvin Jennings. An older photo, but she recognized his narrow white tie and direct gaze.

Leslie had turned the volume up, and Ilka realized they were watching a segment in honor of Jennings.

"The final breakthrough in the case occurred just before Jennings's death," the TV newscaster said. He then talked about how a female former member of the cult had agreed to testify against the cult leader.

Suddenly Lydia appeared on screen, standing beside a uniformed police officer. In a small separate screen in the upper right corner, Isiah Burnes was being led away in handcuffs. Ilka saw the tears on Artie's cheeks.

Jane-Maya appeared on the screen. "A life in hell is now over," said the female journalist standing beside her. "A life of violence, fear, tyranny, and serious sexual abuse of children. How do you feel right now?"

She shoved the microphone in front of Jane-Maya, who was wearing a buttoned-up pastel-green dress.

"Do the girls know about this?" Ilka was looking at Leslie, but Mary Ann was the one who nodded.

"They've spoken with their mother, but they grew up without TV, and she asked us not to let them see the news."

"I'm fine." Jane-Maya cleared her throat then looked straight into the camera, saying that she had agreed to testify against Isiah Burnes. "It's time that all the monstrous things he's done come out. Mostly, though, I'm looking forward to seeing my girls."

The newscaster explained that Jane-Maya's girls had managed to escape and were now in safety, staying with friends of the family.

Friends, Ilka thought. She looked around at the others. However natural the word sounded when spoken by the newscaster, the fact was that all of them huddled around the iPad had joined forces to protect Jane-Maya's children, even though they didn't know her. They stood together. Together with Lydia, together with each other. The realization, the warm feeling kept growing in her until she had to escape for a moment. She needed some fresh air. And a cigarette.

On her way to the door Ilka stopped at a mention of the Rodriguez brothers from the television. The newscaster reported that substantial evidence Calvin Jennings had compiled against the two surviving brothers had been found in one of Isiah Burnes's cars. Presented with the evidence, the police immediately dropped all charges against Lydia Rogers. The two men were now in custody.

The news report looped back to the photos of the car chase. Another voice reported that a three-car caravan transporting Isiah Burnes had been stopped earlier that day at a roadblock south of St. Louis.

Ilka lit a cigarette and closed the door behind her, but it immediately opened again. Her father stepped out to join her. They stood in silence for a few moments as she smoked, then he cleared his throat.

"Mary Ann and I have agreed to divorce."

Ilka glanced over at him; she could hear he had more to say.

"She's been very generous." He explained that his wife had decided to share the enormous Fletcher fortune with Amber, Leslie, and him.

Ilka whistled under her breath. "Well. Things are certainly looking up for the funeral home's future."

He nodded. "I'm moving into Amber's house when she and Tom take over the ranch."

"What about Dorothy?" She turned to him. "Why don't you move in with her?"

He smiled. "At our age it's best to live separately. It's something that happens over the years, you become a bit eccentric, and it can be difficult for others to live with."

Ilka smiled back, but his face had turned somber again.

"Artie won't go back to the hospital."

He leaned against the wall and frowned. "He wants to go back to his place. Of course, we can pay for physical therapy at home, and for driving him back and forth to the hospital when it's necessary, but one of us needs to stay with him. He can't lie out there in bed alone."

Ilka felt his eyes on her. She nodded.

After a few more seconds he said, "Would you consider doing it? Even though that would mean you'd have to move out there?"

She nodded again. Mostly to herself. "I'll stay until he gets back on his feet."

The worry disappeared from his face.

They stood in silence for a few minutes.

"You've grown up to be the person I imagined, the woman I'd hoped you'd be. I'm sorry that—"

"Stop, please. Just let it go."

And he did.

"When I was a kid, I dreamed about having brothers or sisters," she said. "I dreamed we were one big family, and there was always someone to talk to. Someone to sit around the table with. People don't always get the families they dream about. But I have all of you now, and that's good enough for me."

The family she was talking about included Artie and Lydia. And even Mary Ann. Ilka crushed her cigarette with her foot. She was feeling a bit sentimental and was about to tell him how much it meant to her that they had found each other. All of them.

But before she could speak, her father cleared his throat again and pulled out a folded-up sheet of paper from his back pocket.

"Have you heard about Dazzling Star?" He handed her a photo of a dark-brown trotter crossing the finish line as a winner.

Ilka shook her head and skimmed the article below.

"I saw him run as a two-year-old, and I've been keeping my eye on him. And now, after all this with Mary Ann and the money, I'm thinking about buying him."

Ilka looked up.

"He's running this weekend. You want to come along? We can see how he does before we make an offer."

They stood looking at each other for the longest time. Then Ilka folded the paper back up and nodded.

ACKNOWLEDGMENTS

My trilogy about the undertaker's daughter has been so much fun, truly an exhilarating journey. My heartfelt thanks go out to all of you for how warmly you've welcomed Ilka, and for following along with us.

The Third Sister is a work of fiction. Many settings in the book exist in the real world, but I've also taken the liberty of creating locales, reshaping them, moving them around to make them fit my story. My travels to Racine and Key West have been fascinating, but my characters are not based on real people. Their names and everything about them sprang out of my imagination.

The same goes for God's Will. It was inspired by actual cults and true events, but the cult and everything that transpired in the book are fictional.

Again, I'd like to extend my gratitude to Christina Gauguin, the undertaker at Elholm Mortuary. She was my first contact with the undertaking business and has since taken time to answer all my questions.

This book could never have been written without the help of Benee Knauer. Her help with research in the United States has been indispensable.

I lived in the US for eighteen months while writing the Family Secrets trilogy. I would like to thank the enormous Danish network over there for your incredible support, both for my books and for me personally.

My team at my publisher, People's Press, deserves a big thank-you. Thanks for working with me, thanks for supporting me from the very start of this trilogy. A special thanks goes out to my gifted editor, Lisbeth Møller-Madsen, who always knew precisely where I wanted to go with Ilka.

Thank you so much, Elisa Lykke, for being a wonderful PR agent. You have a sharp eye for knowing what's best for me. It's meant so very, very much to be able to work so closely with you.

And I want to thank Malene Kierkegaard from the Plot Workshop for her many hours of work helping me get everything into place. I'm so grateful for how committed you've been, how willing you were to keep at it until I brought out everything in the story I'd wanted.

A warm thanks goes out to the very talented Lotte Thorsen, who spent a week with me in New York to find out what was hidden behind the sister's habit. Your ideas helped get the whole project off the ground. Thank you.

A very special and loving thanks to Lars and Andreas. You two keep my entire life and everything around me from unraveling. Thank you.

And my loving thanks go out to my son, Adam. Everything is better when you're here. You are my biggest support and my greatest joy.

Finally, my heartfelt thanks go out to my fantastic, loyal readers and followers. You are the ones who make the stories live for me, who simply make me want to write. Thanks for always cheering me on. I'm so grateful that you want to read what I write. *Thank you!*

—Sara Blaedel

ABOUT THE AUTHOR

Sara Blaedel's interest in story, writing, and especially crime fiction was nurtured from a young age, long before Scandinavian crime fiction took the world by storm. Today she is Denmark's "Queen of Crime" and is published in thirty-seven countries. Her series featuring police detective Louise Rick is adored the world over, and her new Family Secrets series has launched to great critical success.

The daughter of a renowned Danish journalist and an actress whose career included roles in theater, radio, TV, and movies, Sara grew up surrounded by a constant flow of professional writers and performers visiting the Blaedel home. Despite her struggle with dyslexia, books gave Sara a world in which to escape when her introverted nature demanded an exit from the hustle and bustle of life.

Sara tried a number of careers, from a restaurant apprenticeship to graphic design, before she started a publishing company called Sara B, where she published Danish translations of American crime fiction.

Publishing ultimately led Sara to journalism, and she covered a wide range of stories, from criminal trials to the premiere of *Star Wars: Episode I*. It was during this time—and while skiing in Norway—that Sara started brewing the ideas for her first novel. In 2004 Louise Rick and her friend Camilla Lind were introduced in *Grønt Støv* (*Green Dust*), and Sara won the Danish Academy for Crime Fiction's debut prize.

Originally from Denmark, Sara has lived in New York but now spends most of her time in Copenhagen with her family. She has always loved animals; she still enjoys horse riding and shares her home with her cat and golden retriever. When she isn't busy committing brutal murders on the page, she is an ambassador with Save the Children and serves on the jury of a documentary film competition.